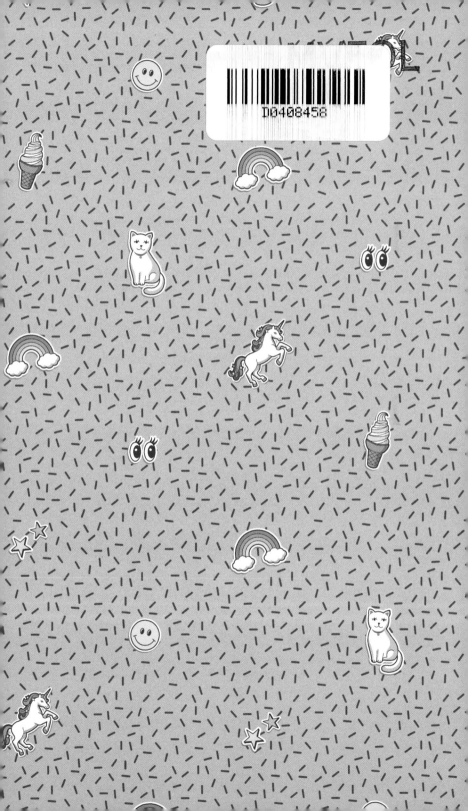

THIS
IS NOT
THE
JESS
SHOW

Also by Anna Carey

Eve

Once

Rise

Blackbird

Deadfall

this is not
the JESS SHOW

ANNA CAREY

QUIRK BOOKS
PHILADELPHIA

Library of Congress Cataloging in Publication Data
Carey, Anna, author.
This is not the Jess show / Anna Carey.
Summary: "When strange things start happening in Jess Flynn's hometown of Swickley, the high-school junior suspects reality isn't as it seems and seeks to uncover the truth about her family, her friends, and her town"—Provided by publisher.
CYAC: Reality—Fiction. | Secrets—Fiction. |
Family life—Fiction. | High schools—Fiction. | Schools—Fiction. |
Dating (Social customs)—Fiction.
LCC PZ7.C21 Thi 2020 | DDC [Fic]—dc23   2020007413

ISBN: 978-1-68369-197-6

Printed in the United States of America

Typeset in Gotham Rounded, Lulo, and Sabon

Cover illustration by Tim O'Brien
Cover design by Andie Reid
Production management by John J. McGurk

Quirk Books
215 Church Street
Philadelphia, PA 19106
quirkbooks.com

10 9 8 7 6 5 4 3 2 1

For Clay

1

Three things happened the week I found out. *Titanic* won a bunch of Oscars, and my sister and I stayed up late to watch because we'd never miss a chance to see Leo in a tux. Meanwhile every news anchor was talking about the president, and everywhere I went people repeated that phrase, how he "didn't have sexual relations with that woman." I probably should have cared (president, impeachment, important stuff) but another, more pressing matter, had consumed me: I'd fallen in love with my best friend.

Tyler. Also known as Ty, Scruggs, or Tyler Michael Scruggs. Formerly known as Bugs, Bugsy Scruggsy, or Fire Crotch (more on that later). We'd managed to be friends for six whole years with no feelings whatsoever. We'd never got weird with each other, even when we were in the throes of puberty and I was having vivid dreams about hooking up with Zack Morris. Growing up, Tyler had these huge buckteeth and moppy, rust-colored hair. When kids weren't making fun of his smile, they were heckling him for being a ginger, as if that alone were a sin against humanity. It had taken five years of braces to get his two front teeth back inside his head, but now those braces were gone and his smile was kind of . . . well, perfect. Now he was five eight, and his hair was longer and a little darker, and it fell into his eyes when he played the drums. Now he worked out.

I rolled over in bed, my eyes squeezed shut. This thing with Tyler had gotten into my bloodstream and infected my brain. I was never alone because I was always imagining him right beside me. I couldn't stop thinking about the way the sleeves of his tee shirt strained against his biceps. How he closed his eyes and tilted his head back when he played the drums, and you could see the veins in his forearms. He was still the tiniest bit bucktoothed, but now he rested the tip of his tongue against the bottom of them when he was deep in thought. Now it was totally hot.

There was a knock on my door. My dad pressed his face into the room, his cheek on the doorframe à la *The Shining*.

"Jess, what are you doing?" he asked. "It's almost seven. Kristen's going to be here soon."

"I'm alive. I'm moving."

But I didn't actually move until he closed the door behind him.

I turned over, watching the tops of the trees sway with the wind. A squirrel ran across the telephone wire. It was the end of March and the cold air had just broken, giving way to spring, so I'd slept with my window open for the first time in months. I got up and searched for my jeans and my pink, fuzzy turtleneck, trying not to obsess about the fact that I had band today with Tyler.

Someone was shouting something. It was so far off I couldn't make out the words right away, but it was the relentlessness of it, the repetition that drew me in. It was as steady and sure as a beating heart. *Power* was the first word I heard with any certainty. The next was harder to make out but it sounded like *Forages. Forages, power, forages, power,* on and on like that. The words repeated on an endless loop, but when I stepped into the hallway they sounded farther away.

"The TV's not on downstairs, is it?"

My dad was sitting on the bottom step now, his broad shoulders hunched forward as he laced up his work boots. The back of his jacket read FLYNN PEST CONTROL in block letters.

"No. Why?" He picked at a knot with his fingers.

"Never mind."

I walked across the hall. Sara was sitting up in bed, a blood pressure cuff on her arm. Lydia, her nurse, had arrived early that day, and the room filled with the *thwick thwick thwick* of the pump. She put on her glasses to read the gauge.

"Did you hear that?" I asked.

"What?" Sara's black hair was messy at the crown, where it rubbed against the pillow. Lydia didn't look up until she'd marked Sara's blood pressure on her notepad and pulled the stethoscope out of each ear. We were all quiet for a moment, straining to hear past the machine by Sara's bed, which hissed and sighed like a living, breathing thing.

"That bird? The chirping?" Lydia asked.

"No, it was different . . ." I went to the window and opened it, but the words were much harder to hear now, over everything else.

"My faculties must be going. The beginning of the end," Lydia said, the hint of a smile at the corner of her mouth. "Forty is approaching . . ."

"Forty isn't old." I knew she was kidding, though.

She sorted Sara's pills into piles on the nightstand. Lydia always had an easy way about her, breezing through even the most chaotic days in our house. She was my mom's best friend, and she'd been a part of our family for as long as I could remember. When I was kid I'd lie awake, listening to faint laughter downstairs as they talked at the kitchen table. She was our live-in nanny when we were really little. When we got older Sara and I would spend hours with her after school, digging up bugs in her backyard while my parents were still at work. Lydia was two years into her nursing degree when Sara got sick, and she'd wanted to go into private nursing, so it made sense that she'd be the one to care for Sara as the disease progressed. She'd be there when we couldn't.

"What did it sound like?" Sara asked.

Before I could answer a leaf blower started up outside, drowning out my thoughts. Then my dad appeared in the doorway.

"You're not even dressed yet? Jess, come on."

"I know, I know," I said on my way back across the hall. I pulled on the fuzzy turtleneck and paused, trying to hear the strange chanting again, but the leaf blower was still blasting, and the house was noisier now that everyone was starting their day. My mom must've turned on the radio in the kitchen. "Waterfalls" by TLC floated up the stairs, the lyrics muffled by my bedroom door.

I went through the motions of getting ready, on autopilot as I stepped into my jeans and brushed my hair. I was still standing at the window when Kristen pulled up and honked the horn.

2

"You're like the guy from that song, 'Lady in Red.'" Amber glanced back at me as she unbuckled her seatbelt. "It's like, really? You've known her this whole time and you're only into her now, after seeing her in a red dress? Isn't that a little . . . fickle?"

"Or maybe it's totally normal," I said, pushing out into the upperclassmen parking lot. Amber and Kristen were really good friends in a lot of ways, but they had this weird habit of dissecting everything I felt. I couldn't sneeze without it turning into a discussion.

"I just didn't realize I liked him until I did," I said.

Kristen tied her flannel around her waist. Her long, curly brown hair was still recovering from last spring, when she got too enthusiastic with the Sun In.

"Until you saw him with his shirt off," she smirked.

The thing is . . . she wasn't wrong. It had all started the last week of August, when it was so humid you couldn't walk

12

from the car to the house without your shirt sticking to your back. I worked that summer at the Swickley YMCA, playing the keyboard for the Seniors Sing! choir, but on Thursdays and Fridays I was off. Those empty hours were filled with *Saved by the Bell* reruns and swimming in Amber's pool, which was in-ground and heated to a perfect eighty-five degrees. We stayed in the water until our fingers were wrinkly and our eyes were bloodshot from the chlorine.

Ty had called me that morning, bored out of his mind. Driftwood Day Camp had ended and so had his reign as assistant to the Music Director. He'd known Amber and Kristen almost as long as I had, but it wasn't an obvious thing, me inviting him over to Amber's house. I had to beep her, then wait for her to call me back so I could ask, and she said he could come if he picked up a bottle of Dr. Pepper on the way.

He'd already started dressing differently by then, trading in his old polos for vintage tee shirts he'd found at Goodwill, ones that said ITHACA IS GORGES or ORLANDO in loopy, '80s font. When he came through the back gate he seemed taller, and he was tan from a summer spent outside, his shaggy hair overdue for a cut. He was the same Ty I'd known for six years, whom I'd defended in gym class when people called him Fire Crotch or Bugsy Scruggsy. The same Ty who'd stayed up late with me, lying in the treehouse in my backyard after Sara was diagnosed with Guignard's Disease. The same Ty who only said sorry, *I'm so sorry*, knowing that the silence was what I needed. But he was different, too. He came through the gate and hugged me, and something felt different.

"I can't believe you're into Bugs, I mean, it's *Bugs*." Amber pulled her braids down in front of one shoulder. She'd worn her hair that way ever since *Clueless* came out—Dionne Davenport was her style icon.

"He's gotten so full of himself too," Kristen said. "It's painful to be around."

"I don't think he's full of himself," I said. "Besides, this is high school. People reinvent themselves all the time."

I didn't go on, but I didn't have to. Just two years before, Kristen had gone through her own Love Potion No. 9 transformation, saying goodbye to her glasses and the vast majority of her body hair, and returning freshman year with boobs. She'd started September by making out with Kyle Sawicki, captain of the JV lacrosse team, as if that alone could announce: SEE, I'M DIFFERENT!! I never gave her shit for changing. But Amber and Kristen had distanced themselves from Ty almost as soon as he started working out. They kept saying he was conceited, and it felt like he was trying too hard, and didn't I find it all a little annoying?

"Where is everyone?" I asked, as we passed the tenth empty parking spot on our way inside the school. The lot was half empty.

"Haven't you heard? There's some kind of flu going around..." Amber spun her pearl earring between her fingers.

"Paul Tamberino has been barfing for three days straight," Kristen said. "Fever, chills, the whole thing. We should be wearing hazmat suits."

She pushed through the back door, which had SPRING

FORMAL fliers taped on it. She held it open just long enough for Amber and me to pass through, then rubbed her hand against the front of her jeans. It was seven twenty-six, just four minutes before first period, but the hall was practically empty. No Max Pembroke and Hannah Herlihy making out at the lockers by the auditorium. No sophomore girls standing in front of the vending machines, pretending to be engrossed in a snack selection as they waited for the senior guys to pass through. No Mrs. Ramirez telling people they needed to hurry up, get to class.

"Half the school is out," I said. "It's a stomach flu?"

"Just the regular one, but really, really awful," Kristen said. "Things coming out of either end, nonstop. They said that—"

"Ew, Kristen, repulsive." Amber winced. "We get it, it's bad."

"Jess asked!" Kristen turned left down the hall, then spun around and walked backward, pulling her tee shirt up over her face so it covered her nose and mouth, as if that alone could protect her from germs. "Stay safe out there."

"Just remember: Lady in Red," Amber said, before starting toward her Physics classroom. "She was the same person she was before the dress."

"It's not a Lady in Red situation. I swear."

But was it? There was something about Amber's declarations that always made me unsure. Amber was the only one of us who'd dated anyone seriously. She and Chris Arnold had gone out for six months last year, and she'd decided to break up with him because he said "I love you" and she knew immediately she'd never say it back.

I took the stairs down to the music wing. I passed a bunch of juniors I recognized, but it was as if all the underclassmen had vanished. I hadn't seen the school this empty since the tornado in 1996, right at the end of my freshman year. It touched down one night in May, and my family huddled in the basement, listening to it barrel through like a freight train, exploding trees and cars and mailboxes in its wake. The entire block behind the library was destroyed, including Kristen's house. I'd volunteered every Saturday for weeks, digging personal items out of the debris. I'd found Kristen's third-grade picture under a bathtub.

When I got to band, half the seats were empty, and Tyler wasn't in the percussion section. Emily Hanrahan and Kima Johnson, two girls I'd known since elementary school, were the only flutes. The sophomores who sat behind them were out and most of the woodwind section was missing too. A woman with red glasses sat at Mr. Betts's desk.

I went to the music closet, but Tyler wasn't there either. My mom had been on the phone all weekend, so I was only able to sign onto AOL for five minutes on Saturday, and he hadn't been on. I hated thinking he might be sick too, that I might not see him for a whole week, maybe more. He didn't stop by our house as often as he had when we were younger, and I looked forward to every class we had together—on Thursdays especially, when he sat next to me in study hall and we spent the period passing notes back and forth.

My keyboard was on the top shelf and I had to yank it out inch by inch, sliding it across the wood so that it didn't fall on my head. The band room had a grand piano that I sometimes played, but Mr. Betts preferred the keyboard this year, considering the medley we were performing. It was a mash-up of all these sitcom theme songs—*Perfect Strangers*, *Friends*, *Full House*, *The Simpsons*, and *Family Matters*. He liked how the piano solo at the beginning of *Family Matters* sounded on the keyboard. It was poppy, electronic, and closer to the original. I didn't have a problem with the actual composition, but part of me knew he was going to make us do something cheesy, like wear sunglasses or shimmy our shoulders at the break. He was always adding what he called "dramatic flair," even though it felt more third grade than eleventh.

I'd gotten the keyboard halfway out when someone rushed in to help.

"Hey, sorry." I turned and Tyler was right beside me, lowering the thing to the ground. "I was waiting for you by your locker, but then I remembered you don't go to your locker Monday mornings until second period, so then I came here—whatever, it's stupid. Hi."

I smiled. "Hi."

His snare drum was against the wall, behind us, but he didn't go for it. Instead he just stood there and brushed his bangs out of his eyes. He wore a vintage Eagles tee shirt with a zip-up hoodie over it, and he was standing so close I could smell his shampoo, this new peppermint one he'd started using. One of his drumsticks was in his back pocket and he turned the other between his fingers.

He was completely unrecognizable from the gawky boy

I'd met in fourth grade. We'd only interacted because I'd tried to throw a kickball to Kristen and it had flown past her and smacked Tyler in the head. I'd felt so bad, I'd asked him to play with us, and then he started coming over after school.

"You weren't online this weekend," he said.

"My mom had a work emergency. She never got off the phone."

"Oh." Tyler shrugged. We usually IMed at least Friday or Saturday night, just blabbering on about stupid stuff, like Mr. Betts's new toupee.

I thought he might say something else, but he just drummed on the side of the storage shelf, tapping out a quick rhythm. His cheeks were turning this splotchy pink color. They only did that when he was nervous.

"What's wrong?"

"Nothing, no." He shrugged.

"Ty, say it."

"I guess I just missed you?"

It was a question. He looked up and gave me this half smile, then started laughing. "Fine, I said it. I missed you, whatever. You're my everything, Jess Flynn, it's torture without you, blah blah blah. You happy now?"

"Extremely," I said, and I felt the fire in my cheeks, all the blood rushing to my face at once. "I have that effect on people . . ."

He turned and grabbed the snare drum, carrying it in front of him as he walked out. He stopped right beside me, leaning in so his lips were just a few inches from my ear, and I could feel his breath on my neck. His freckles always disappeared during the winter, but when we were really close I could see the faint remnants of them along the bridge of his nose.

"You definitely have that effect on me."

Only this time, when he said it, he didn't laugh or make it a joke. His hazel eyes met mine and there was a moment when I was sure he would kiss me, right there, in the storage closet. Every inch of my body was suddenly awake waiting for him.

But then he turned and walked to the back of the room. He looked back twice, smiling at me over his shoulder. Something had changed. He wasn't the same person who'd slept next to me that night in the treehouse, when we were eleven, scanning the trees with a flashlight, looking for bears (even though we both knew Swickley didn't have any). The air between us was charged, and I noticed every time he brushed my shoulder or the back of my hand.

I set up the keyboard stand behind the clarinet section, feeling Tyler's eyes on me the whole time. When I looked up his cheeks were still pink and splotchy. I kept running through the conversation. It was like I'd been possessed by someone older and more confident. *I have that effect on people.*

The sub pulled her gray hair back with a checkered scrunchie, then tapped the conductor's baton against her music stand. A French horn player stopped halfway through her scale. The class was still only about half full.

"I'm Mrs. Kowalsky, your sub for the next few days. I know we don't have a full band, and we're missing almost all of the saxophones . . ." She glanced at Ajay Sethi, who looked particularly lonely surrounded by empty chairs. "But let's do our best. Starting from the top."

She rapped the baton against the stand again, then brought it up in front of her face.

Even after the first song began, the trumpets blaring the first notes of the *Friends* theme, our eyes kept finding each other. The whole period I was thinking of Tyler's mouth, how red his lips got when he blushed. I kept wondering what it would be like to kiss him.

3

"We can't risk Sara getting sick." Lydia pushed a heaping pile of salad onto her plate. "I think I've sprayed every inch of this house with Lysol."

Sara pushed her mashed potatoes around with her fork. She was still in her pajamas, even though it was after six o'clock. My dad always carried her downstairs for dinner, singing "Here she comes, Miss America . . ." the whole way.

"That seems kind of unlikely," Sara said, "considering I see the same four people every day."

"I had to move all the Reyes's new furniture into storage," my mom went on. "The new dining set, every lamp and table I bought for the living room. We were supposed to be putting the finishing touches on tomorrow, but Vicki's sick, and I wasn't about to risk it. We won't be done for another two weeks. That's if we're lucky."

My mom was one of Swickley's most popular interior designers. Her business grew organically after she renovated our house. She'd spent a whole year huddled over fabric swatches and paint chips, a measuring tape glued to her hand. She was the one who'd chosen the gray Formica dining table we were eating at. She'd paired it with these asymmetrical chairs that look like someone hacked them in half with a machete. Our living room was painted pale turquoise, but even with the fuchsia carpeting and black media cabinet, it somehow all worked. When she insisted on pink walls in the kitchen we fought back with everything we had. I suggested five other options; Sara said it would feel like swimming in a bottle of Pepto-Bismol. It wasn't until Amber and Kristen came to see it after school that I realized it wasn't as horrible as we'd thought. Maybe it was even kind of . . . cool?

"I'm just hoping I don't lose too much time," my mom went on. "The kitchen renovation on Oakcrest is a complete disaster. There's only one guy left on the crew. Everyone else called in sick. It took him six hours just to install the sink. I can't even imagine what I'm going to have to deal with tomorrow."

"Sounds rough," I said. She was getting into that hyper-focused place where all she could do was talk about work. I turned to my dad, hoping he'd derail her, but he was cutting his steak with the precision of a neurosurgeon. He held up a tender piece, studying it on his fork before taking a bite.

In the past few years my dad's conversational skills had shrunk to short phrases, as if it took too much effort to form any kind of imaginative or complicated thought. My mom addressed it without addressing it, saying that he was "under a lot of stress" and "having a hard time with Sara's illness" or, my favorite, that he was "a man of few words." It was a horrible masculine cliché, but the only time he seemed genuinely excited about anything was when he talked about the Swickley High varsity baseball team. He'd been the head coach since I was a kid. I'd formed all these theories about sports being a socially acceptable way for men to talk about their feelings, to scream and cry and rage against the world. I was certain that when he teared up after the team lost the championships last fall, it was really about losing control, and how he felt about everything our family was going through.

Mostly, though, I just missed him.

"Oh, I should show you the design for the Hill Lane project," my mom barreled on. She looked from me to Sara, but I couldn't figure out who she was talking to. "You'd love the master bedroom. All florals. Simple. I usually resist florals because it feels grandma-ish, but what Betsy Baker wants, Betsy Baker gets. That woman is a force."

The table was quiet and for a second I thought I heard it again, that same chanting from the other morning. It was hard to be sure because the stereo in the kitchen was still on. The radio station played a Dave Matthews song I hadn't heard before. Something about not drinking the water.

"Forages . . ." I stared down at my plate, to the last grisly bits of meat. "That just means to look for food, right? It's not like there's some other obscure definition?"

My mom tilted her head and studied me. "Where'd that come from?"

"I just . . ." I started. "I heard it the other morning. It sounded like it was coming from outside, like someone yelling. Forages, power. Forages, power. Over and over like that. But then I couldn't hear it anymore."

"That's what you were asking about yesterday?" Sara said.

"And for a minute or two today, right when I got up."

Sara turned to Lydia. Her dark brows knitted together the way they did when she was pissed. Lydia stared straight ahead. It was like she was purposely ignoring her.

"What?" I asked. "What's wrong?"

"Very strange . . ." My mom said it in this chipper, high-pitched voice. "Does anyone want more steak? There's two more pieces."

"I'm good," I said.

It wasn't the type of conversation my mom was interested in. She would've been happier if I'd engaged with her on her Oakcrest kitchen design, or if I'd told some funny, meaningful story about school. The thing about having a mom who obsessed over the tiniest aesthetic details of our house was that her obsession extended to all the people in it. She was always suggesting new hairstyles (*you should grow out your bangs, shorter cuts are harder to pull off*), and one time she'd bought me a whole pile of new clothes without asking. She'd paired different skirts and sweaters together and had all the blouses tailored to my frame. Everything I said and did and wore had to be just right.

I stacked Sara's and Lydia's plates and started into the kitchen. Sara was glancing sideways at Lydia again, like she might say something else, but she didn't. I wondered if she'd heard the words too, or if she was just responding to my

mom's obsessive need to control the conversation. I'd have
to ask her when we were alone.

Sometimes just being in a ten-foot radius of my mother
was enough to make me feel anxious. When I was thirteen
I begged her to let me take guitar lessons, though she went on
and on about how I was such a beautiful piano player—why
did I want to change instruments? *Sam*, she said to my dad.
Tell her what a waste that would be. It had taken months to
wear her down, but she finally agreed that if I kept playing
the piano I could also take guitar. I'd do both.

But six lessons in my guitar teacher, Harry, had what my
parents described as a "psychotic break." He'd been showing me how to play "Landslide" when he paused, staring at
the mirror that hung across from our sofa. He asked if I'd
ever wondered about the nature of reality. Did I ever feel, in
my gut, that there was more to this world? That things were
oppressively surface level? Did I ever feel trapped in someone else's delusion?

I wasn't used to people asking my opinion, so I had to
really think about it. *Sometimes things feel weird . . . like
I don't have control*, I said. *Like I'm trapped. Is that what
you mean?* I started to tell him about my mom, and how she
needed to know where I was every second of every day, but
then my dad walked in. He'd heard the whole conversation
from the kitchen.

Harry never came back to our house. When we went to
Mel's Music a week later, they said he'd moved in with his
mother in New Jersey. *He'd been hearing things*, an egg-
shaped man behind the counter said. His gray beard was

so long it made him look like Rip Van Winkle. *He wasn't well . . . in the head, you know?*

I rinsed the dishes and went downstairs. I looked at my reflection in the mirror above our sofa, trying to see what Harry saw in it. Maybe I was smart enough not to say it out loud, but I still *did* question "the nature of reality." I did feel like everything was surface level. And now I was hearing things, too.

He wasn't well . . . in the head, you know?

I was starting to feel like I did.

Kristen pulled on her jeans, never taking her eyes off me. She was always the slowest to change after gym class, lingering in her bra, her flannel shirt balled in her hand, or using those seven minutes before the bell to launch into some in-depth conversation that would inevitably spill into the hall. I couldn't help but wonder if it was because her boobs were three times the size of mine and Amber's.

"You're being so annoying," I said. "Come on. Out with it."

Kristen peered around the corner of the gym lockers, checking the shower to make sure no one was there. The tiled room was only used for storage, but sometimes girls sat on the stacked gymnastics mats and smoked out the window.

"Fine . . . Patrick Kramer is going to ask you to Spring Formal." Kristen drew out the sentence, pausing after each word.

"She heard it from Patrick's best friend," Amber said, clipping her overalls in front. "It's like he wanted it to get back to you."

"Patrick Kramer," I repeated. It wasn't enough that he was six foot three and started on the varsity soccer team. Last February he'd been at the Empire State Building when a guy opened fire on the observation deck, and he'd jumped in front of a group of third graders, bringing them all to the ground. No one was hurt. He'd given interviews to STV News. He'd been in every paper, with headlines like "Young Hero Saves Third Grade Class" and "Bravery at the Empire State Building." I might've liked him based on that alone, but it was more than a year later and he was still trying to work it into every conversation, as if everyone hadn't already discussed it ad nauseam.

"Patrick and I are complete opposites. And we've only ever talked like, a handful of times. Mostly about Physics homework."

"You don't need to talk to enjoy his abs." Kristen turned and folded her arms around her body, making sucking noises as she ran her hands up and down her sides. We laughed, but that wasn't enough for her, and she kept going, grabbing her own butt until I nudged her to stop.

"It just feels out of nowhere."

"Apparently he's liked you since Homecoming. And I double-checked to make sure he wasn't talking about Jess Aberdeen, Jess Thompson, or Jess Weinberg." Kristen finally pulled on her baby doll tee, then plopped down on the bench to lace up her Doc Martens. She didn't take anything too seriously—crushes, homework, even the SATs. With Sara sick, I wouldn't leave Swickley after graduation—I couldn't.

The only thing that made me feel better was the idea that Kristen might be here with me.

"He's just not my type. Besides, things are finally happening with Ty."

"If things were going to happen with Ty, they would've happened already." Amber pointed her lip gloss wand at me. "Seriously, Jess, you've known him since fourth grade."

"It's not easy to go from friends to something more," I said. Ty wasn't a Patrick Kramer, one of these guys who tried to shove their tongue down your throat as soon as they got you alone. "He's probably only just realized I like him."

"I mean, I knew as soon as he left my house that day." Amber raised one eyebrow. With a swipe of berry lip gloss she looked flawless—not like she'd spent the last forty minutes playing a vicious game of badminton.

"Well, he wants to ask you this Friday," Kristen said. "Jen Klein's having people over."

"Friday? Two days from now?"

It felt too soon to have to make a decision. Saying yes to Patrick meant saying no to Ty, even if he hadn't officially asked me anything yet. I couldn't do that. I didn't want to.

"He's hoping you'll come . . ." Amber said. "And, to be honest, we are too. It's been like, a hundred years since you hung out on a weekend."

I'd been to those parties before. Weaving through the crush of sweaty, flailing bodies. Cigarette smoke and people spilling shit on you and feeling awkward because I was never wearing the right thing. I'd always admired how Amber could walk into a room and make anyone her friend, how she wasn't preoccupied by what people thought of her. Whenever someone complimented me I doubted it was genuine, and lately everywhere I went I felt skinless—overexposed.

"Come on, Millie loves parties," Kristen said, threading her arm through mine. Millie was Kristen's 1990 Volvo station wagon. She was pee-yellow, with ripped leather seats, but she was our portal to freedom.

"So are you in or what?" Amber finally asked, pulling on her backpack. "We'll get dressed up, arrive fashionably late. Make a big entrance. Maybe I'll steal some wine coolers from our basement fridge."

Even if I didn't like Patrick Kramer, and I didn't want to go to Spring Formal with him, there were other perfectly good reasons to go to Jen Klein's party. Tyler lived three houses down from her. It wouldn't take much for him to stop by, even for just a little bit.

"Hmmm . . ." I smirked. "What time do you wanna pick me up?"

"That's the Jess I know and love." Amber wrapped her arms around me and planted a sticky kiss on my cheek.

"We're going to a partaaaaaaay," Kristen said as we started out of the locker room. She did a spin, then a slide, but it all looked more Elaine-from-*Seinfeld* than Britney Spears.

Amber grabbed my hand and we both dipped down to one side, then back up. We'd been in dance class together when we were kids, and we still sometimes did bits of our old routines. She hopped forward, leading me, when something fell out of the bottom of her backpack. It skidded across the tile and under one of the wood benches.

"I got it," I said, kneeling.

The flat silver cartridge was just smaller than my hand, with shiny black glass on one side and metal on the other. I turned it over and pressed a button. Nothing happened.

"What's this?" I glanced up at Amber.

Suddenly it blinked on, and I caught a glimpse of something behind the glass. But then Amber grabbed the cartridge out of my hands and started fiddling with her backpack, where a mesh pocket had come undone.

She didn't respond until it was tucked away and everything was zipped shut. "What?" she said.

I stared at her. "That thing that fell out of your bag."

She adjusted the knapsack so it was in front of her, her arms wrapped around it like a fake belly. She was already a few steps ahead of me when she finally spoke.

"It's just . . ." Her words were slow and deliberate. "I found it in my dad's briefcase. I was going to ask Mr. Henriquez if he knows what it is."

"Mr. Henriquez? The Tech teacher?" I asked.

"I don't know," Amber shrugged. "It's just weird. My dad's had that job forever, and he barely says anything about it. I've never seen his office. He's never home for dinner. Then I find this."

I glanced sideways at Kristen, but she was staring at the floor. It seemed like they'd already discussed the weird contraption, whatever it was, but neither of them wanted to tell me anything. What did Amber think Mr. Henriquez was going to say? And what was she implying, exactly? That her dad was a spy? That he was having an affair?

"So you think . . ." I waited for the answer.

"I don't know what to think."

We pushed into the hall just as the bell rang. Amber waved to a few girls on the dance team. She was heading to History and I had Calc next, which meant we only had until the last set of gym doors before we went opposite ways.

"Can I see it?"

"Look, Jess, I really don't want to talk about this anymore," she said, heading down the stairs. "I gotta go. I'll meet you guys in the parking lot after school."

I looked to Kristen, hoping she'd explain what the hell just happened, but she was walking toward the science wing. Her flannel was tied around her waist, her books stacked in one arm as she waved at me over her shoulder.

"What was that about?" I called after her.

"You know Amber . . ." Kristen just shrugged.

Then she slipped into the AP Bio room, leaving me to replay the moment in the locker room over again, wondering why the two of them were being secretive about it. I tried to remember what the thing looked like. I'd seen that logo before, I knew I had, but on the school's computers. Behind the glass, this one had been sleek and silvery.

An apple with a bite out of it.

I could hear every word of "Not the Doctor" through Sara's bedroom door. After it became too difficult for her to go outside, she'd become obsessed with my CD collection. Tori Amos and the Indigo Girls, Jewel and Fiona Apple. We'd sit in her room listening to them, or sometimes I'd bring in my guitar and we'd have a sing-along. Lately it was Alanis Morissette. Just the week before I had to explain to her what it meant to "wine, dine, sixty-nine" someone.

I rested my head against the doorframe. She was sitting up in bed, the lyric book in her hand, memorizing the words to the song.

"Don't worry, I'm being super careful with them," she said, as she patted the CD case beside her. It was six inches thick. "I haven't even scratched one. Mint condition."

"I trust you."

"You sure you don't want to stay home tonight?" she

asked. "The new TGIF lineup is just riveting. I'm sure *Sabrina* can compete with Jen Klein's party."

"If anyone can, it's Sabrina."

Fuller, our terrier, was whining beside the bed. He was too arthritic to get up on his own, so I snuggled him to my chest and slid in beside her, letting him lick my chin.

When they first delivered the hospital bed, I'd hated it. It was too big for the room, and even though Sara was fourteen, she looked like a child inside it. But now I'd gotten used to tucking in next to her and watching TV, or just lying back and staring at the white Christmas lights we'd strung across the ceiling. Fuller would curl up with us and we'd rub his belly and count the spatter of gray spots across his chest.

"I would definitely rather do that. But I promised Amber and Kristen I'd go. Don't tell Mom it's a party . . . I said we're seeing *The Wedding Singer* again."

Tubes snaked underneath Sara's flannel pajamas, a metal clamp biting down on her finger. *Guignard's Disease.* When I'd heard those two words I didn't realize they'd hold so much power over us, that from then on we'd be consumed by tests and prescription bottles and whirring machines. It was a rare blood disease—so uncommon that only a few dozen cases had been documented. Sara was too weak to walk anymore, and the doctors recommended palliative care to keep her comfortable as the disease progressed. We never talked about what that phrase really meant, that the disease kept progressing, that Sara kept getting sicker. That there was no cure.

"You're going because *Tyler* will be there," Sara said, smiling.

I rolled my eyes. "Well, I did tell him about it. I'm hoping we can hang out without it being a big deal or whatever."

"It's still a big deal."

Amber and Kristen knew I liked Tyler, but Sara was the one who heard all the minutiae: how he'd poked me in the side when he walked past me in study hall, or how he had snuck into my lunch period just to say hi. We'd spent the other night analyzing our interaction in the storage closet, and what it all meant. *You definitely have that effect on me.*

Tyler was flirting, that was obvious. The question was how far he'd take it and if there was something real there. I'd heard a rumor he'd dated a girl from his camp over the summer, but he'd never mentioned it to me then or since, and Sara and I had interpreted that as its own sign. Maybe we weren't just friends.

"This would all be a lot easier if Mom wasn't watching my every move."

"You can't start sneaking out again."

"I'm not an idiot."

Last year, in an attempt to get around my curfew, I'd started sneaking out the door by the garage. I'd pretend I was just staying up late, watching TV, then I'd leave for an hour or two at a time. Kristen and Amber would pick me up one block over and sometimes we'd go to a party, but mostly Henrietta Park, where the upperclassmen hung out.

It all ended one night in May. I must've left the door

unlocked, because when I came home the whole first floor of our house had been burglarized. The television was gone, and so was our brand-new stereo system, along with my mother's engagement ring, which had been sitting in the soap dish next to the sink. The police had been there until five in the morning, taking notes and dusting for fingerprints, and as soon as they left, my mom broke into tears. I'd felt so guilty that I eventually confessed everything. After our neighbors heard about what happened, they hired a private alarm company to do regular rounds. Now you couldn't go anywhere without seeing one of the white and red SWICKLEY ALARMS cars driving by.

It didn't matter how many times I'd said I was sorry and promised it would never happen again. My mom's list of rules had grown, and there was always this unspoken suspicion between us. I could do the dishes every night and rake the leaves and wear the green corduroy skirt she had gotten me, telling her how much I loved it, but she'd never trust me again. Not really.

"The other night at dinner," I started. "Were you just annoyed at Mom? Why were you looking at Lydia like that?"

"Like what?"

"Like you were pissed about something."

I rubbed the back of Fuller's head, careful to avoid his right ear, where our neighbor's German shepherd had bitten him last week. Now two purple stitches kept the skin together.

"I wasn't mad . . ." She squinted like she couldn't quite see me, even though there were three different lights on.

36

"I guess I just didn't know what you were talking about the other day. You were serious about hearing that stuff?"

"Why wouldn't I be serious?" I asked. "You must've heard it too, right?"

"Yeah, I heard it." She was still looking at me like she didn't know who I was.

"So?"

She didn't say anything for a good thirty seconds, just tilted her head to the side and studied me. Then she shrugged. "I don't know?"

Sara had shone brightest when she was a kid, running around the house singing the opening of *Beauty and the Beast*, a dishrag tied around her head like she was some maiden from the French countryside. It was hard to watch her lately, how she always seemed frail, how thin she looked now that she'd lost the baby fat in her cheeks. Sometimes it seemed like she wasn't listening to what I said, like she was only half there.

Fuller lifted his nose and licked my cheek. It was almost seven thirty. Amber and Kristen were supposed to be here any minute. "Have you ever seen this thing, it's this silver and glass like . . . cartridge? This big . . . ?"

Sara watched me size it up with my hands. "I don't think so?"

"It fell out of Amber's backpack, and then she got all weird when I asked her about it. She's lying about it for some reason, and now Kristen won't tell me anything either. It's like they both know something I don't."

"I feel like it's always something with them."

It was true. At some point in the last few years Amber and Kristen had gotten closer, and I'd drifted further outside our three-person orbit, laughing along to jokes I didn't really understand. We still ate lunch together every day, and they still came over after school sometimes to see Sara and bring her Dunkin Donuts. But things were different. I'd thought about it dozens of times, trying to pinpoint how exactly it had happened, and when this space had ballooned between us. Was it because that middle-school awkwardness had clung to me so much longer, because I had to wait for my period, then my first kiss? Or was it after I got in trouble and started spending most weekends at home?

"It had an apple logo on it," I tried.

"I'm not sure," Sara said, but she was still giving me a strange look. "But I haven't left the house in a year, so I'm probably not the best person to ask . . ."

It seemed like she was about to say more, but then the door opened a crack. My mom pushed in with a tray balanced on her forearm. Sara called it the mush buffet, because she could only eat soft foods now, like mashed sweet potatoes and applesauce and vanilla pudding.

"Potato and leek soup," my mom said, maneuvering around the bed. She set the tray down on Sara's dresser, then adjusted her pillow in nearly the same way I'd done minutes earlier. She was studying the machines when I heard Millie outside. Kristen always gave two short, peppy beeps.

"That's my ride."

"What time is the movie?" my mom asked.

"Eight. I'll come home right after."

"The roads are still a little slippery, so make sure Kristen drives slowly. And call us if anything happens."

I rolled my eyes. "Nothing is going to happen."

"Things happen," my mom repeated. "Flat tires, car accidents. I still think we should get you a beeper."

"Why? So Kristen can beep me BOOBS?"

"What's BOOBS?" my mom asked.

Sara started laughing.

"80085," I said.

"Boobs? Huh?" My mom still didn't get it. "Just be careful."

I grabbed my denim jacket and headed for the door.

"What about some lip gloss?" my mom asked, like she was puzzled I hadn't thought of it myself. "A little mascara?"

"Mom, we're just going to the movies."

But she held up a finger to signal *one sec*, then started down the hall to her bedroom. She was always doing this. Attacking me with a mascara wand or a compact right before I left the house. It wasn't enough that I was wearing the red plaid skirt she'd bought me, or the hoop earrings she and my dad gave me for my Sweet Sixteen. She always adjusted the metal clips that held my bangs in place, or combed through my hair with her fingers, tousling it at the roots.

"Can you believe this?" I said, turning to Sara.

"Yup. It checks out."

My mom strode in with two silver lipstick tubes in her hand, and a neon-pink mascara wand. She compared each shade of lipstick against my complexion and then went with the darker, purplish color, dabbing it on my bottom lip.

"Okay, that's enough. Can I go now?" I asked.

"It just makes your features pop. A little goes a long way," she said. "Doesn't it, Sara?"

"Ummm . . . I guess?" Sara said.

My mom ignored me, twisting the mascara wand out of the tube and holding it up in front of my right eye, waiting for me to lean forward. I gave in, staring up at the ceiling fan until it was finally over.

"I'm really going now." I didn't wait for permission this time. I hugged Sara and kissed my mom on the cheek before slipping down the stairs.

"You look great," she called after me. "Love that color on you!"

I'd already opened the back door, about to slide in, when I realized shotgun was free. Kristen was the only one in the car.

"Where's Amber?"

"Grounded."

"Since when do her parents ground her?"

Kristen tugged on a curl, pulling it completely straight. It had been raining hard all afternoon, but now there was a break in the storm clouds. Only the occasional gust of water hit the windshield.

"Her dad found out she took that thing from his briefcase," Kristen said. "I guess it was some kind of prototype that was supposed to be top secret. A disk drive or something. You didn't say anything to anyone, did you?"

It didn't look like any drive I'd ever seen. I shook my head, even if it was (kind of) a lie. I hadn't gotten specific with Sara.

"You still want to go?" I asked. "You don't think it'll be weird?"

We'd never been to a party without Amber. She'd been class president for the last two years and knew everyone, moving easily between groups, chatting about an upcoming volleyball game or making jokes about Joey Plink's new haircut. One lunch period, a line had formed to talk to her. Maybe it was just three people, and maybe they were chatting with each other so it wasn't as obvious, but it was an actual line.

"I don't know, I guess I figure why not?" Kristen looked in the rearview mirror. "Creeper Alert: your mom is still watching us."

Kristen came to a complete stop at the stop sign on the corner, lingering there for a full five seconds longer than normal. When I turned back I spotted my mom's silhouette in the upstairs window. She'd always been overprotective, but since Sara's illness her anxiety had gotten worse, and after the burglary there was this whole other layer of paranoia. If I was a minute late for my ten thirty curfew she began calling my friends' houses, waking their parents. Lately I practiced driving in the Home Depot parking lot only once a month, sneaking off with my dad because she insisted I wasn't ready to take my license test, that I wouldn't have a car while I still lived at home.

As Sara's world got smaller, mine had too, the edges of it shrinking first to our town, and now to certain streets and certain places. Henrietta Park was too dangerous once the sun went down, or so my mom said, but my friends and I still went there to eat our Taco Bell drive-thru. I wasn't supposed to get into a car with anyone who was drunk (obvious) or anyone who wasn't Kristen or a parent (less obvious), and since the break-in I had to report to my parents' room, in my pajamas, every night before bed, just to confirm that I was in fact home. She'd even put a set of Christmas bells on the outside of my doorknob so she'd wake up if I snuck out. Maybe I'd deserved it, but still. While every other junior was driving into the city or breaking curfew at Maple Cove, I was waiting on AOL for someone, anyone, to appear on my buddy list.

"You're the only friend she'll let me drive with," I said.

"Well I *am* known for my rigorous safety standards." Kristin, accelerated over a speed bump. Millie caught air and I grabbed onto the handle above the door, laughing.

"That was messed up."

We passed the mall, the Weezer CD skipping as we took another bump at full speed. The parking lot was empty. We only saw one other car on the road, a lone Ford Taurus with a busted front headlight. Part of me wondered if it was the flu going around our small town, but it was hard to know for sure. The streets of Swickley were always desolate at night, as if everyone had an early bedtime. *It's not totally dead*, Amber would say. *You just have to know where to go.*

"It just doesn't make any sense," I said. "She was being so secretive about that stupid thing, and it's like . . . why? Who cares?"

"I'm just telling you what Amber told me, and her parents have been fighting lately and . . . I don't know. Maybe there's something else going on. Don't get all bent out of shape about it." Kristen shrugged.

"I'm not all bent out of shape about it. Why do you always take her side?"

"Why do you always think I'm taking her side? Maybe there aren't any sides," she said. "Ugh, you made me miss my turn!"

She hooked a right at the 7-Eleven, its windows dark, a CLOSED sign on the front door. Then we looped around the block so we could go back to the light. We drove the rest of the way in silence. When we got to Jen's house we parked down the street so the party wouldn't be as obvious, but a few kids were already outside, staggering up the lawn.

"Is that Chris Arnold?" Kristen squinted out the windshield, trying to change the subject. "He's wasted."

It was Chris Arnold, and he was wasted. He'd always been much taller and bigger than the other guys in our grade, but he looked almost comical now, as one of his friends helped him walk. His legs came up to the guy's chest.

In the quiet of the car it all seemed so stupid. Ty hadn't said he was definitely coming, and now that Amber was out, why were we even here? I'd tried every drink there was—beer, wine, shots, cocktails with weird names like Sex in the Driveway and the Sassafras Slinger—but I'd never once gotten drunk. While everyone else was hooking up in closets or playing beer pong I was usually planted on the couch, petting the cat. I might've said as much, but Kristen was already out of the car.

I could feel her staring at me through the driver's side window, waiting. Eventually she tapped on the glass. I looked over and her nose was pressed against it so I could see up her nostrils. Her eyes were wild, like she was a pig monster from the woods, ready to gobble me up.

"You're a psycho," I said, but it was what got me out of the car. We were both laughing as we walked toward the house.

There was no sign of Tyler. I kept watching the kitchen door like I could will him into appearing, but a half hour passed and nothing. The party was small, only twenty or so people, and mostly other juniors that I knew. Kristen and I stood in the narrow space between the island and the stove. I'd been drinking some pink concoction for the past hour, but I didn't feel anything. I couldn't even taste the liquor in it.

"And then the guy was all: what's the secret password. He literally said that, '*secret password*'." Kim Kennedy leaned over the counter and tipped the fake ID back and forth in the light, showing us the hologram. She'd bought it in December, when her parents took her to New York City to see the Rockettes. "He wouldn't let me into the back room until I told him."

"So what was it?" a sophomore with a mushroom cut asked.

Kim paused dramatically. "New England Clam Chowder."

"New England Clam Chowder," Mushroom Cut repeat-ed. "From *Ace Ventura*? You're lying."

"Why would I lie about that?" Then, before anyone could question her, Kim snatched the ID and tucked it back in her wallet. The music changed, and that cheesy Savage Garden song came on. Z100 was playing it every hour.

"Hey, I wanted to see," a familiar voice said.

The group was suddenly quiet, and it wasn't until I turned that I realized Patrick Kramer was standing right behind me. He was in his iconic red and black North Face fleece, his hands pushed deep into its pockets. Okay, he was good looking—like Joey Lawrence if he was taller and had darker hair. I knew why Kristen and Amber wanted me to want him, but everything about him was just so . . . blah.

Kim passed the ID to him and he inspected it, looking at her, then to the photo, like he was some bouncer at a club.

"Decent," he finally said.

"I haven't had any problems."

Patrick smiled, but no one else said anything. He was usually trailed by at least three guys from the varsity soc-cer team. When they moved in a pack it was impossible to approach them, and we didn't know what to do with him now that he was alone. He kept glancing around the room, then pressing his lips together, like he was waiting on line in a bank.

Kim said something to Kristen, and then everyone broke off into side conversations. I tried to maneuver myself closer to Kristen but she inched away, separating me and Patrick from the group.

"You don't come out much," he finally said.

I probably should've made up something that sounded mysterious or cool, but it was Patrick Kramer. It didn't feel worth it.

"I was grounded for six months. Now it's been down-graded to close surveillance," I said. "After my house was broken into? You probably heard?"

"Oh, right. You're over in the flower streets, Honeysuckle Court, Rose Lane. That's why those Swickley Alarm cars are everywhere."

"I don't feel like I missed out on much. I mean, this isn't really my scene . . ."

I swirled the pink concoction around my cup.

"So what is your scene?" Patrick moved closer, dipping down so we were eye level. I had a jolt of nervousness, like I was taking a test I hadn't prepared for. Kristen was right . . . Patrick Kramer was flirting with me.

"I kind of like the Wolf Den, that place on Main Street where they have live music twice a week." My voice got all weird and pitchy. "It's sixteen and over now to get in."

Patrick leaned against the wall and stared off, like I'd just said something incredibly profound. I was 99 percent sure he'd never been to the Wolf Den, but even if I was right, he didn't ask about it.

"Yeah, I don't think this is my scene either. It can be hard to relate. Everyone's getting high, or talking about stupid meaningless stuff, like the yearbook superlatives. I feel really separate sometimes, like I'm watching a movie of it all, that it's all happening in front of me but I'm not part of it. Especially after last year."

He didn't look at me as he said it, and I knew that was my cue. We were supposed to have some deep conversation about what happened that day at the Empire State Building. *You're a hero*, I'd say, resting my hand on his chest. *Tell me what it's like.*

"I have to uh . . . go to the bathroom . . ." I slipped past him, immediately wishing I'd found a better excuse, that I'd said anything but that. I just wanted to get rid of him, not make it seem like I had explosive diarrhea.

A few guys from the basketball team were playing quarters on the kitchen table. It was unclear where the bathroom was, so I wandered through the first floor for a minute, finally trying a door off the living room. It was locked.

"There's another one upstairs," Neel Nair, a hot senior from my Spanish elective, said as he passed. His breath smelled like bong smoke.

Jen Klein didn't seem to care that her friends had started a dance party in the living room. She messed with the stereo, switching on "Baby Got Back." It was cliché and obvious but everyone was just drunk enough to love it, doing this silly stomping dance. Chris Arnold slammed into the wall as I went up the stairs.

The bathroom linked Jen's bedroom with her older sister's—the kind I'd only seen on *90210*, where Brandon and Brenda Walsh ran into each other brushing their teeth. I closed the door behind me and locked it, enjoying the quiet comfort of being alone. I could've stayed in there for hours, reading the stack of *YM* magazines next to the sink, or just lying on the furry bathmat and listening to music. At home the bathroom felt like the only place I could relax. Maybe it was how good the acoustics were when I sang, or maybe it was that no one bothered me when I was taking a bath or drying my hair, but those private spaces always calmed me.

I smoothed on my lip gloss, careful to blend it to the corners, taking my time. I had this horrible feeling Patrick would be waiting for me right where I'd left him, and Kristen had no interest in helping me dodge the Spring Formal invite.

Then someone was at the door, two quick knocks echoing in the bathroom. At first I worried it was Patrick, so I ignored it, but then I got paranoid people were waiting outside and they'd think I was doing something weird. When I peeked out there was only one person there. He inspected the CD tower by Jen's bed, running a hand through his mop of red hair. Tyler.

I just stood there, unable to speak.

"Jess! It's you . . ."

"It's me."

Then he smiled that smile, and everything switched on inside me. I was suddenly hyperaware of the strip of exposed skin by my waist, where my sweater cropped up, or the spot where my hoop earring brushed against my neck. I wanted to go back into the bathroom and reapply my lip gloss and pinch color into my cheeks.

"Who knew Jen Klein was obsessed with Chumba-wamba?" His finger rested on some CD spines in the middle of the stack. "I didn't even realize they had other bad songs."

"I actually wouldn't mind that stupid song if it wasn't so lazy," I said, stepping toward him. "Have you ever listened to the lyrics? It's the same two verses over and over again. He says the same line three dozen times."

"But also, what is the guy in the song even doing?" Ty was still smiling as he said it. "He drinks four drinks in a row, all different. Like, I'm no bartender dude, but I'm pretty sure mixing a whiskey drink and a vodka drink and a lager drink, then chasing it down with hard cider, is not going to be good."

Did I love him? Was it possible to love someone you'd never even kissed?

"You hiding out in there?" Ty asked, glancing over my shoulder into the bathroom. He had on this green flannel that he was obsessed with and a vintage Tears for Fears tee shirt underneath, the fabric faded from so many wears.

"Maybe. Don't tell anyone."

"You kept my secret about that weird cat statue."

"The statue! I forgot about that." I laughed.

"That's how good you are at keeping secrets."

When I was younger, my mom bought this abstract cat statue and displayed it on a pedestal in our den. Ty and I were rolling around inside a refrigerator box, pretending it was a carnival ride, when we slammed right into it, knocking it to the floor. I put the head back on with Crazy Glue. You could only tell it was broken if you held it an inch from your face.

"What is that?" he asked, peering at the pink stuff in my cup.

"Some weird lemonade drink. Wanna try?"

"With that rave review?"

Ty stepped closer. That one small movement sent me spinning, and even though I could still hear the music from the party, we were suddenly in another universe, one all our own. I'd spent so much time wondering what it meant that Ty always stopped by my locker on his way to gym, or that he'd volunteered to play drums for me last month in the talent show. Did he feel anything when he threw his arm over my shoulder as we walked down the hall, or was it just another version of the hundreds of other hugs he'd given me over the years? He answered me now with this smile, with the way he let the silence linger between us.

"You look . . . nice."

"Nice?"

"Pretty."

And then he shrugged this tiny, awkward shrug, like he couldn't help himself—like he'd had to say it. I laughed, because it seemed like the only thing to do, but then he leaned in closer. His lips touched down on mine and he kissed me slowly, carefully, like he was just learning how. His hand wandered to my hair, his fingers getting tangled inside it. His breath warmed my skin. As we kissed, my hands found their way to his back, and I tried to pull him closer, but no matter how close we were, it wasn't enough.

At some point the overhead light flicked on. Jen Klein stood in the doorway, a Zima in her hand. Her eyes were bulging out of her face—the melodramatic, drunk version of someone in shock.

"You guys aren't supposed to be in here," she said, stepping forward. She shooed us away like dogs. "Come on, get out of here. Get out."

Tyler and I ducked around her, bursting into laughter as we ran down the stairs. She yelled something else that I couldn't quite hear. His hand found mine and squeezed tight.

I could have survived on that memory for years. I kept reliving it over and again in my mind, slowing it down to savor the tiniest details. There was the moment Tyler stepped toward me, and that question: *Nice? Pretty.* I rewrote the dialogue so I was sharper, funnier. Every version started and ended just as it had on Friday night, but they were each special in their own way, and I never got tired of any of them.

"You're doing it again," Sara said. "That smiley, staring off into space thing."

"Sorry." I pressed the picture of Fuller against her wall. I'd taken it a few weeks ago—it was the closest he'd ever come to being photogenic. "Here? Or lower?"

"That's great." She was sitting up in bed, watching me cut and tape and organize.

"I'm just distracted. Tyler hasn't been online all weekend."

When we rejoined the party on Friday, Kristen already

had her jacket on and was ushering me out the door, muttering something about curfews and Kim trying to be a club kid instead of accepting that she wasn't any cooler than the rest of us. Tyler and I still hadn't had a chance to establish what we were now. After that kiss, after his hands were in my hair, after it was so clear we were more than just friends.

"Well, he obviously likes you," Sara said. "Why would he kiss you if he didn't like you?"

"But why would you avoid someone you like?" I asked, rolling a piece of tape onto the back of the photo. I made sure it was straight before I smoothed it on the bottom-right corner of Sara's collage.

"There's no way he's avoiding you." She squinted at the wall. "How do you want to put the dried flowers up?"

I stepped back to assess my work. Sara had spent all of seventh grade hanging up different postcards and mementos, magazine spreads and polaroid pictures. Raffle tickets from the Swickley carnival and a hand-drawn playbill for *Annie*, her elementary school play. There was a whole collage of disposable camera photos—her and her friends at a Valentine's Day party and a pretty one of Sara in her black-and-white recital outfit. My favorite was a particularly silly photo-booth strip she and I had taken two years ago, before she'd gotten really sick. In one picture she was sticking out her tongue and in the next she was pressing it to my cheek.

"I'll tape the stems," I said, and tucked the ends of the dried roses underneath a *Bop* collage of Devon Sawa and Andrew Keegan. Fuller was sprawled out on the floor beside me, twitching and huffing in sleep.

"He's always been in love with you," Sara said.

"I don't know about that . . ."

"Oh please! He's always looked at you with those googly love eyes."

"Googly love eyes?"

Sara leaned forward, her gaze unfocused and just the slightest bit cross-eyed. She smiled so wide it looked like she was wearing a rubber mask. I took a step to the right, then the left, but everywhere I went she kept staring at me.

"That's really creepy. Stop."

She laughed, then sat back in bed. "I'm just saying. If you really want to be with Ty, I think you'll be with Ty."

"But how do you know?"

"I just have a feeling."

"So you're psychic now?"

"Maybe." She closed her eyes, pretending to be in a trance. "I see homemade chocolate chip cookies in my future. I see them on a tray with milk."

"It's almost ten o'clock. I am not baking you cookies." I laughed. But I was already considering it, weighing how much time it would take, if we had any chocolate chips. Lately it felt like there wasn't anything Sara couldn't get me to do.

"It was worth a try."

I stepped back and felt something underneath my bare foot. I knew what it was before I even looked. Sara was obsessed with Lisa Frank, and it was maddening how those stickers turned up everywhere. I'd find them in the medicine cabinet, underneath plates, and clinging to Fuller's butt. I'd once cut a neon dolphin out of his fur.

"Seriously?" I raised my eyebrows as I peeled the rainbow unicorn off my heel.

"I've gotten better," she said. "I've been trying to keep them all in that sticker book you got me."

I smiled so she would know I wasn't genuinely mad. But when I moved to throw it away she yelped.

"Just give it to me, I'll put it in here," she said.

She grabbed one of the books off her nightstand. Sara read more than anyone I knew, including Miss Thomas, our Swickley High librarian. After she'd blown through all the Baby Sitters Club books and everything Christopher Pike, she'd moved on to adult books like *The God of Small Things* and *Tuesdays with Morrie* (which she said was horribly cheesy). She'd even had our mom's friend from London send her an advance copy of something called Harry Potter, which had only been published in England. As she pressed the unicorn onto a back page, I studied the cover.

"The Philosopher's Stone?" I asked. "Isn't this a little young for you?"

Sara paused, holding the sticker book in the air. She squinted at me, like she was confused, but then the expression passed. "It's really great. I have a feeling it's going to be huge. There are supposed to be seven."

"You have a feeling about a lot of things," I said.

Sara tilted her head to one side as she smoothed the sticker back into the book. Then she pointed to a picture of us that our dad had taken when we were kids. We were rolling around in the grass, our eyes squeezed shut as we laughed. It was tucked beside the carnival tickets.

"Do you remember the park we went to that time? It was near the old library, before it closed."

"Kind of?"

I wasn't even sure that's where the photo was taken, but I vaguely recalled a huge park we went to once as kids. We'd raced to the end of the tree line, to where the grass met the woods.

"It had that garden. There was that fairy statue in the middle of it."

It felt so far away, but I could almost see it—the stone fairy with her wings tucked behind her back. I'd wandered off. There had been something strange about the trees there, but I couldn't remember what. Our parents had called for me and I felt like I'd done something bad, that I was about to get in trouble. Had I?

"What made you think of that?" I asked, adding a few cards to the top of the collage. One of Sara's friends from music camp had sent her a postcard that said MULLETS ROCK.

"I don't know." Sara fiddled with her blanket, smoothing it down over her legs.

There was a strange, persistent silence. I expected her to say something else, to elaborate, but she didn't. We'd been having moments like this more regularly lately. Awkward pauses and her saying something I couldn't decipher, then not following up with an explanation. Part of me wondered if it was a sign her disease was progressing, or one of the consequences of her being at home alone all day, with no one to talk to but Lydia.

"Okay, out with it," I said.

"Nothing, what?"

"Nothing? That's your response?"

Another long silence, then she started picking off her nail polish, as if I might forget what we'd been talking about.

"You're being really weird," I said.

"I'm not."

I rolled my eyes at her, but she was still chipping away at the polish, pastel-green flakes now scattered over the blanket. I went to the end of the bed and tried to see the wall the way she saw it. The pieces we'd added spread out above her dresser, but there was still so much blank space by the door.

"We have to find more things to add," I said.

"When it gets warmer, maybe we can go out and take more pictures," Sara said, finally looking up. She pointed to the space. "That whole area needs something. It's starting to feel lopsided."

We kept putting things off for when Sara felt better, for when things improved. We'd have a picnic in the backyard and we had to go to the mall so she could finally get her ears pierced. There were still so many memories to be made. There were pictures that needed to be taken and printed and hung up.

"I think we might have some chocolate chips left," I said, turning to her.

"For the cookies?" She smiled, and the dimple appeared in her right cheek.

"For the cookies," I repeated, then squeezed her feet under the blanket. "Just give me a minute to check."

Monday, last period. There was only one minute left and Tyler was next door, in American History, a single wall separating us. If the timing worked out right we'd run into each other after class, but that meant something different now. We'd only spoken for a few minutes in band, and he hadn't stopped by my locker the entire day. When we passed each other after third period, he just waved.

A wave.

Like I was some sophomore hall monitor.

It was possible he'd heard about Patrick Kramer. People had seen us talking at Jen's party, and if Amber and Kristen knew the rumor about the Spring Formal invite, it may have gotten back to Ty, too. Maybe I should've just told him I liked him, declared it in some formal way. But wasn't making out with him enough? How could he possibly think I'd have any interest in Patrick Kramer?

When the bell rang I grabbed my Discman from my

backpack and put on Ani DiFranco, blasting it so loud it overpowered every thought. "Untouchable Face" hit the chorus just as I passed the cafeteria. Half the school was still out sick, and the halls felt so much lonelier than they normally did. I was right by the water fountain when I felt a tap on my shoulder. Tyler had caught up to me. I could only vaguely understand what he was saying, his lips mouthing each word as I tugged off my headphones.

"What'd you say?"

"I just said . . . wait up. Actually I said it like"—he raised his eyebrows and kind of yelled it—"Jess, wait up!"

Then he smiled.

Like that, we were back there, and I could feel him nuzzling into my neck, and I remembered how his hands had cupped my chin, his thumbs against my cheekbones. He had smiled while we kissed, and it had made it so much better but so much harder to actually kiss.

"Did you want a ride home? I know Kristen usually takes you or whatever, but I thought maybe . . ." Tyler nodded to the junior parking lot behind us. He always drove to school, even though his neighborhood was just a two-minute walk through the trees behind the north gym. My mom would lose it if she saw me in his ancient Chevy Blazer, with the huge dent in the side.

"Kristen has a Spanish Honor Society meeting, so I was going to take the bus. You're sure it's not out of your way?"

He laughed. "It's definitely out of my way, but I knew that."

I was smiling so much it was hard to look at him.

"Okay, perfect."

Except for the part about my mom, and not wanting to die in a rollover accident, but I wasn't going to mention that.

"Want me to carry those?"

He nodded to my textbooks, which I'd tucked under one arm. Maybe it was stupid, but it felt like a sign. Carrying your books was a very boyfriend thing to do. Wasn't there so much more to that question?

"You sure?"

"Don't let them tell you chivalry's dead."

"Who?"

"I don't know, the same people who say 'great minds think alike' or 'follow your heart.' They're saying things all the time."

"Oh, I know them. They also said 'nothing in life is free' and 'love is blind.'"

"Love is definitely not blind. They were wrong about that," Ty said, and for the first time I noticed it—the googly love eyes. He was staring at me like he could see through my clothes.

I passed the books to him and he hugged them to his chest.

We took a detour on the way home, stopping at Maple Cove, which Tyler loved almost as much as I did. It was still too cold to sit on the sand, so we stretched out on a warped picnic table, our shoulders pressed together. We stared up at the sky, watching a flock of birds change direction overhead. Our breath appeared and disappeared in front of us.

"But really," I said, "how many sweater vests do you think Ian Grand owns? If you open up his closet, are there just stacks and stacks of them?"

"It's like he decided that was his style. Forget JNCOs, forget Sambas: sweater vests."

"Sara went through a sweater vest phase," I said. "Right after she saw *Clueless*."

"Yeah, a little different . . ." Tyler tipped his head to the side so he could see my face. "How is she doing?"

"Do you want the real answer or the fake answer?"

"Both."

"The fake answer is: she's good, her spirits are up, and the doctors say she's stable." The back of my throat was tight, and I wanted to believe it. It sounded so much better than the truth. "The real answer is that it feels like we're all on this train we can't get off of. And we can see that there's another train up ahead and we're going to crash into it if we don't do something, if something doesn't change. But we can't switch tracks and we don't have control of the steering, and so we're all just bracing for it. I keep wishing I could just slow everything down, like maybe if I had enough time they'd figure out a cure, or there'd be some medicine that really helped her. Maybe there'd be another way."

I pressed my hands deep into my pockets, working an old

candy wrapper into a ball. I felt like someone was choking me. My throat was still tight, and the heat rose behind my eyes, a wash of tears blurring my vision. I started counting. I counted seven birds cutting across the clouds. I counted the three picnic tables on the beach, one lifeguard stand, and five trash cans. I only stopped when the back of my throat released and I felt further away from it, from anything that could hurt me.

I'd gotten so good at Not Crying. I could compete in the Not Crying Olympics. I could give lectures on the cause. When Sara had gotten sick I couldn't let her see me cry, so I started counting. In the doctor's office, at the hospital, in her bedroom. When the sadness threatened to overtake me I'd count the chairs lining the wall, the overhead lights. I once counted sixty-two slats in a set of vertical blinds.

"Even if my mom would let me go away to college, which is doubtful, I'm not going to leave Sara," I said. "I just can't be away from home right now."

His head was still turned to the side, but I didn't want to look at him. Not yet. I counted the freckles on the back of my hand—six—until I felt steady and sure.

"I know I told everyone I was going to UCLA," I said. "California, the absolute farthest point from New York, from Swickley. Palm trees and endless sunshine and whatever. It just all seems a little silly now."

"It's not silly. We wouldn't have electricity or movies or museums filled with great art if people didn't dream. Like, where would we be if Matisse thought dreaming was silly?"

He propped his head on his hand and then I had to face him. A tiny leaf was stuck in his hair but it looked so cute that I couldn't bring myself to brush it away.

"Where are you going to apply next year?" I asked.

"There aren't a ton of schools with music programs, or not the kind I'd want to go to. New School in the city, Miami, Berklee, LA College of Music. I don't know, we'll see."

The thought of going away, of getting out of our small town for years at a time . . . it didn't seem possible. I'd heard the whispered conversations behind my parents' bedroom door. My mom had grown her business to twice the size it had been just a year before, but it still wasn't enough to keep up with a barrage of medical bills. I'd found six different credit cards in her desk drawer, all too maxed out to actually use.

"Why California?" he asked me.

"Because of *Unsolved Mysteries*."

Tyler's brows drew together. "*Unsolved Mysteries*? The TV show?"

"Come on, it's a great show," Then I dipped my voice a few octaves, putting on my best Robert Stack impression: "*Join me . . . you may be able to help solve a mystery.*"

"Okay, now I'm really confused."

"I just saw this segment—no murder or anything—about this couple who was running scams there. That's not actually the point. The point is that they lived on the beach and it had all these palm trees and this cool lifeguard house, and it just . . . it felt like a place I needed to be. I mean, I've never even seen the ocean. Part of me has always wondered what it would be like to live right next to it."

I didn't mention the other, unspoken dream that was tangled up in that. Being on stage, just myself and a guitar, the audience barely visible beyond the spotlights. I'd heard about the clubs in Los Angeles—the Viper Room, Largo, the Troubadour. Maybe I wasn't ready to play there yet, but I could be in the next few years, if I was ever able to get the money together to go.

"You seem happy here, though," he said. "Like there are definitely kids at school who have it really rough, but you have Amber and Kristen, and everyone just really likes you. But not in that obnoxious, popular-girl way."

"There are worse places, yeah. But I can't help feeling trapped, like there's so much more than this. I mean, this town is, like, five square miles. The place is totally dead at night. And I can't even remember the last time I left. It's a big deal when I go to the Blockbuster on the other side of Main Street."

Tyler lay back on the table, moving closer to me. He inched his hand toward mine until the backs of them were touching, and then I let my fingers curl around his, enjoying how good it felt to be close again.

"Big things can happen in small towns," Tyler said, squeezing my hand. "Even places like Swickley."

"Oh yeah? What kind of things?"

"I don't know. People make art, music. People fall in love."

The words sat there, between us. All the blood rushed into my cheeks, and my chest felt so full, I thought I might float into the sky. Maybe there was still something for me here.

"We should watch *Unsolved Mysteries* together some-time," I said, fighting back a smile.

"I am always down to watch *Unsolved Mysteries* with you."

He leaned into me and I leaned into him.

Then we were kissing again.

10

When we pulled into the driveway, my dad's work van was the only car there. FLYNN PEST CONTROL, it said in big letters on the side. LICENSED TO KILL. LITERALLY. There was a picture of my dad wielding his backpack sprayer. Lydia must've left early, because her Corolla wasn't parked on the street like it normally was. It would be another hour until my mom got home.

Tyler was still holding my hand. He hadn't let go of it the entire ride home. "What if we just stay here?" he asked, staring up at the house. The sky had gone dark, the moon just visible above the trees, a spattering of stars beyond it.

"In the driveway?" I laughed.

"In this car. We could order pizza, tip the seats back, and sleep. Skip school tomorrow and listen to every CD in my glove compartment. Get Chinese food and have my little brother drop off some clothes. We'd only go inside to use the bathroom and the phone."

"My parents would not like that."

"We'll sneak through the back door."

"Start homeschooling each other," I said with a smirk. "Drink rainwater. Give our college applications to the mailman."

"Come on, don't leave," he said when I finally reached for the door.

"I'll see you tomorrow, promise." I kissed him before jumping down from the Blazer. I waited at my front door, watching as he pulled out the driveway and up the block. My cheeks were sore from smiling so much.

Fuller didn't greet me the way he normally did, his tiny butt wiggling like crazy. The house was quiet. I glanced up the stairs and noticed Sara's door was open, but her room was dark. She wasn't blasting her stereo. The television was off.

"Dad?" I started into the kitchen. The light above the stove cast ominous shadows. He was at our table, his chin resting on his hands. If we were religious I would've thought he was praying, but as soon as he turned toward me I saw that his face was flushed, his eyes red and watery.

"What's wrong? What happened?"

"Lydia couldn't wake Sara up. We had to call an ambulance." He was already wearing his jacket. His boots were on and the car keys were already on the table. Before I could ask anything he grabbed them, wrapping one arm around me as he ushered us to the door. "We have to meet your mom at the hospital."

I barely had time to put my backpack down.

~~~~~~

"I don't understand," I said. "She was fine this morning. It seemed like she was having a good day. A really good day."

My mom was sitting on the edge of the bed so I stood awkwardly beside it, not sure where to put my hands. I didn't want to think too much about the private room we were in, with its windows looking into the woods, or the armchair that folded down into a cot. They'd never given us one that was so nice, and I didn't want that—I didn't want to settle in. Sara was supposed to be going home soon.

"They think it's pneumonia." My mom was looking past me, her eyes unfocused.

"But she didn't seem sick this morning."

"It came on quick," Lydia said, and leaned forward in the armchair, her elbows on her knees. "She was exhausted so I let her rest. I just let her rest and then she wouldn't wake up."

Sara's skin was pale and damp, long strands of hair sticking to her face and neck. My dad paced back and forth, watching her as though she might wake up at any moment and explain things to him.

"I'm going to find the doctor," he finally said.

Sara's nose and mouth were covered by a plastic face mask, the machines whirring beside her. My instinct was to do what I always did at home—adjust her bed, her pillow. Get a few snacks from the kitchen so she never had to ask for them. But now, here, there was no way to help.

We'd come close before, but this wasn't supposed to be it. It couldn't be. She still had time, probably years, they'd said, and we had made plans. We hadn't been on a boat together since we were kids, and her doctor said she could go when it got warmer. She'd use a wheelchair but they said we could take her out on the lake. We wanted to write songs together, me on the guitar and her singing, the lyrics pulled from her poetry. We were supposed to have a John Hughes marathon next week.

I folded the thin blue blanket up from her feet, letting it cover her waist. There was no room for me in her bed, so I curled up on the floor beside the armchair.

11

Sara and I had agreed: Claudia Kishi was the coolest babysitter in the Baby-Sitters Club. It wasn't just that she had great style, with feather earrings, a snake bracelet, and suspenders that held up purple pants. She had all the things we wanted: Unrealized artistic talent that was certain to be realized at some point in the future, in some remarkable way. A best friend from Manhattan. Junk food hidden in desk drawers and shoeboxes. A prime spot in a love triangle. Her own phone line.

Long after Mary Anne, Dawn, and the others had faded in our memories, Claudia was the one who stayed with us, informing our decisions. Long after the series had been packed in boxes and deposited in the attic, she was the reason we'd bought the hollowed-out book from the Blackwell's garage sale and then stuffed it with Charms lollipops. We'd hidden Warheads in my blue plastic piggy bank, and Big League Chew in the back of our pillowcases. The first thing I did that night, when I came home from the hospital, was dig a Baby Ruth bar out of the inside of my patent-leather umbrella and eat it in bed.

I'd been the last one to talk to my sister that morning. I'd said goodbye to her after my parents left for work and before Lydia arrived, checking if she needed me to pop in a video or bring her something. I'd been so nervous about seeing Tyler and what that would or wouldn't mean that I must not have realized something was wrong. There was no way she'd go from talking, laughing even, to not being able to speak or open her eyes. What had I missed?

I didn't want to move, but I couldn't stop thinking of Sara in that room, being prodded with needles. When I closed my eyes, I saw her in the hospital bed. It wasn't until after nine, when I was desperate for a distraction, that I finally went downstairs in search of real food.

A frenetic, rambling voice drifted into the kitchen, and I knew my dad was medicating the way he always did, by watching baseball. He was so obsessed with the Red Sox I could identify the different announcers without looking at the screen. My mom had stayed with Sara, and the house suddenly felt huge with just us there.

The top shelf of the fridge was packed with medications. I couldn't pronounce any of the names. There were amber pill bottles and large saline bags that Lydia hooked up to Sara's IV. Vitamins and creams. I grabbed supplies to make a turkey sandwich. I peeled a few pieces of meat from the stack and folded them on the bread, then took some of the extra, smaller pieces for Fuller.

"Fuller, I've got turkey for you," I called, as if he'd understand. He was usually right there as soon as I opened the fridge door.

He didn't come. Actually, he hadn't greeted me after school either, and not after we'd gotten back from the hospital. No one had even mentioned letting him out or walking him since we'd gotten home. His bowl was still full of kibble.

I went to the top of the den stairs. "Dad, are the Kowalskis watching Fuller?" It took my dad a few seconds to register I was talking.

"Fuller? No, he's here somewhere. Did you check the usual places?"

"Not yet . . ."

"Maybe upstairs?"

He looked at me, then back at the TV.

I went upstairs, assuming he was just waiting for Sara to come home, but when I flicked on her light his crate was empty. He wasn't curled up under the bed. Then I checked and double-checked my room. Sometimes he liked the chaise by my parents' dresser, but he wasn't there either.

"He's not here," I said, returning to the den. My heart was pounding now, and I could feel my voice getting thin with nerves. "I can't find him anywhere."

My dad got up, but he was still watching the TV until he reached the stairs. His eyes flicked over the obvious places, the kibble bowl and the back door, where Fuller sometimes waited, whining at the glass to come in. Then he went into the living room and knelt on the floor.

"Bingo," he said. "He's probably just scared. It was a long day for all of us."

Sure enough, Fuller was curled into a tight ball under the back corner of the couch. His eyes were open but he didn't move, even when he saw me. My dad kissed me on the head and went back to the den.

"Fuller, it's okay," I tried. "I have a treat for you in the kitchen. Come here."

Treat was one of the few words that Fuller understood, but he didn't perk up when I said it. I inched closer until I could just barely reach him. He hated being dragged anywhere or being forced to do anything, but it was just too depressing— the thought that Fuller was depressed. I needed him.

As soon as I touched his front leg he let out a low growl, his whole body trembling with it. "It's okay, buddy," I reassured him. I tucked a hand under each of his front legs and tried to slide him out. He squirmed and growled some more.

"What's wrong?" I asked. "You're shaking. Are you sick?"

His nails scratched at the wood floor, his paws working furiously to keep him in place. I slid him just an inch farther and he bit down hard on my hand. It was so startling I pulled back, and he darted straight across the living room and under the dining table.

I looked at my hand, stunned. He'd gotten the fleshy bit around my thumb and it was already bleeding, the skin broken in two different places. I yanked a tissue from the box on the coffee table and wrapped it around the wound before going back to him.

"Bad," I said in my sternest voice. "Bad Fuller."

He sunk in on himself, both of his paws splayed out in front of him. When I knelt down, reprimanding him again, he flipped onto his back in submission. He knew he'd done something really horrible.

That's when I noticed his chest. Instead of seven small, speckled grey spots, there was only one. His ears were different too. The skin on the right one was perfect—the two stitches were gone and there was no scar. How was that possible?

I leaned back against the wall, trying to steady myself. I don't know how long I stayed there, silent, the world continuing on around me.

That wasn't my dog.

12

"Dad . . . something is really wrong."

I stood at the top of the den stairs, watching the light from the television flicker across his face. He didn't register me. Instead he leaned in and raised his fists, tracking something in the game.

"Yes, yes," he muttered. "Go, go, yes!"

He jabbed the air. Cheers filled the room. The announcer said something about it being a tied game, and the Red Sox having a good night.

"Did you need something, Jess?" he said, finally noticing me there. He lowered the volume with the remote so he could hear better.

"That dog . . . it isn't Fuller. He doesn't have the spots on his stomach and he hates me, he bit my hand." It didn't feel like enough somehow, so I added, "The scar on his ear is gone."

My dad rubbed his temple, as if a sudden migraine was coming on.

"You're sure?" he finally said.

"Am I sure? Yeah, I'm sure," I said. "I know my dog."

"That's um . . ." He stared at the floor, like the answer might be printed on the carpet. "That's really odd. I don't know what to tell you."

I thought he was going to say something else, but he just shrugged and turned his attention back to the game. I stared at him. Why was he being so weird? He wasn't concerned that Fuller was missing? That some random dog was in our house?

I tore up the stairs, the sound of the game following me. He'd already raised the volume back to its normal can't-hear-yourself-think level. I tried to go through my routine like nothing had happened. I put on my pajamas and lay in bed, listening to *Love Phones* on my stereo until the house was quiet and dark. *Love Phones* always made me forget my problems because the caller's problems were so absurd. Like the girl whose new boyfriend asked her to dress up like a horse. I listened to hours of it, then the whole *Tidal* album start to finish, but the entire time I kept thinking about the imposter Fuller under the couch.

Was it some kind of stress-induced hallucination? How could Fuller . . . not be Fuller?

It must've been three a.m. by the time my mom's head-lights flashed across my bedroom wall. I pushed off the covers and ran downstairs, but it took forever for her to get to the front door.

"Christ, Jess! You scared me."

She squinted against the foyer light. There were gray

circles under her eyes and her sweater was creased across the front. She carried her purse like there was a bowling ball inside it.

"How's Sara doing?" I followed her into the kitchen. She opened the fridge and stared into it, her face a mask of strange, ghostly light.

"She's stable. They told me to go home and get some rest." She glanced at her watch, then pulled out some left-over pasta. "I'm going to go back at eight. I couldn't sleep there, but I can't imagine I'll be able to sleep here either."

"So she's going to be okay?"

"They don't know."

She didn't look at me as she said it. Instead she grabbed a fork and ate right from the Tupperware, leaning against the sink for support. She picked around the pasta to get the cheesy bits of tomato and broccoli. It had been years since I'd seen her eat carbs.

"Something happened while you were out. With Fuller."

"Please don't tell me he got into a fight again."

Part of me wondered if she'd been the one who'd done it. If Fuller had died right now, would she lie to protect me? Would she go as far as replacing him so I didn't have to deal with that loss, on top of everything else? But her expression was an open door. She watched me, taking another bite, waiting for my answer.

"He bit me." I held up my hand, showing her the tissue that was still wrapped around my thumb.

"He bit you? Are you all right?"

I nodded.

"He must be stressed. The paramedics coming through, all the commotion."

"But it's not just that. His ear . . . it's like nothing ever happened. The stitches are gone."

"I knew that vet was good." She gestured with her fork. "He was like a plastic surgeon, the way he stitched Fuller up. They must've been the dissolvable kind."

She closed the Tupperware and slid it back into the fridge.

"No—you're not getting it. It's not Fuller. There isn't even a scar. And there aren't any spots on his chest, not like before. Someone did something to the real Fuller. He's gone."

"What do you mean, the real Fuller?" She smiled as she said it, like I'd just told her some cheesy joke.

"He's gone. There's some random, fake Fuller in our house. A straight-up Fuller imposter."

"Jess, come on. I'm too tired for this."

"Seriously. It's like . . . it's like someone replaced him. Come here."

I gestured for her to follow me to the living room, back to the couch and the mound of white fur beneath it. We were still a foot away from him when he started growling.

"See?" I said. "Fuller would never do that."

Mom shook her head. "He's probably still anxious about everything that happened today. No one replaced Fuller, Jess. I promise."

I didn't want to do it, but I had to. I reached under the couch for him, but as soon as I got within two feet he went wild, each bark louder than the last. She plugged her ears with her fingers until I pulled my hand away.

"See? He hates me. And his ear is fine—it's not even the same shape. The real Fuller's flops over a little bit at the end. I'm telling you, someone did something to him. Why would he suddenly not have a scar? Those spots on his chest didn't just disappear—this isn't—"

That was it. My mom stood, brushing off her jeans. She was a tiny person, with ropey biceps and high, full cheekbones. People said we looked alike, but I couldn't see it. She was prettier, thinner, and more elegant than I was. She was blond and never did anything to her eyebrows, but they somehow always managed to look perfect. Now she was studying my face like it was something strange and ugly.

"I don't know, okay, Jess? I don't know," she said. "But maybe you could be a bit more sensitive. Today has been one of the worst days of my life and you know what? It may only get worse from here. So I don't know why his ear is different, but I don't really care."

"I wasn't being insensitive." My eyes were suddenly burning, and I could feel the weight of the day behind them. How empty the house was when I came home. The inside of the car, still and silent, as my dad drove the seven minutes to the hospital. Sara in that bed. I ran my hand over the couch cushion, counting the tiny black stitches along the seam. I'd gotten to eight before she said anything.

"I can't do this," my mom said. She gestured at me, at the couch.

"You can't do what? You can't . . . talk to me? You can't be my mother?"

"Oh, stop being so dramatic," she snapped. Then she turned back toward the kitchen. "I'm just tired, Jess. I'm beyond tired . . . I'm running on empty."

When I got to the doorway she was at the fridge again, examining one of Sara's medicine bottles. She read and re-read the label, then opened it and counted the pills inside.

"I'm sorry," I said. And I was. She looked miserable as she checked another bottle and then held one of the saline bags up to the light. She was doing what I'd done. She was trying to figure out where things went wrong.

"I really can't handle any more stress. Just . . . please don't bring it up again."

She stared at me, and there was nothing behind her eyes. If she had even said just a little more, or explained what she thought had happened, maybe I wouldn't have felt the bottomless, horrible feeling I felt then. *Please don't bring it up again?*

She was lying. I knew she was lying to me.

I climbed the stairs like a ghost, unable to focus on anything in front of me. I found myself in Sara's room, and then I was turning on the light beside her bed. The sheets were a tangled mess. A plastic cup and tissue box had fallen on the floor, probably when the paramedics had gotten her. My bare foot sucked against the thin, sticky layer of apple juice.

The collage was almost exactly as it had been that morning. Pressed flowers, the *Annie* playbill, that photo strip of me and Sara from the Swickley carnival, two years ago. My eyes went to the blank space on the right. Someone had adjusted the pictures around it so it wasn't as noticeable, but there was no way I'd miss it. There was no way I wouldn't have realized it was gone.

The most perfect, photogenic picture of Fuller had disappeared. I bent down to check the floor, but it was clear. It wasn't stuck behind the postcard below it, either.

I peered into the hall, but Mom wasn't there. The light in the kitchen was on and I could hear the sink running. I moved my hand to the black-and-white photo strip of Sara and me, as though that was what I'd always come here for—as if it was the only thing I'd wanted. I peeled it off the wall, then picked the rolled tape off the back, making sure I didn't crease it. I couldn't risk this memory disappearing, or being stolen, or whatever the hell had happened to the photo of Fuller.

It was the only thing tethering me to reality.

13

I'd finally fallen asleep when I heard the car horn. With everything that had happened yesterday, I'd forgotten to tell Kristen not to pick me up.

My dad peeked his head into my room. He had on a collared shirt and his hair was combed in place. He looked like he'd been awake for hours. "You don't have to go to school if you don't want to. Mom's at the hospital. I was going to head over in a few."

Kristen beeped again, and I wanted to throw something out the window at her. Why didn't she realize that beeping incessantly was rude? It hadn't been more than, like, thirty seconds.

"Or you could come meet us this afternoon," my dad said. "Your call."

I glanced at my reflection in the mirror above my dresser. My hair was a little tangled in the back, but all it would take was a quick change and I'd be ready. I'd still have to explain to Ms. Chen why I hadn't written any of the Cold War responses in my History workbook.

"I guess I could use the distraction . . ." I wiped the sleep from my eyes and grabbed my striped turtleneck from my closet. My dad was waiting in the doorway, like he wasn't sure if I was serious. "Will you tell them I'm coming?"

The backseat was piled with Kristen's field hockey stuff, the beat-up stick threaded through the handles of the bag. I slid it over and buckled in. Everything smelled like wet grass.

"You look like butt." Amber twisted in her seat to get a better view of me. They'd already stopped at Walter's for her extra-large coffee, and she held it with both hands, sipping it like hot cocoa.

"Your alarm didn't go off?" Kristen asked. I met her gaze in the rearview mirror.

I raked the back of my hair with my fingers, trying to get the knots out. It wasn't until we were halfway down the street that I realized I'd forgotten to brush my teeth. I was certain my breath smelled.

"Sorry. I slept three hours last night. Not even." It was only a half-second pause, but I hesitated before I said the rest. There was no way to have the conversation without it changing everything. "It's Sara."

"Oh no, Jess, I'm sorry," Amber said. "And I didn't mean—you look—"

"I do look like butt," I laughed. "I know I do."

"What happened? You don't have to talk about it if you don't want to." Kristen was watching me so intensely in the rearview she didn't notice the stop sign. She had to slam on her brakes to make it.

That's the thing, though. Talking always made me feel better, like handing off bricks one by one until the weight of everything isn't just on me. I'd never turned down the chance to tell Kristen and Amber what I was thinking. About Sara, about anything.

So I started with my dad, and what the house was like when I came home last night. How the paramedics had been there while I was out, and how Sara wouldn't wake up, and the hospital room and that horrible mask that they'd put over her face. I told them about the dog that definitely wasn't Fuller, and the fight with my mom. I don't know why, but I stopped right before the part about the missing photograph. Would it sound too weird? Like I was . . . maybe losing my mind a little?

"My mom was lying about it. And I don't know if something happened. Maybe he got hit by a car, or maybe they just had to put him down . . ." My chest felt tight, and I tried to push it away, the thought that I was never going to see Fuller again. ". . . maybe she didn't want to tell me. I mean, he *was* really old. Maybe she didn't think I could handle it."

"That sounds a little extreme," Amber finally said. We'd just pulled into the school's long, winding driveway. The upperclassmen parking lot was still half empty.

"I don't know how else to explain it."

Kristen threw the Volvo into park and stared out the windshield. Kevin Pak and Liz Woodward were sitting on the back bumper of Kevin's Miata, making out. Kristen didn't seem to register them.

"You've just had to deal with a lot lately," she finally said. "Your mom is definitely anxious and overprotective, and she still seems pretty pissed about the break-in. But she's not a liar. At least I don't think she is?"

"So then what happened? Where is Fuller, and who is this other dog?" I leaned forward, resting my hands on their seats.

Amber glanced sideways at Kristen, and it was so subtle I wouldn't have noticed it unless I was right there, right next to them. "What was that?"

"What was what?" Amber shrugged.

"You just gave Kristen this look, like I'm being weird or something."

"You just told us your mom found another dog and replaced your real dog, because she's trying to trick you," Amber said.

"Okay, when you put it like that it sounds wild. But that doesn't mean it didn't actually happen," I said.

Amber picked at her glittery nail polish. "You've just been on edge lately," she said. "I feel awful about what's going on with Sara, and we want to be there for you, seriously. We do. It's just . . . I don't know what happened, but I really doubt that's it."

She grabbed her backpack and got out of the car. Kristen fiddled with the bag in the back, pulling out some gym clothes before heading toward the school's front entrance. I followed behind them. At some point Amber changed the subject, pointing out the faded chalk *1998*s on the sidewalk— remnants of the senior prank. I just nodded, feeling like I couldn't say anything right. I knew what I'd seen. I knew I wasn't imagining it. I'd been certain that they'd believe me. Why did Amber and Kristen always feel the need to dissect everything until it was a confusing mess? Didn't they know I'd never make this up?

I still felt so separate from them, even now. They were supposed to be my best friends, but lately everything was off. I'd told them a dozen times about the fact that I 1) had feelings for Tyler and 2) had kissed him the night of Jen Klein's party, but they still kept bringing up Patrick Kramer and that stupid Spring Formal invite. It was absurd. On the ride home from Jen's, Kristen had asked two questions about me making out with Tyler, my best guy friend since fourth grade, and ten questions about the three-minute interaction I'd had with Patrick. In the past few days Amber had only mentioned Tyler once, offhandedly, and Kristen hadn't mentioned him at all. Why couldn't they at least pretend to be happy for me?

As we walked inside, I stared at the back of Amber's Kipling bag. The tiny monkey swung back and forth with each step. It hadn't even been a week since that thing had fallen out of her backpack, and she'd made all these excuses, trying to explain it away. I still couldn't get a straight answer from either of them about what it was.

And she thought *I* was the one being weird?

14

You can feel when people have been talking about you. After fourth period the air was thick with it, and everywhere I went someone stared at me just a half second too long, or gave me one of those conciliatory, pressed-lip smiles. I had History second period and I'd made the mistake of talking to Mrs. Chen as the bell rang, the class scrambling to find their seats. Someone must've overheard what I'd said, because the news had spread like lice.

It just seemed like another drama for kids to play out. They picked their roles and created storylines that weren't there. *Poor Jess Flynn, did you hear about her sister?* Or *I know their family, our moms are friends. Sara hasn't left her room in months.* There's nothing like tragedy to reveal the grossest sides of people.

I spun through my locker combo, trying to ignore Deiondre Matthews, a senior who played the clarinet. His locker was a few down and he kept glancing over, giving me this deep, sympathetic stare, like he was hoping to get my attention. I tugged hard on the lock and it popped open. Our school only had half-sized lockers, otherwise I might've crawled inside and stayed there.

Scott Wolf gazed out from the collage on the locker's back wall. Kristen and Amber decorated the inside of it for my birthday, and it had really just become a Scott Wolf shrine, which I tried to pretend was ironic. There were magazine pictures of him from *Party of Five* and *White Squall*, and *Teen Beat* posters of him smiling that dimpled smile. A paper dialogue bubble by one said I LOVE YOU, JESSICA FLYNN.

"Jess, there you are. I've been looking for you."

Patrick Kramer was walking toward me. Unless I stuffed everything in my locker and sprinted in the opposite direction, there was no way to avoid this.

"Patrick, hey. I was actually just leaving. Don't want to be late for lunch."

"Lunch?"

Then he was right next to me. I angled the locker door so he wouldn't see the Scott Wolf collage. "Yeah, the early bird gets the . . . I don't know what I'm saying."

"I heard about your sister. I'm really sorry."

He put his hand on my shoulder and I was trapped. He wasn't going to leave until I said something.

"Thanks. I really should go, though."

"I'm here for you if you want to talk."

"That's okay, I don't want to talk."

Not to you, I thought.

He leaned down so his face was inches from mine and

stared out from under a thick curtain of black lashes. His hair had a natural wave to it, and his complexion was smooth and bright. He looked like he'd stepped out of a J.Crew catalog.

"You don't have to go through this alone," he said.

He was hoping I'd open up, reveal how hard it had all been—that this would be the moment we finally bonded. But instead I smiled and said, "Okay, thanks, Patrick."

I put my hand over his hand, then slipped it off my shoulder. The hall was clearing out and there was no easy way to escape him, so I just closed my locker and started walking away. It wasn't until I was outside, cutting across the school's back lawn, that I was sure I was free.

Upperclassmen could go off campus for lunch, but there were really only two choices—McDonald's or Jerry's, this pizza place with an owner who was five hundred years old and spit when he talked. I went through the break in the chain-link fence and over a few strip malls to TCBY, because I was pretty sure no one would be there. That, and because frozen yogurt has great healing properties, like vitamin C or homemade chicken noodle soup. It's a fact.

For some reason Chris Arnold, Amber's ex, was working behind the counter. I felt bad for him. He was so tall he always hunched forward, like he was trying to make himself shrink to fit the space.

"You work here?" I asked. "What happened to the

curly-haired guy?"

"I just started," he said. "He uh . . . got the flu. He's still real sick."

"But don't you have to go to class? It's the middle of the school day."

"Yeah, it's this new part-time thing where you can work during your lunch hour. I actually combined it with my study hall so now I work two periods straight, then after school."

Was that even legal? I wanted to ask him more but the door jingled open behind me. I braced myself to see Kristen and Amber, or the cheerleading squad, or worse—Patrick Kramer. But when I turned around it was Tyler. He tucked both his thumbs under his backpack straps, pulling them away from his chest.

"Did you follow me?" I asked.

"Maybe."

He put his backpack on a table by the door. Before I knew it I was hugging him, my face buried in his sweatshirt. I felt normal for the first time all day.

"You heard then."

"I heard, yeah. How are you doing?"

Horrible. I feel like everyone's talking about it. I'm terrified she won't wake up. Part of me wants to be at the hospital, and part of me wants to be at school, because the hospital is the most depressing place, consumed by third-circle-of-hell-level waiting.

"I'm okay," I said instead.

"I don't believe you."

"Fine, I'm miserable. Everything feels off."

"Do you want to see her? I could drive you to the hospital."

"I can't go back there right now."

We stood facing each other, an aggressively cheerful Backstreet Boys song blasting over the radio. He dug his hands deep into the pocket of his sweatshirt and shrugged, like he wasn't sure what to say. I wanted to hug him again but I didn't know how.

"You were going to eat TCBY for lunch?" he asked.

"Don't say it with so much judgment."

"No, no! It's a good choice, considering the circumstances. But we could also go to my house and I could make us grilled cheese sandwiches. It's kind of my specialty."

"You're suggesting we cut?" I raised my eyebrows.

Tyler glanced around the dingy, tiled room. Chris was trying to transfer rainbow sprinkles from a two-gallon jug into a plastic dish that was obviously too small. Half of them scattered across the floor. He seemed too preoccupied to notice what I'd said.

"Yeah, I'm suggesting that. Don't say it with so much judgment."

I smiled and slipped past him, racing him to the door. He maneuvered around me and got there first, putting his hands on the doorframe to block my way. I tried to squeeze through the narrow space, but everywhere I went he threw up his knee or moved his hip and penned me in. It took me punching him in the side before we broke off, laughing.

~~~~~~

In the entire history of our friendship, I'd only been to Tyler's house a handful of times, and we'd mainly stayed in the backyard. Whenever we hung out, it was usually at my house or during school, when we'd sit at the picnic tables outside the cafeteria. After his mom got remarried I stopped suggesting it, because his cheeks would immediately do that red splotchy thing, and he'd fumble out an *um, uh, there's nothing to do there.* He didn't need to explain it. I knew he'd tried to be out as much as possible, that his stepdad's mere presence was enough to make him nervous. Craig had once called him a loser for getting a B on a math test.

"My not-so-secret secret ingredient is a tomato slice," he said, plopping one down on top of the cheese and bread. He slid the whole sandwich onto the pan and we waited, watching as it sizzled against the heat.

"I've never had the Ty Scruggs signature grilled cheese. Today is a big day."

The place was different than I'd remembered it. The living room had two floral sofas and was barely decorated except for the fireplace, which had a Buddha statue and candles. In front of it was a meditation spot for Ty's mom, with a circular pillow on the floor and a pile of burnt incense. She taught at Om Yoga on River Street.

"You know my dad's talking about tearing down the treehouse?" I said.

Ty froze, holding the spatula in midair. "He can't. That

place is a national monument. It would be like destroying Mount Rushmore."

"He's says the wood's all rotted. That it's becoming a safety hazard."

"But we were just up there a month ago when we watched *Pulp Fiction*. It seemed fine."

"That's what I said. Sara tried to lay a guilt trip on him, like it was an attack on her childhood. Remember when she used to crush us in Monopoly? She was like, eight, and she was already smarter than us."

Tyler pressed the sandwich down with the spatula. He didn't look at me when he spoke. "I don't want to say I understand what you're going through, because I don't. I'm just sorry. About everything."

"You didn't do it," I said, letting out a low laugh.

Tyler turned his back to me as he opened a cabinet and pulled out plates. There were only four of everything inside—four plates, four mugs, four bowls. The upper shelves were empty. I swiveled around on the kitchen stool. The fridge didn't have a single magnet on it—no photos, no calendar pinned in place. The bookcase had a few vases and a framed picture of a sunset, but I didn't remember it feeling so bare.

"You guys don't really have any photos out . . ."

He just shrugged. "We're not big photo people."

"Where do you keep your drum set?" I asked.

"Oh, I forgot to tell you. Something strange happened . . . one of the stands got messed up, so I took them to this special music guy to fix them." He pushed one of the plates across the counter at me. The sandwich sat in two perfect halves, the cheese oozing over the edge of the bread.

"It's not just the stuff with Sara . . ." I picked up the sandwich, holding it like a prop. "This thing happened last night with Fuller. With my dog. He was acting weird, and I know how this is going to sound . . . but it wasn't him. There's this dog in my house, but it's not Fuller."

I hadn't meant it to be a test, not really, but his reaction scared me. His cheeks flushed. He kept his eyes down, and when he finally spoke, his voice was pitchy and strained. "That is really weird. That doesn't sound right?"

"And two different mornings I woke up and heard people yelling, like chanting or something. Amber and Kristen keep acting like everything is completely normal, like I'm the one who's being weird. It's like I don't even know them anymore. Everything feels off."

Tyler chewed the first bite of sandwich, not saying anything until he'd swallowed it down. He pushed around some crumbs on the plate with the tip of his finger. "I really do care about you, Jess."

"Um . . . I know?"

Why was he saying that now, when I hadn't even been talking about us? Sara being sick had nothing to do with him. And why would he feel bad if Fuller was replaced, if I'd heard something strange?

Why was he acting like we were over before we'd even begun?

"I really do," he repeated.

He covered my hand with his hand, and I didn't have the sweet, buzzy feeling I used to. Everything in me went cold.

I tried to smile and tilt my head to one side, like it was the same as it had always been between us, but I didn't feel it. Something was wrong.

Tyler leaned in and put his other palm against my cheek. Then his lips pressed down on mine. We only kissed for a few seconds before I pulled away, trying to fake a smile, because I was worried he'd already felt my hand shaking under his.

He leaned in so his lips were next to my ear, his head resting on mine. His breath was hot on my skin.

"Let's go sit on the couch," he whispered. "Come on."

"I need a minute," I said, stepping back. Then I turned and walked across the kitchen. I tried to keep my breaths steady as I went down the stairs to the bathroom.

15

The stillness of the bathroom was dizzying. I double-checked the lock and opened the medicine cabinet, already suspecting what I'd find. There wasn't a single toothbrush or bottle of Tylenol. At home, our bathrooms were filled with years' worth of junk. Half-empty tubes of hand cream and old mascaras and Snoopy Band-Aids. I knelt in front of Tyler's sink and checked the cabinet, but it was empty, too. No plunger, no hair dryer. Not even an extra roll of toilet paper. I ran my fingers along each of the empty shelves.

What the fuck was going on?

"Jess? You okay? You need anything?"

Tyler was right outside the door. There was no trash can or hand towel. The metal bar beside the sink was bare. I took a deep breath, trying to calm myself, then opened the door and let him inside.

"What's wrong?" he asked, his voice low and quiet. "You're scaring me."

I locked the door and stood in front of it, blocking his way out. If he'd looked nervous before, it was even worse now. His arms were crossed tight against his chest like it was twenty degrees.

"You don't have anything in your medicine cabinet," I said, my voice barely a whisper.

"Oh, yeah, we don't really use this bathroom. Why?"

"So if I went upstairs right now, and I checked the other bathroom, the medicine cabinet would be full?"

He hesitated for a fraction of a second, then let out a low laugh.

"Why are you so obsessed with my medicine cabinet?" he asked. "That's weird, Jess. You shouldn't be looking in there."

"There's not a single photo in your entire house," I said.

"We're not really picture people. Come on, we shouldn't even be talking about this."

"This? What do you mean, *this*?"

He reached for the faucet and twisted it on. The tiled room filled with the sound of rushing water. For a few seconds we just stood there and watched it, how it pooled above the drain.

We were alone, in an empty house, and he was worried someone could hear us. Why else would he do that? Why else would he let the faucet run?

"There's a *this*," I finally said.

"Yeah, I guess?"

He ran his fingers up under his bangs and brushed away

a thin layer of sweat. He was cringing as he spoke, as if it physically hurt him to say the words.

"Have you ever wondered about the nature of reality?" I asked. "That's what my old guitar teacher asked me once. He was acting weird, and he wanted to know if I thought there was something more to this. To my life, to Swickley. Lately I've been wondering . . . I think he was trying to warn me."

"You sound—"

"Right?"

Tyler stepped to one side, but I met him there. He tried to maneuver around me but I pressed my back against the door.

"Every year, right around March, I get this horrible feeling in the pit of my stomach, because I know something is coming. Every single year, it feels like everything is building toward this catastrophe I'm never able to avoid. Eighth-grade Sara was diagnosed with Guignard's. Then the following year the town was hit by the tornado. Sophomore year our house was broken into. And now . . . what? Sara's going to die? Is that's what's going to happen? That's what everything's building up to this year?"

"I can't talk to you about this, it's . . . I just can't." He clasped his hands together, and he seemed panicked now. "Let's just go back outside and finish our sandwiches. I can't have this conversation. Please."

"If you don't tell me what's going on in three seconds . . ." I said. "I'm going to run out there and say I know. I'm going to yell that you told me—"

"Jesus, Jess!" He held the side of his head like he'd just been struck with a brick. "Lower your voice. They'll hear you," he whispered.

I stared at him, and my whole body went cold.

"Who is *they*?" I whispered.

Tyler twisted on the other knob of the faucet, doubling the sound. There was a long, stiff silence, and then he finally spoke.

"The producers." he said it quietly, as if that meant something to me. "They hide the cameras and mics in all sorts of things—mirrors, computers, chalkboards, streetlights. They've planted mics in bushes and on trees. I think there's one on your backpack."

"What do you mean? Producers?"

"They're the ones in charge of everything. Everything's being recorded, all the time. Except, you know . . . not in here. Not in bathrooms. I think they decided the audience doesn't need to see every single thing." He smirked.

"What for? They're making . . . ?"

He bit on the side of his nail, working at the cuticle. "They record hours of footage, all day long, then they edit it into this two-hour long show. It's aired every single night, for an audience. People watch it on TV, on their devices, whatever. When we go back outside we'll be on camera again."

He studied me, waiting for my reaction. He'd said it all so simply, like, yeah, those persistent feelings of dread you've had since you were kid are totally legitimate. Everything you know is a lie. Everyone you know is a lie. It's all completely fake.

I could have punched him in the face.

"So you're saying . . . that our town is kind of like *The Real World*?" I said. "Or *Road Rules*? Swickley is a version of reality, but it's not real. Things that happen here are kind of . . . orchestrated. They're creating the drama. Or did that tornado actually happen—was that real?"

He shook his head. "I can't talk about this anymore. I've said too much already."

"You don't have a choice now." I jabbed him in the chest. He rubbed the spot where I'd hit him, as if it was immediately sore. "I already know. It's over."

"You think they're just going to let you out of here?" Tyler almost laughed as he said it. "There are hundreds of millions of people watching, from all over the world. You think they're just going to give that all up?"

Hundreds of millions of people. A rush of secret, shameful moments came to me, one after the next. Jumping on the trampoline in Kristen's backyard and laughing so hard that I peed my pants. How I'd just stood there, silent, when James Ford poured a beer over Billy Barrett's head. The day my mom handed me *Human Sexuality*, a book with a tattered blue cover, with graphic illustrations of male and female genitalia. And worse, the nights I'd pull the blanket over my head and read it with my Hello Kitty flashlight, studying the pages and pages of sex positions.

My throat felt tight, and I counted the tiles on the floor until I was sure I wasn't going to cry. I didn't have time to be a self-hating mess. As tempting as it was to think and rethink through everything I had and hadn't done in front of the cameras, we only had a few minutes before we had to go back outside. It was possible they already suspected something was off.

"You need to tell me everything you know. The flu—it's not . . . people aren't sick, are they? All the people I don't really talk to, the ones I don't really know, it's like they've disappeared . . ."

"It's an actors strike. The extras, the ones with no lines or less than a few lines an episode—they're renegotiating their contract. It was only supposed to be three or four days, but it keeps dragging on."

He was talking, but the words floated past, and I only half heard what he said. Instead I had the clearest vision of my mom—tiny, thin, with her high cheekbones and perfectly sun-kissed hair. Her nose was so much smaller than mine, the tip of it dainty and refined. We didn't look anything like each other, and I thought now of the gym set up in our basement, of waking every morning to the dull thumping of her feet on the treadmill.

"So what are you saying? Everyone—you, Amber, Kristen, my parents—you're all . . . actors?"

Tyler practically smiled as I said it. "I mean, I like to think of myself as an actor, yeah. But not formally trained, no."

I sat down on the edge of the bathtub, working my fingers through my hair. I tugged out one of the metal clips that held back my bangs and kept popping it open and closed, trying to calm myself down. When Tyler didn't say anything else I stared up at him.

"I need to know everything. I'm serious, tell me everything from the beginning. And if you leave a single thing out, I swear I'll go to the producers and say you were the one who told me the truth. That you sabotaged them."

He chewed at his nail. He was quiet for a moment, then he slouched against the vanity. "Everything? You sure you want to hear this?"

I nodded.

I'd never been so sure in my life.

16

"Start with my parents," I said.

Tyler sighed, then his finger dropped away from his mouth.

"Okay, so your mom . . ." he said. "Helene Hart is her name, she studied acting in London, she has a master's and everything. She's kind of a force. A brand. She got famous online from doing all this interior design, fashion and life-style stuff. I never saw them, but apparently she used to do these long confessional videos about her personal life. That's why they pitched her this. She'd been on and off with Carter for years—"

"Carter?"

"Carter Boon, your dad. He was still playing for the Red Sox when she met him, but he's been retired for ages. They were always breaking up and getting back together, and then suddenly they were *on* in a big way. She made this whole twenty-minute video announcing her pregnancy. They were really popular then, with everyone following your birth and them being a new family and everything. When you were three they started the show. They signed these fifteen-year contracts saying it would run until you were eighteen. Initially they were the leads, but then they were in this really bad place, the fighting was so intense that the producers had to edit a lot out because they didn't want to completely ruin the brand. I think it was around that time that Sara was cast as your younger sister. Things were better after that."

Sara was cast as your younger sister. I had to go back to it, turning the words over like I was translating from another language. She was *cast*, not born. I remembered them bringing Sara home from the hospital, though. It was hazy, but it was there—the memory of sitting down on our living room sofa and holding her for the first time. She was my baby sister.

"Sara's family gave her up for adoption?"

"Ohhhh . . ." Tyler's mouth was a perfect circle. "Yeah . . . this might sound strange, but Lydia? Your family friend? That's Sara's mom. I think her dad died before she was even born."

Lydia. We'd always joked that they looked alike, but Lydia had freckled skin and huge gray eyes. I knew she dyed her hair, I could see her dark roots, but Sara had a completely different complexion. She must've looked like her dad, because she had full eyebrows and wavy black hair.

"The show was always supposed to be more about the family, and your parents' dynamic, but the last few years there's been rumors that Carter and Helene hate each other's guts and are just waiting out their contracts. Besides, I think the audience likes you better now. Since seventh grade, and that whole fight with Kristen where she stopped talking to you, and there was all that drama around the Bon Voyage dance? Suddenly the fan base exploded. Teenagers were watching with their parents, whole families were following along."

Tyler sat down beside me on the edge of the tub. He was almost unrecognizable. I felt like I was shrinking into myself and he was somehow taking up more space, coming alive. He casually threw out these names and phrases I'd never heard, and he was smiling—actually smiling—as he told me all about the people in my life who'd been lying to me.

"Mr. Henriquez? Jen Klein? Kim?" I asked, trying to think of the most normal, genuine people I knew. "They're all acting?"

"They're all guest stars, smaller parts. I was only supposed to be an extra on the set. Like, just another one of the nameless, faceless people who populate the town. But then you hit me in the head with that ball in fourth grade. That was my big break."

I felt like I might puke.

"Guignard's Disease," I said. "It's made up. It's not real."

Tyler didn't say anything. He just sat there, his elbows on his knees.

"They just made it up, and there was no real way I could know . . ." I said. My hands felt numb. I tried to shake the blood back into them, but I couldn't. "But that means Sara isn't really dying. She's going to be okay?"

Tyler waved me off. "Technically she is dying, at least for the purpose of the show. She's being written off. This season is supposed to be about you coming to terms with Sara's sickness, and soon her death. She might've had a chance if puberty hadn't hit her so hard. People hate watching her now, like really, really can't stand her. She's garbage for ratings. The audience just finds her really annoying and gawky and—"

"Will you stop?" I said.

He looked like I'd pushed him. It was hard to listen, when everything he did and said was so completely different from who he was before. Even his voice had somehow changed. It was higher pitched and faster, almost frenetic as he spoke.

"So Fuller died, and they replaced him with another dog . . ."

"I don't know," he shrugged. "There's a rumor one of the disgruntled extras snuck into the set and stole him, just to screw over the producers. They thought they'd hold him hostage and the producers would freak, but they ended up just finding another dog that looked like him."

"They didn't think I'd notice?"

I kept counting the fourteen tiles on the floor, trying to steady myself. Fuller. Helene Hart. Carter Boon. My parents had names and lives I knew nothing about. My dad hadn't spent the past twenty years building a successful extermination company, he'd been coasting on a reality-television contract. He wasn't stoic, he just couldn't stand being around us. My mom was using me to build her lifestyle brand. It had started as early as I could remember, the constant photos, the outfits she'd bring home that she'd want me to pose in. We couldn't do anything—go to the park or bake cookies— without it being this huge production.

They were liars.

They were both gross, manipulative liars.

Even over the rush of the faucet I could hear it, the sound of a car pulling up the gravel driveway. When I opened my eyes Tyler seemed panicked. The front door slammed shut. Someone was home.

"It's my stepdad."

"Is he . . ." I whispered. "He's an actor?"

Tyler nodded, but before he could say anything else Craig was in the kitchen, his voice clearer now. He was calling to him. To us.

"Tyler! Tyler Michael Scruggs! What the hell are you doing home?"

17

The bathroom felt impossibly small. For the first time I noticed there was no window—the door was the only way out. Even with the faucet running I worried they had heard us, that somehow the producers already knew that I knew.

"Why is he home? It's not a coincidence, right?" I asked. "Are there mics in here? Could they have heard what we said?"

My fingers went to my throat, and I felt along the collar of the sweater, then down over the front, checking if it was possible I had a mic on me, like the ones I'd seen talk-show hosts wear. I studied the buttons on my jeans and squeezed the little metal grommet thing at the seam, but they felt normal. At least I thought they did.

"I'm not stupid," he said. "There aren't any microphones in bathrooms, not these at least. I think they have a few right by the sinks in the girls' bathroom at school, and they definitely have some in the locker rooms, cameras too. But not here."

I thought about tugging off my gym clothes on camera, or Kristen talking to me in her bra as she took ten minutes to flip her tee shirt inside out. I felt sick. He must've noticed my expression because he added, "They have a female editor who cuts out the visuals whenever you're changing. It goes to a black screen. Some of the actresses are older, like eighteen or twenty, so they show those shots sometimes."

As if that made it any better.

I pressed my ear to the door, trying to gauge where Craig was. I couldn't hear much beyond the rushing water, just the occasional creak of a wooden floorboard, or what sounded like the refrigerator opening and closing. Tyler squeezed next to me. He checked and rechecked the doorknob, making sure it was locked.

"Look, I don't know how much time I have left on the show," he said. "You're supposed to date Patrick Kramer. You were always supposed to date Patrick Kramer, that was the plan from the beginning. The audience likes him better."

It was the way Tyler said it, like it was a truth neither of us could escape. We'd just have to accept what the producers wanted, what the audience wanted, as if that was the most important thing. What about what I wanted? Didn't that matter? Why couldn't I set my own course now, knowing what I knew?

"Who cares if the audience likes him better?"

"I know, right? You don't have to explain it to me. But

I guess he tests really well with teen girls and the over-forty set, which is kind of creepy if you think about it." Tyler's face scrunched tight, like it enraged him to even think about Patrick. "Males ages eighteen to thirty-four like him too, which is really annoying, because he's so vanilla. I mean, what do people see in him? He's like a cartoon version of what a high-school guy should be."

"He has no personality."

"I know." Tyler leaned in close, and I could feel the warmth of his breath. Only everything between us was different now.

"I mean, I feel like that moment in the storage closet was beyond romantic, right? That's the kind of stuff all classic nineties TV shows have. Joey and Dawson from *Dawson's Creek*, like every scene in *90210*. The kiss in Jen Klein's bedroom felt real, didn't it?"

I tried to back away but I knocked against the sink. There was nowhere to go. I couldn't believe I'd ever kissed him. That I'd ever *liked* him.

"Are you serious?" I finally said.

"You don't even know the whole story," he went on. "Patrick and his family already have a contract for a spin-off show. They live inside the set in this huge, decked-out house, with all this fancy tech and crap, while the rest of us commute in every day like a bunch of plebs. And you haven't even been over there yet, that's the worst part. You haven't even set foot in there, and they're living large."

There were footsteps on the kitchen stairs. His stepdad's

voice was getting closer, and even over the water I could hear him repeat Tyler's name. Tyler grabbed my hand. I stared down at it, as if it wasn't part of my body.

"You know how people are always walking in on us, how Jen interrupted?" he said. He didn't wait for my answer. "And then they sped up the whole Sara storyline, making her slip into the coma last night, because they thought that would throw me off. But they didn't count on you having real feelings for me. You really do like me better than Patrick. They can't stop this, no matter how hard they try. I'm a real player now."

"I don't get it. What's your point?"

Tyler held my hand up. He was clutching it now, holding it tight between both of his, and then he did the grossest thing. He pressed it to his cheek.

"They're threatening me," he said, closing his eyes for a moment. "I know this is going to absolutely crush you, Jess, but they want me off the show. They're never going to let a ginger be the love interest, and they refuse to let me dye my hair. Now they say I'm distracting you too much, and they want you with Patrick, even though—for the record—I've really grown my following in the last two months and it's only a matter of time before I have more followers than Patrick. Seriously."

"Following? What do you mean?"

There was a knock on the bathroom door. Tyler's stepdad was right outside now—I could hear him clearly.

"Tyler? You in there?"

The doorknob turned half an inch, then stopped.

"One second, *Craig*!" Tyler called out, like he was delivering the punchline of a joke. Then he lowered his voice to a whisper. "They're pissed that I went rogue. That I dared become more than the shitty little best friend part they assigned me. They're going to write me off. Boarding school. Maybe ol' Craig here will have to move home to Michigan to take care of his dying mother. Some crap like that. But you can change it, Jess—you can force them to keep me here. I told you everything you asked, I answered every single question. And from now on I'll make sure you have whatever info you want, and then you'll be in on everything. Let's just act like we're going to go back to being friends for a while. We can just slow this all down and pretend we had a change of heart. Then I get to stay, and you're in on everything moving forward. We'll plan and decide on things together. Like business partners. Isn't that genius?"

It was like I wasn't there. He wasn't asking me, he was telling me how it would be, how we would be together. When I stood up my legs felt unsteady. He'd spent years pretending to be my friend, and the last three months luring me into a fake relationship. He'd been to my house hundreds of times. After Sara had gotten sick he'd brought her a basket of candy and *YM* magazines and gave this whole shy, rambling speech telling her he hoped it "lifted her spirits." Then we'd had a movie marathon in the treehouse, as if watching *Dazed and Confused* for the third time could replace all my bad thoughts with good ones.

I'd been so excited when he'd offered to help me with the talent show. One time we'd stayed up late, practicing in the garage for an hour after our bassist went home. We made Bagel Bites and I played him a song I'd written on my guitar. I'd believed him when he'd told me I was "crazy talented" and "really something else." He'd actually said that, in this low, breathy voice I didn't recognize. *You're really something else, Jess Flynn. Do you know that?*

"Just date Patrick Kramer for a little bit." Tyler kept going, squeezing my hand tight. "Or what about a love triangle? People are obsessed with love triangles. You date Patrick and I fall back, become the best friend again. Steady. Dependable. I'll pretend I'm waiting in the wings, the unsung hero type. But then they'll get what they want and I'll get to stay."

I tugged my hand out from between his and turned the faucet off. Tyler was still staring at me.

"So . . ." he started. "What do you think?"

This was his version of sincere. He actually thought he was being considerate, kind. He thought we were a team.

"I think you can go fuck yourself," I said.

Then I swung the door open and stepped out into the den, where Tyler's stepdad was waiting. He acted surprised to see me.

18

When I was eight my family planned a vacation to Disney World. Sara and I had been obsessed with the commercials, and every time they came on we'd call each other into the room, like they contained the meaning of life. Circling, overhead shots of Mickey perched on the Epcot Center globe or waving from the top of Cinderella's castle. *Imagine yourself here*, the voice would say, and there'd be an explosion of confetti and lights and music as all the characters came together to dance.

And we *did* imagine ourselves there. Day and night that's all we imagined or talked about, long after those commercials stopped playing, and we couldn't find them on any station, ever. Sara wanted to meet Snow White and I wanted to meet Mickey, mostly because he was the big boss, the mouse behind the madness. We didn't drop it, even when my parents said it was too expensive, and even when that summer came and went. We never stopped asking to go to Disney World.

One Christmas we got a few presents from Santa, though we were skeptical of him by then. Go-Go My Walking Pup, one or two Littlest Pet Shop toys. And then a box with a slip of paper in it. I was the one who read the note aloud to Sara, the tiny folded scrap with my mom's handwriting printed in red pen. *A TRIP TO DISNEY WORLD!!!* We were going in March, over school break, and that night we both pulled down our suitcases and started packing. We didn't care that it was more than two months away.

I don't remember when exactly my dad started talking about being afraid to fly. The story was that he'd only been on a plane once, when he was in high school, and one of the engines had blown out. That was all background noise to us. We were asking our mom to buy us sunglasses and trying to decide which ride we would go on first. It wasn't until the morning we were leaving that I noticed something was wrong. He didn't get out of bed. My mom was hovering over him, coaxing him to breathe. She said he'd gotten sick—panic attacks—and we couldn't go. She was sorry but we'd have to cancel the trip.

Sara and I had asked the question to each other, a dozen times, but neither of us ever had the courage to ask our mom. Why couldn't we just go without him? Why couldn't he stay at home? Why did our dad's fear of flying prevent us from going anywhere as a family, from ever being able to travel?

"You're being so quiet," Tyler said, glancing sideways at me, then back at the road.

He'd volunteered to drive me the two miles to the hospital. I didn't refuse because I was stranded, and I was also acutely aware that we were back on camera, back to every-one watching us. I had to pretend to be normal . . . at least until I could figure out what to do next.

It was impossible to focus, though. All the memories were rewriting themselves, taking on new meaning. My dad wasn't scared of flying, it was another lie they'd made up so I'd never wonder why I hadn't been on a plane or even seen an airport. My mom had to play the overprotective, nervous type so she could keep a close eye on me. Otherwise I might decide to borrow the car and leave Swickley one night, only to find I couldn't.

And then there was Sara. She'd never looked like either of my parents. She had someone else's square jaw. Someone else's deep-set brown eyes.

I kept going back to what happened right after the Disney trip was canceled. I'd gotten up to go to the bathroom in the middle of the night and heard faint sniffling coming from Sara's room. When I'd gone in and brushed the hair out of her eyes it was wet. She'd been crying, sobbing really, and the whole top of her nightgown was damp with tears.

I just really wanted to go, Jess, she'd said through choked breaths. *I thought we were really going. Why did they lie to us?* Her sadness had felt so real, so intense, that I had to fight off my own tears. I snuggled in beside her and stayed like that, listening to her breaths until she fell asleep. She was only a kid then, she was only ever a kid. I remembered play-ing with her under our kitchen table before she could even talk. Was it possible she'd had as much choice as I'd had? Had she known Lydia was her mother? If the disease had been made up, if she was pretending to be sick, they must've told her the truth at some point . . . but how? When? And why hadn't she told me?

Looking back, it felt like she'd been trying to communicate something lately, but I still couldn't decipher what. She'd been acting strange. Then she kept talking about that park we'd gone to as kids . . .

"Could you just say something?" Tyler asked. "You're freaking me out."

"I just have a lot on my mind."

Tyler nodded, as though he understood. "Sorry about Craig. You get why I never have people over, right? You'd think I'd murdered someone, not cut a few classes at the end of the day."

I let the silence linger between us. I tried not to be obvious, but my gaze kept returning to the air vent by the car door, to the small, round object just an inch inside it. It almost looked like there was a marble, smooth and glassy, lodged deep in the grate. Was that one of the cameras?

He turned the corner onto Newton Avenue, a three-mile stretch of shops and office buildings. Swickley had always felt small and quaint, a place where you passed the same white-haired woman in the supermarket that you'd seen coming out of the Lemon Tree that morning. (Her name was Mildred, and she was widowed three years ago when her husband died of a heart attack. Or at least that's what she'd told me.) I realized now I'd never actually seen a map of the town, but there were so many dead ends and cul-de-sacs on the outskirts, and when I was riding my bike I sometimes got that strange, turned-around feeling, like I was lost in a corn maze.

Everyone in Swickley loved Swickley, though. It sometimes felt like a prerequisite for living here. They said we were lucky. They said we had everything—culture, nature, a coffee shop that served homemade apple pie and root beer floats. They said our sprawling, man-made lake made it impossible to miss the ocean, and wasn't it amazing how there was always some fair coming to town, or a concert at the pavilion near the beach?

I knew the tree in Swickley Square that bent awkwardly toward Town Hall, one branch so low that people sat and ate lunch there. Fortune House, the Chinese restaurant on Arbor Mist Road, that had been shuttered since I was a kid. I'd been to every store in the Willow Creek Mall, knew each body mist in Garden Botanika and every weird contraption at Gadgets & Gizmos. Swickley had always been as familiar as my own face.

"It kills me to say it," Tyler started, as he pulled off Newton Avenue, onto that last stretch before the hospital. "But maybe you're right. Maybe we should just be friends for now."

He waited for a response, but I wouldn't give him one. He was still preoccupied with what was going to happen to him. His role, his storyline.

"You're under a lot of stress right now with everything that's happening with Sara," he said, throwing the Chevy Blazer into park outside the hospital's main entrance. I'd never really thought about it before, but the building was much smaller than ones I'd seen on TV. There was only one floor with a dozen or so rooms.

"I really care about you, Jess," he went on, and he took my hand again, sandwiching it between his own. "I'm here for you, even if it means we can't be together right now. I know you have feelings for Patrick, and I'm not going to stand in your way. You deserve to be happy more than anybody."

From how he positioned himself, I guessed the main camera was hidden in the Steven Tyler bobblehead on the dashboard. The plastic stand it was on was weirdly transparent. He gazed into my eyes, putting on a decent impression of a caring, best friend type, but he didn't care about me at all. If he wanted a new story, I would give him one.

"I don't think we can even be friends anymore." I pulled back my hand. "Not after what you said in the bathroom. It was so . . . *disturbing*."

It wasn't a lie.

"I . . . I don't know what you mean." Tyler's voice was pitchy, and the red splotches that always appeared when he was nervous began to spread over his face and neck.

"You know what you said."

There was no turning back now. He could try to explain it away, but it didn't matter. I'd effectively written him off the show.

"Jess, don't do this," he said, and he was practically begging. "I don't even know what you're so upset about. We can figure this out, it's just . . . it's a misunderstanding. A big misunderstanding."

I jumped down from the Blazer and stood there, holding the door open just long enough to finish the thought.

"Seriously, don't call me. Don't try to talk to me. I never want to see you again. Ever."

Then I slammed the door shut, his voice muted behind the glass.

Knowing didn't make it any easier. When I walked into the hospital room and saw Sara there, hooked up to all those machines, heat rose behind my eyes. It felt real, no matter how many times I told myself it wasn't. Sara looked like she was in pain.

My dad paced in front of the bed. All I saw now was his mess of black hair, which had somehow gotten thicker and darker over the years. He was supposedly fifty but he looked younger, his skin taut and dewy, and he was constantly working out, his shirt stretched over his chest. My mom had been sitting in the armchair beside Sara. She stood to greet me, and it wasn't until she was coming forward, her arms outstretched, that I realized I'd have to hug her. There was no way to avoid it.

She clutched me tight, her chin nestling into my shoulder. Helene Hart. It had always been about her, hadn't it? Every aspect of my life, every choice I thought I'd made on my own, she'd always been behind it. In fifth grade she sent me to a child psychologist when I couldn't sleep, explaining that I was just worried about starting middle school, that

I had a hard time adjusting to change. She'd made a huge deal about my Sweet Sixteen, throwing me a candy-themed surprise party at Bell's Landing, this fancy banquet hall, even though I'd insisted I wanted something small. The green corduroy shift dress was a costume, one of many, and I was always playing the part of the artistic daughter, whether I realized it or not. She'd made me practice the piano for an hour every single day. She'd insisted.

And for what? So I'd make better television? Because she wanted me to be more dynamic, more interesting . . . more worthy?

Then there was the stolen engagement ring, which was taken during the burglary. That stupid engagement ring, which, looking back, probably wasn't even real. She had raged at me that night, pacing the kitchen, her eyes bloodshot from hours of crying. *How could you do this, Jess?* she kept repeating. *How could you be so irresponsible? This was a complete betrayal.*

A complete betrayal.

When I pulled back I couldn't look my mom in the eye.

"How's she doing?" I managed.

"It's touch-and-go," she said, pulling her oversized cardigan tight around her. "They've been running all these tests, but . . . there's still nothing conclusive."

"This damn disease." My dad gripped the end of the bed. He pounded a fist against it. "Why, goddamn it, why . . ."

It was melodramatic, even for the situation. He was huffing a little bit, breathing deep, his eyes fixed on the ground. I'd always thought he was out of touch with his feelings, but now I saw him for who he was: a bad actor. Like, really bad.

"Can I have a minute alone with her?" I asked.

My mom didn't say anything right away. She just dabbed her nose with a tissue, her eyes on the floor as she let out a long, exhausted breath.

"I guess we could use a little break," she said. "I think the only thing I've eaten today is a blueberry muffin."

She hadn't eaten a blueberry muffin, that was an absolute lie, but I didn't contradict her. I just let her pull my dad away, her arm tucked around him. I waited until I heard the clink of the lock before I did anything.

It was impossible to look for the cameras and mics without being obvious. It felt like they could be anywhere, everywhere. My best guess was the black box below the television, which was supposed to be where the cable connected—it had a large front panel with tinted plastic. The sheets seemed too thin to have a mic in them, so I ran my hand along the side of the bed, then rested it on the top, checking if there was something stuck to the frame. I didn't feel anything, but I couldn't be sure.

When I touched Sara's forehead, it was warm and damp.

"I'm here, it's me. Jess," I said.

The shadows beneath her eyes were a strange purplish color. I put my palm on her cheek and brushed the pad of my thumb against her cheekbone, getting close enough to be certain. I sat down next to her on the bed and waited a few minutes, pretending to just savor those moments with her. Then I stared down at my hand.

There was a deep-purple smudge on the side of my thumb. Makeup.

I took her hand in both of mine. The IV was taped down on the back of it, but now that I looked closer there was no needle, no pinprick of blood where it had broken the skin. I swiped my hand across her forehead again and then leaned down, my lips just an inch from her ear. I tried to speak low enough so only she could hear me.

"I know," I said. "I found out the truth. Is it safe to talk to you here? Squeeze my hand once if yes, twice if no."

She tensed her grip. It was so subtle at first I thought I'd imagined it. I leaned in closer, and brushed the hair away from her face, positioning myself so our hands were hidden between us.

"You were trying to tell me about that park. Something about what happened that day . . ."

Her face was still. She didn't move, she didn't squeeze my hand. We'd had so many years together, nights conspiring in the treehouse out back, or sitting in her bed, analyzing the lyrics to every song on the Oasis album. There'd been so much time and now there was none. We couldn't even talk to each other.

"Is it too late?" I finally asked. "Are you really leaving? I'll never see you again?"

The words caught in my throat. It wasn't fair. I didn't want to be left behind.

I waited, and she squeezed my hand twice. *No.*

"So you're going to be okay?"

She squeezed my hand again, twice. *No.*

That horrible, choking feeling came over me again. I counted the buttons on the machine beside her bed—twelve—and waited until it passed. It was excruciating, not being able to say it out loud, to just tell her everything that had happened at Tyler's. That I knew now, about the cameras and the strike and my parents constructing this world as an extension of themselves, of some kind of brand. We could finally have a real conversation and instead I just sat there. I had to keep pretending.

After a long silence she pinched my palm so hard I almost yelped.

"What?" I whispered. "I don't know what I'm supposed to do. I need you to tell me."

Another pinch, and this time she used her nails, digging them into my skin until I had to squeeze back to get her to stop. If we'd been in any other situation I would've seriously gone after her. Growing up we'd never fought in that I-punch-you-you-punch-me-back way most siblings did. We were scrappier, more underhanded. I'd once poured a glass of ice water down the back of her tee shirt. She'd once written JESS WUZ HERE on the headrest of my mom's Honda. Permanent ink.

"I swear to God, Sar—"

Then she pinched me a few times in a row, quick and light, and I realized she was trying to get my attention. Desperately trying to communicate one last important message.

Before I could say anything else, a fast, insistent beep sounded from one of the machines beside her bed. The screens flashed different lights and graphs I didn't understand, and maybe nobody did. Then the door swung open and a rush of nurses and doctors came in.

"Get back, back," one of them yelled.

A nurse grabbed my arm and led me away from the bed. She was wearing a paper mask over her nose and mouth, but I recognized her wiry gray hair and the checkered scrunchie that held it in place. She was the same actress who'd subbed for Mr. Betts in band.

"You're going to have to leave," she said, barely looking at me.

The last time I saw Sara, a woman in a long white coat was hovering over her. The crowd of nurses surrounded them, pressing buttons on machines and pulling the blankets off her legs. The doctor laced her hands together, pounding away at Sara's heart.

19

My dad paced the length of the waiting room. We were the only people in there, and with every minute that passed he seemed more agitated. He kept rubbing his hands together, working at the palms with his thumbs.

"They didn't say anything?" he said. "Nothing?"

"No, they just told me to leave."

It was the second time he'd asked me. I slumped lower in my chair, letting my head fall back against the wall. It had been at least an hour. My mom was crying, but in an artful way. Every time a tear slipped out of the corner of her eye she swiped at it, then blotted her cheek with the sleeve of her sweater. I had to give her credit . . . she was good.

My dad banged his palm against the nurses' station until a woman came down the hallway. A paper mask covered her mouth, and she pulled it down around her neck to talk to him. She was the same nurse who'd checked us in, the same nurse who'd brought my mom tea yesterday and helped pull the sheets off of Sara just before, when the doctor rushed in. I was starting to think there were only five other people in the entire building.

"Mr. Flynn, I'll give you news as soon as I have it," she said. "You have to sit tight."

"I don't have to do anything," he grumbled, then he slammed his palm down on the counter again. The nurse gave my mom a simmering look, like *you married this person?* Then she disappeared back down the hall.

"I can't lose her, Jo," he said to my mom as he kept shaking his head. "We can't lose her."

"We're not going to."

"I just . . ." he said, pacing again, "I know I haven't always been there for you and the girls, not in the way I should have been. I know that now. But I deserve a second chance." He knelt in front of my mom and me and grabbed each of our hands. "I want a second chance."

I sat up, trying to seem moved, but it was all so exhausting. I just nodded and tried to stay focused on him.

"She's going to be okay," my mom said, to no one in particular.

"Why did it take me so long to realize it?" he sputtered. "Why did it take this to know? I've just been pulling back, trying to protect myself. Trying not . . . to *feel* anything. And now it's too late. Sara might never know how much I love her. I didn't say it enough, I never . . ."

My mom rested her forehead against his. She let herself cry, the tears coming so fast she didn't bother to wipe them away.

"It's okay," I said, giving him two small pats on the back. "It's going to be okay."

I was trying so hard to stay present, to seem engaged, that I didn't see Lydia coming across the parking lot until the automatic doors slid back with a *whoosh*. She held her hair away from her face with one hand, gripping her head like she was in pain.

"I just listened to my messages," she said. "I got here as fast as I could."

My mom stood and hugged her, and I let Lydia kiss my forehead and pull me tight to her chest. We'd sometimes joked that she looked like Sara's cousin (*her sophisticated, supermodel cousin*, Lydia had specified) but now it was all I could see. They had the same thick, dark brows and the same nose. Sara had someone else's eyes and mouth, but they were related. It was so obvious now that they were related.

"What did they say?" she asked. "What happened?"

"Jess was in the room with her and the machines started going off," my mom said.

"And then the doctors and nurses came in and told me I had to leave," I explained.

Lydia pulled off her scarf and set it down on the chair. She yanked her arms out of her coat and balled it up, tossing that down too, her striped sweater and jeans a stark contrast to the scrubs she normally wore. Then she went straight to the nurses' station and peered over the counter. She rapped her knuckles against it as she looked down the hall.

"Does anyone want to tell us what the hell is going on?" she called out. "Hello?"

I wondered what would happen once Sara was officially off the show. If Lydia—or whatever her real name was—was Sara's mother, it was only a matter of time before she left, too. How long would it take before they were both out of our lives forever?

It was harder to be angry with Lydia. I'd always liked her. Maybe I even loved her—at least I'd told her I did. She'd always been easier to talk to than my mom, and she didn't seem personally offended by my inability to style my hair or pull together dynamic outfits. She'd brought Sara into the show when she was just a baby, and I didn't understand why, but part of me wanted to. There was no way to talk to her now, though, not with my parents around. It all felt too risky.

My dad stood, and when I looked at his profile, I remembered being ten and him coming home one night with two black eyes and a splint over his nose. They said he'd gotten clocked in the face at his baseball game. Four weeks later his nose was smaller, straighter, and missing the bump that had always been on the bridge. I'd told myself that was normal.

"She's so sick," he said, his voice low, breaking.

"But she was stable," Lydia said, turning toward him. "Just this morning she was stable."

"I wasn't there for her," my dad repeated. "I haven't been there and I should have. Now it's too late."

He stepped forward and they hugged, and he began weeping, his back heaving with each choked breath. My mom clutched my hands and watched like it was an Oprah-level breakthrough. It occurred to me that this had probably been orchestrated for the show, that this was a big scene for my dad, who barely spoke more than three sentences at a time. I scanned the hall, wondering if the lines had been written by someone, or if he was just making it up as he went. Who were the producers Tyler had talked about? Was it one of the nurses? Carol Pembroke, our next-door neighbor?

I tried to fix my expression into something normal. I don't know how much time had passed before the doctor appeared at the end of the hallway and pulled down her mask. DR. CHUNG was embroidered in loopy script on the pocket of her white coat. She wore a paper operating cap, even though it didn't make sense that they'd operate on Sara. I knew what she was about to say before she even said it.

"I'm so sorry," she said. "We did everything we could, but it wasn't enough. She's gone."

When we finally left the hospital the sun was coming up. The streets were empty, and as my dad took each turn, passing rows and rows of dark windows, I'd never felt more alone. Sara hadn't died, but it didn't matter—she was gone. Either way, I'd lost her.

"It must be protocol," my mom said, staring straight ahead. "We have to trust the doctors."

"But I wanted to see her." I'd said it so many times in the hours that had passed between then and now. If I could've had just a few more minutes with her, we might've been able to communicate those last important details. She might've been able to tell me just a little more.

I was stuck here, trapped inside the set, and I didn't even know her real name. I had no idea if she was sad to leave the show, or if she'd hated it these past few years, pretending to be someone she wasn't. Was she as angry at Lydia as I was with my mom? Where was she going now that she was leaving? What was beyond the set?

She'd lied to me about her sickness. She'd lied about the show. They piled up, a thousand daily betrayals, and still . . . some things were impossible to fake. When Sara was little, right after Lydia had stopped living with us, she'd wake up in the middle of the night. It was my bed she'd crawl into. She'd tell me about whatever nightmare she'd had (usually involving Freddy Krueger) and I would rub her back until she fell asleep again. I'd been the one who'd taught her how to ride her bike. I'd run behind her, gripping the seat, and hadn't let go until she screamed for me to. Then she'd circled me, laughing. She'd been so proud of herself.

"I still can't believe she's gone," my dad said.

He'd sat and meticulously filled out all the paperwork. Then he'd called the one funeral home in town and started planning the service.

"You can talk to us," my mom said. "I don't want you bottling it all up."

It took me a minute to realize she was speaking to me—I hadn't said much since the doctor told us what had happened. *An infection*, she'd said. *It was resistant to the antibiotics.* It felt safer to stay silent, to act like the last two days had sent me somewhere else, that I was numb. But if I didn't give them some kind of reaction soon, they'd suspect something was off.

"It's so surreal," I said. "It all happened so quickly."

My dad pulled into the driveway and we sat there for a long while, listening to the birds waking up. My mom let her chin fall and the tears came faster. I tried to think of sad things—Fuller in some stranger's house, without me to help him get up on the bed. Sara leaving the set and never coming back. Losing any chance at a carefree, normal life. There'd be no more lazy beach days at the lake, no sticking my head out of Kristen's sunroof as she did donuts in the Blockbuster parking lot. No crushing on anyone, ever, because it couldn't be trusted. No Spring Formal. No prom.

I thought through all of it, willing myself to cry, but I couldn't. Maybe I'd gotten too good at Not Crying. Or maybe I was just too angry.

What I really wanted was to rage at them, to tell them what liars and hypocrites they were, how when I tried to feel anything for them I couldn't. No sympathy, no love. It was physically uncomfortable when my mom touched me, her hands like fire against my skin. I hated my dad for sleepwalking through the past five years, as though there weren't any repercussions to what was happening. I wanted to be free of both of them.

I just needed to get away, as far away as I could.

"We're going to get through this." My dad rested a meaty palm on my mom's shoulder, then turned back to look at me. "We're still a family. We're a strong family."

"My Sara," my mom said softly. "My baby."

We sat there listening to each of her choked breaths.

Next door, Carol Pembroke stood in her kitchen making eggs. She was in her bathrobe and foam curlers. Sara always said Carol looked like Weird Al Yankovic's stunt double, and once I saw it I was never able to unsee it.

"I miss her already," I finally said.

That was the sentence that broke me, because it was the truth of the truth. The only real thing. The back of my throat tightened and then my eyes were full and for the first time in a long time I thought I might actually cry, exposed for every camera to see. I pushed my way out of the car and ran inside.

"Jessica! Jessica, wait!" my dad called up the stairs after me. My mom trailed in behind him, her face swollen and red. She barely looked up.

"I just need some privacy," I said, before locking myself in my room. But there were cameras everywhere, anywhere. I knew that now. They could be hidden in the mirror above my dresser or in the back of my TV, in the light above my bed or behind the *Romeo + Juliet* poster on my wall.

I threw myself down on the bed and pulled the covers over my face. The exhaustion of the past twelve hours made my head swim, and now I couldn't stop crying, even if I wanted to. I needed to get out of this place, no matter how impossible it seemed.

I had to at least try.

20

I woke up in my outfit from the night before. At some point I must've tugged off my shoes and socks and kicked the blankets into a ball by my feet. The sun streamed in through the curtains, bright and blinding. It had to be past noon.

When I went out into the hall Sara's bedroom door was closed. I heard my parents' voices beyond it. It wasn't until I pushed inside that I realized what was happening.

Lydia and my mom were sorting Sara's clothes into piles, and Lydia had a duffel bag where she occasionally tucked a sweater or a pair of jeans. My dad knelt over a drawer filled with Sara's junk—old diaries, half-full bottles of GAP perfume, and a bunch of Baby-Sitters Club dolls she'd never given away, though she'd promised them to her friend Alison's little sister. He had the whole thing out, on the floor, leaving a gaping hole in the top of the dresser.

My mom's fingers moved methodically through a pair of Sara's jeans. They dipped into the front pockets before going to the back, then pinched the bottom hems as if something might be sewn inside them. She only stopped when she noticed me standing in the doorway, watching her. She quickly grabbed one of Sara's favorite sweatshirts, a blue hoodie from her friend Laurie's bat mitzvah, and pressed it to her face.

"It still smells like her," she said, taking a deep, lingering breath. "I think I'll keep this one."

"Why are you going through her things?" I asked.

Because you have to make sure Sara hasn't left anything behind, I thought. That she hasn't accidentally written something in one of those diaries that reveals the show or brought something into the set that she shouldn't have.

"I feel closer to her here," my dad said, holding up one of her diaries. "I don't know what to do with half this stuff, though. Part of me wants to read these, just to see her handwriting again. See what she was thinking. Part of me knows I shouldn't."

"Here, let me help . . ." I reached for the second drawer in the dresser, about to pull it out, when my dad covered my hand with his.

"No, Jess, you rest," he said. He was still in his pajama pants, a red plaid pair we gave him for his birthday last year. "We'll do this alone."

Alone. Without you. The word stung, even if he hadn't meant it to.

"I'm going to run some of this back to the hospital. Maybe drop that bag at Goodwill," Lydia said, unplugging one of the machines from the wall. It had this accordion-like contraption inside it, and I'd always thought it looked a little cartoonish, the plastic a bright blue and yellow. She grabbed the blood pressure cuff and the thermometer off the dresser. "The agency wants to place me again, but I'm not ready for that. I'm going to take some time off after the funeral. I could use some space to wrap my head around everything . . ." She trailed off, her gaze meeting mine. She crossed her arms tight across her chest and there was something in her expression that I couldn't quite place. Did she feel sorry for me? Did she regret it, even a little, that they were putting me through this?

"You took such good care of her," my mom said. "Such good care. We'll never be able to repay you, Lydia."

I walked over to Sara's stereo. My giant CD case was sitting beside it. Sara had loved flipping through the heavy sleeves, sometimes stopping to pull out a lyric book and read it, other times switching whatever music she was listening to. *Jagged Little Pill* was still in the stereo.

"Can I at least take my CDs back?" I asked. "We used to listen to them together."

My dad turned to my mom, waiting for her to answer. She took a deep breath before she spoke. "I guess that's okay, sure. You keep those."

I pulled the Alanis CD out of the stereo and flipped through the giant binder, looking for the lyric book that matched it. I'd organized everything in alphabetical order, according to the band or musician's name, and I always put the CD right beside the lyric book. But when I got to the place where the *Jagged Little Pill* book should have been, it wasn't there. In its spot was one of Sara's Lisa Frank stickers—a purple kitten sitting on a rainbow heart.

"Everything all right?" my dad asked.

My sister died but she's not actually dead, I wanted to say. *And instead of giving a shit that you've been lying to me for my whole life, and it's all culminated in this most despicable lie, which would've been enough to warrant twenty years of therapy, you're still acting out this narrative of the grieving father. You're still worried I'm going to notice something's off. That I might discover what a complete and utter monster you are.*

"Yeah." I shoved the CD in and closed the binder. "Just had to find the right spot."

"I keep thinking she's going to be back any minute," my mom said. "That she's going to walk in that door and be annoyed. *Why are you going through my stuff?*"

Her Sara impression was spot-on.

"She loved watching the birds," my dad said, pointing to the window facing the Pembrokes' house. "She was my sweet bird, she was my—"

He lowered his head, hiding his face from view. His back shook and he kept muttering "sweet bird, sweet bird." He was probably wondering if it seemed believable, if he was angled right to give the cameras a good shot.

Neither one of them cared what I was thinking or feeling, or the fact that to me, Sara wasn't just another actor on the show. She was never coming back. This wasn't just another plot twist, her death was real. This was my life.

Lydia tucked one of Sara's nicer sweaters into the duffel bag. I wondered if they'd discussed it before, what Sara wanted to take with her and what she would leave, or if Lydia was just choosing the best items out of her wardrobe. *Goodwill?* I wanted to say. *You sure about that?*

"The next week is going to be impossible." Lydia folded up another sweater.

"Impossible," my mom repeated.

They both turned to me, like they were hoping I'd add something meaningful to the conversation, but I just stood there, hugging the CD book to my chest.

"Impossible," I added, hoping that would suffice.

"You can talk to us, Jess," my mom said. "Really."

She put her hand over her heart as she said it. Her chin did this weird puckered thing, like she was dangerously close to breaking into sobs. It was still all about the manipulation, about getting me to say and do something for the cameras. She started crying and I felt nothing for her, not even the slightest pull of empathy.

"I know," I said. "It's just a lot. I think I'm going to go lie down."

Lydia gave a small nod. My dad was still staring out the window, presumably at the birds, while my mom turned back to the closet and pulled out another pile of clothes.

When I got to my room I set the CDs on my dresser and curled up beneath the floral comforter, pulling the edge of it up so it covered my entire head. Sunlight streamed through the fabric and I could see everything inside. The way the stuffing clumped together in places, or how some stitching was coming loose in one square.

Sara knew I'd be pissed if she lost one of my lyric books—and besides, she hardly ever left her room. There was no place for her to lose it. She had to have put the sticker there on purpose.

But why? What had she been trying to tell me?

21

I turned over in bed, making sure every inch of my body was still covered. The cameras had seen me throw tantrums and scream. They'd heard every ungenerous thing I'd ever said about anyone. They'd captured me lip-syncing to Backstreet Boys songs with a hairbrush microphone and trying on bathing suits—it didn't matter if some editor had blacked out the footage so no one saw me naked. The last thing they deserved was more.

If this was a set, then there was everything outside of it. Towns I'd never heard of. New York City, which had always been so close and so far away, then completely off-limits after Patrick Kramer and the shooting at the Empire State Building, when my mom had declared it "unsafe." Niagara Falls. California. Thailand, which I'd seen pictures of in a book and always wanted to go to. It would never be an option as long as I stayed here, pretending I didn't know. As the years passed there would only be more reasons and excuses for me to remain in Swickley. I was trapped.

The thought of what was beyond the wall, beyond this . . . a life without so many limitations and rules and expectations. A life that was free of my parents and their lies. It wasn't a choice now—I couldn't stay caged.

I peered out from under the comforter. The sky beyond my window was a perfect, flat blue. The sun hit the clouds in this way that made them look like something you could eat. I wasn't sure how many hours had passed. I'd drifted in and out of sleep, trying to dull my thoughts. At some point my parents came in and left a bowl of soup on my desk, but instead I reached for the bag of Twizzlers hidden in the back of my throw pillow. I ate them in pairs, satisfied by the chewy tug of each bite.

My room was mine, wasn't it? I'd stuck each glow-in-the-dark star to the ceiling, re-creating the Big Dipper in the corner. I'd helped my mom pick out the lavender curtains and the wicker armchair and ottoman. I'd covered the corkboard above my desk with photos and a giant yin/yang sticker, and I'd hung my guitar on the wall beside it. I'd taped up the *Romeo + Juliet* poster myself. But when I saw the framed picture of me, Amber, and Kristen at Homecoming, or the bouquet Tyler had gotten me for the talent show, now dried and tacked to the wall . . . I wasn't sure what was real.

The talent show hadn't even been my idea—it had been my mom's. She'd heard about it through one of her clients and kept telling me I should do it. Then my dad agreed, then Sara, and once I mentioned it to Amber and Kristen, that was it, it was over. Kristen said if I didn't sign up she'd march over to the list outside the auditorium and sign me up herself. But how much had I really wanted it? Everyone had been so insistent, filling my head with a barrage of constant encouragement, it was hard to know where they ended and I began.

I heard the familiar sound of a car pulling into our driveway. Two doors slamming, one after another, and whispered words I couldn't quite make out. The doorbell rang. My mom said something, and then I heard her footsteps on the stairs. I threw the pillow over my head.

"Jess, you have visitors," she said. "Amber and Kristen want to see you."

No one waited to hear what I wanted. Kristen barged in and sat down on the bed, throwing her arms over me, her long curly hair spilling everywhere. I didn't bother to move the pillow. "Ohmygod, Jess," she said. "We're so sorry. So, so sorry."

Amber knelt beside me. Her face appeared in the tiny window between the pillow and the folds of the comforter. "Come on, sit up. Talk to us. We brought you frozen yogurt with cookie dough."

She waved the cup in the air, like just the smell of it could lure me out.

"I just want to sleep."

"Jess, we're worried about you," Kristen repeated. "Please, talk to us. What happened? Sara, she's really . . . I can't believe it . . ."

I didn't want to have some faux-emotional conversation. They were already poking and prodding me, wanting me to tell them every detail of the past day, to reveal my most devastating feelings. The audience needed to see me cry. They all did.

"We're so sorry, Jess," Amber repeated.

I pulled the pillow off and sat up. I was certain my hair was a mess, but I didn't care.

"It's just a lot to take in," I said.

Kristen nodded, like she totally understood. Like she hadn't spent the last eight years lying to me. Maybe it was just a job to her. Maybe she'd been plugging away like a worker on a factory line. Looking back, our entire relationship had existed Monday through Friday between seven a.m. and five p.m., and there'd been huge blocks of time when they were both unreachable. When I'd asked Kristen why she could never eat dinner over my house, she'd said she had food allergies, even though I'd seen her eat everything from cheesecake to pad thai. She and Amber were never online on the weekends, and we hardly ever spoke or saw each other after school unless it had been planned in advance, like when we visited Kristen at the diner. I'd never even had a sleepover with either one of them.

"I can only imagine how you must feel," Amber said. "We thought she was stable. We thought she'd been doing better . . ."

"It all happened really fast."

Kristen smoothed down the comforter with her palm. She pressed her finger into one of the small, lavender flowers. "Your mom called us. She's worried about you."

"Why? Because I haven't broken down yet?" I couldn't hide the edge in my voice.

"Well, yeah," Amber said. "Kind of. She was your sister, Jess."

Was she? Or was she just acting? I wanted to say. The words were right there. I had to fight to hold them in.

"I guess I'm still in shock."

"That makes sense. But you know we're here for you, right? We'd do anything for you, Jess." Kristen squeezed my knee through the blanket. "Just ask."

I stared at the CD case on the floor. There was one thing I couldn't stop thinking about. Maybe it was just a coping mechanism, maybe I was just grasping. But if Sara hadn't been sick, if she'd been completely coherent when she was talking to me, then why'd she bring up that park we'd gone to as kids? We'd been in her room, talking about the Harry Potter book, and she'd pointed to the picture of us rolling around in the grass. She'd asked me if I remembered going there. As many times as I'd replayed the conversation in my head, it didn't make sense.

"There is one thing you could do," I said. "Would you mind giving me a ride?"

22

"You're joking." Amber stared out the window at the tattered tarp. It was strung up between the fence and a lamppost. The gutter was clogged with broken beer bottles and soggy newspapers.

"No way. We can't let you off here," Kristen said. She hadn't put the car in park yet. Instead she peered over the steering wheel, staring at the same homeless encampment Amber was looking at. There were two Toys "R" Us carts against the fence, right beside an office chair with a missing wheel.

I'd forgotten how bad it was on this side of town. The old library had been emptied out and turned into a used-car dealership, its high, open first floor now packed with dented Mazdas and dusty pickup trucks. The park was right next to it, and on the other side was a strip mall with a bail bonds place. The sidewalks were usually crowded with homeless people, some drinking forties out of paper bags, others sleeping under cardboard shelters, but now there was no one. The last time I'd been here was the night of the break-in. Kristen's car had run out of gas, and we had to walk a mile to the Hess station at eleven o'clock at night. It must've been orchestrated, set up so I wouldn't come back until after midnight, only to discover the first floor of the house had been robbed. This "bad neighborhood" on "the other side of the train tracks" was just another way to inject danger into our otherwise peaceful town.

"I'll be fine," I said. "Don't wait for me."

"Don't wait for you?" Amber said, glancing around. "Have you completely lost it, Jess?"

"Sara and I used to come here when we were kids," I said. "I just want to be alone right now."

Amber turned back to Kristen, but neither of them responded. I crossed the sidewalk to where the park entrance should've been. It wasn't obvious at first. Vines and weeds covered the front gate, and an overgrown tree spread its low, cracked branches along the fence. I had to dig to get to the wooden posts, and even then it took a few minutes to find the latch. The gate was locked. A rusty sign hung underneath the weeds, reading: DO NOT ENTER. PARK IS PERMANENTLY CLOSED.

Kristen finally turned the car around and left, but she was going five miles an hour, still watching me in the rearview mirror. The fence wasn't that high, so I wedged my foot above some vines and hoisted myself over. It took a few tries to clear the top, and when I hit the ground on the other side the grass came up above my ankles. It wasn't until I saw the playground, with its warped seesaws and rusted merry-go-round, that the memory of that day finally came into focus.

The park had been full. Screaming kids and parents clustered around the sandbox, swapping stories. Ours had their backs to us as we crept higher on the swings. Sara jumped off in one long graceful arc, and then yelled for me to follow her.

How old had she been? Five, six?

I scanned the edge of the park, looking for the path she'd run down. I went through an arched trellis covered by vines. The tunnel was dark, the sun blocked by the thick mess of leaves above. As I neared the end I saw the statue Sara had mentioned—the stone fairy. She sat in the center of a fountain, wings tucked behind her back. Benches lined the large, square courtyard.

Catch me, Sara had yelled. *Jess, you have to catch me!* I'd chased her through the long tunnel and we'd spilled out on the other side. I'd tagged her once, and then the game turned on its head, with her chasing after me. We'd sprinted all the way to the edge of the woods. Sara stopped but I kept going, darting through the trees, trying to get away. When I was out of breath and could see her on the grass, waiting for me, I finally slowed down and rested against one of the trees. My palm ran along the smooth trunk. The brown plastic didn't have a single variation to it. Even the leaves didn't feel right.

The closer I went to the back of the park, the more trees were like that. I didn't stop until I reached the cinder block wall. It was a towering, impenetrable thing. It must've been twenty feet high. At some point I heard my dad calling for me and I left. When I'd come out my parents were furious. They kept asking me where I'd been, told me I never should've gone in the woods alone. I knew I'd done something wrong, but I wasn't sure what. I was eight or nine then. Old enough that I didn't have to be with them every single second.

I wanted to find that exact spot outside the park, the place where the trees became different, fake, but a high chain-link fence had been put in at the edge of the courtyard. KEEP OUT, a sign said, a skull and crossbones right beneath it. When we asked to go back to the park, my parents had claimed it was closed, that the police had discovered a toxic dump site there.

Sara had been trying to tell me, she'd been trying to re-mind me. Everything I'd suspected was right, true. Why else would she have brought it up like that?

The courtyard was overgrown with weeds. Tall, wiry things that sprouted up in the cracks between bricks. The inside of the fountain was a dark, moldy green and scattered with dead leaves. I wasn't sure what I was looking for until I followed the statue's gaze. When I saw the bright flash of pink and purple I knew immediately what it was. One of Sara's Lisa Frank stickers was on the ground, stuck to the top of a moldy brick.

I knelt in front of it. It was the same sticker she'd put in the CD case—a purple kitten sitting on a rainbow heart. The leaves and weeds around the brick had been cleared away, like someone had recently pulled it out.

It was impossible to know if I was still on camera. The park had presumably been empty for years now, so there wouldn't be a need to have cameras here, and I knew Sara wouldn't have chosen this spot if there were. But I'd made a mistake, telling Amber and Kristen exactly where we were going in advance. I should've just given them directions one street at a time. It was possible the producers had gotten here first and hidden one.

I sat down, trying to seem deep in thought. I peeled off my denim jacket and laid it on the ground, then reached my hand under it and maneuvered the brick free. It was a giant lump beneath my jacket, and I could feel a tin box right beneath it, but it was impossible to see what was inside. I'd found whatever Sara had left me. It was right here.

Frustrated, I peeled back the jacket. It was the Hello Kitty box I'd gotten Sara for her seventh birthday. It was still shiny and new, and when I opened it the missing lyric book was inside. A gray plastic knob sat on top of it.

I glanced over my shoulder, checking to make sure no one was there. I flipped through the lyric book. The pencil marks were subtle enough that I didn't notice them at first. But she'd put a dot under random letters. When I started from the front, ordering the first letters HCN, it didn't add up to anything. It was only when I flipped through from the back to the front that it worked. I pulled a pen from my bag and started writing each letter on my palm.

ARDEN PL
WHER U TGHT ME HOW TO RIDE BKE
RED HOUS

I kept copying the letters down, making my way to the front of the book. Arden Place, the cul-de-sac where we'd learned to ride bikes, was on the edge of town, maybe a twenty-minute walk from the park. There might've been a red house on it, but it had been so long since I'd been there that I couldn't remember. They were clearly directions, though—she was telling me what to do.

MAPLE TREE BEHD TH—

I still had several pages to decode when I heard footsteps.

"What is that?" Amber's voice was flat. "Jess, what are you doing?"

When I turned back she was just a few yards away, trying to see what I was holding. I could already feel how different it was between us, how something had changed. Amber had always floated through life in a way I'd never been capable of. It didn't faze her when she got a B minus on her Calc final, or when Lizzy Hayworth spread rumors that she'd made out with some rando freshman. Nothing could get to Amber . . . except maybe this. Her mouth was twisted to one side and she kept working at the corner of it with her teeth. She knew that I knew.

"Jess, we're all worried about you. Why don't you come here and give me whatever that is. Whatever you found."

"Who's *we*?" I asked.

The question hung in the air between us. *We* wasn't just Kristen and Amber. It was my parents, it was the producers, it was all the people who relied on me to keep the show going. I shut the box and shoved it in my purse. I grabbed my jacket, trying to gather myself up off the ground. She was already coming across the courtyard, closing the distance between us.

23

Amber put herself between me and the exit. She held up both hands in front of her.

"Look, Jess, I'm sure this is a really painful time," she said. "You must be really confused. But I'm worried about you. Kristen's worried about you."

"I'm sure you are," I said.

When I took a few steps to the right she mirrored me, blocking my way out.

"What did you find?" she asked, nodding to my bag. "What is it?"

"You must have an idea. Otherwise you wouldn't have followed me in here."

"I followed you because you demanded to be dropped off in some creepy neighborhood with drug addicts on every corner," Amber said. She gestured around the abandoned park. "Jess, this is not normal."

"Bullshit."

Amber jerked her head back like I'd hit her. "Excuse me?"

"I said it's bullshit, what you're saying is bullshit," I couldn't stop myself now, I didn't care if anyone saw or heard. My hands were trembling and it was hard to hold onto the box. "You want us to be normal again? Tell me the truth. Just this once, tell me everything."

Amber just stood there, and for a moment I actually thought she hadn't heard what I'd said. Finally her expression softened, and she met my gaze. Her eyes were wet. She crossed her arms tight against her chest.

"I'm sorry," she said, her voice so low I could barely hear her. "I'm doing my best. Please, just give me the box and we'll take you home."

She wasn't going to give anything up. Even now, knowing that I knew, she still wanted things to be how they'd always been. But I wasn't the same person I was three days ago. Nothing would ever be the same.

I swung my purse around to the front of my body and un-zipped it, my hand resting on top of the box. Just when her eyes were fixed on it, I darted back toward the right, where the trellis was. I was quick enough to gain a small lead.

"Jess! Stop!" she yelled after me.

I ran as fast as I could, through the tunnel covered in leaves, out past the rusted playground. I saw the fence up ahead. Amber was still running after me, and she was crying now. She whispered into a flat metal device, pressing it against the side of her face, and I realized it was the same thing that had fallen out of her bag that day in the locker room. It was some kind of phone. She paused, saying something to the person on the other end, and I hurled myself over the fence to the other side.

Kristen and Millie were at the curb, the engine still running. The Volvo faced the used-car dealership, so I went behind the back bumper and cut across the street, toward the bail bonds place. As soon as Kristen saw me she peeled out and did a U-turn.

"Jess! What happened to Amber? Jess?" She pulled into the strip-mall parking lot and waved out the window, as if I hadn't noticed her. I took off around the side of the building, not stopping until I reached the road behind it. I tried to remember how to get to Arden Place.

"Excuse me, young lady? Would you mind giving me directions?" a woman with stiff gray hair called from across the street. She had a grocery bag on her arm and she kept waving me down, like I hadn't heard her. I might not have noticed before, but she was wearing a prosthetic nose, I was sure of it. They'd styled her hair in big curls, but I could tell it was the same woman who'd been our sub in band, the same one who'd played the nurse at the hospital.

"Sorry . . ." I doubled my pace, guessing at the right direction.

A pawn shop, a liquor store, and a supermarket I'd never been inside before. I was practically running when I turned the corner into a residential neighborhood. If I was right, Arden Place was north of here. A quiet, dead-end street—the last in a whole row of dead-end streets. But even if I made it, even if I found the red house Sara wanted me to find, what was next?

An elderly man stumbled out of a house up ahead. He was coughing, and as I got closer I noticed thick gray smoke streaming from an upstairs window. He looked familiar too, but I couldn't place him.

"Help! My house is on fire! Please, you—can you call the fire department?" he yelled. I smiled and took off running, pretending he wasn't talking to me. "You—the girl in the plaid dress! The one with the blue purse! Please, stop! Help me!"

If it wasn't obvious before, it was now. I doubled my pace, turning right and taking off down another street. I was almost at the next corner when the Land Rover slowed beside me, then pulled over to the curb. It all happened so fast I barely had time to process it. Patrick Kramer leaned over and opened the passenger door.

"You look like you need a ride," he said. "Come on, get in."

"No thanks."

I crossed the street and tried to lose him. There was no way I was getting in a car with Patrick Kramer. He'd probably drive me to some secluded spot and force me into a conversation about Sara's death, or try to get me to confide in him. He'd want me to cry, and he'd definitely want to see the box she'd hidden. They needed to know what was inside it.

The Land Rover pulled to the other side of the street, trailing me. This time Patrick threw it into park and hopped out.

"Just get in," he said. "I know what happened with Sara."

He reached for my elbow, trying to guide me toward the car, but I wheeled back, punching him hard in the chest. He leaned against the front of the car. I raised my fist again and he flinched.

"Do not touch me, I'm serious," I said.

"Shit, Jess. I'm not trying to hurt you," he said, putting his hand over his heart. "I want to come with you. I want out of the set."

"What?" I said. "You're lying."

"I'm trapped here, just like you."

"Riiiiiiight. Did they kill off your sister too? Or, while your sister was dying but not really dying, did they replace your dog, probably the only authentic creature in this entire set? Did your parents spend their entire lives lying to you so they could create a picture-perfect family for some messed up reality show?" I rolled my eyes, rethinking what he'd said. "And if you've been *trapped*, why didn't you try to get out before now? You think I'm stupid enough to believe this?"

"Because there wasn't a way before this. Come on, we don't have much time. They're coming for you. You should at least believe me on that." My expression must've been flat because he grabbed both my shoulders and squeezed, as if that alone could get a reaction from me. "Look—I know you think I'm boring, and narcissistic, and obsessed with what happened at the Empire State Building, but I'm not. My name isn't even Patrick. It's Kipps Martin!"

Sirens wailed in the distance. When I turned to look down the street, I saw a SWICKLEY ALARMS car coming toward us, a small, pathetic red light blinking on its roof.

He ran back to the driver's side of the Land Rover, leaving me there. The patrol car sped closer. It wasn't a choice—I had to believe him. I climbed in and fastened my seatbelt, relieved when he hit the gas.

24

"Where were you going?" Patrick (Kipps?) asked as he made a U-turn and drove in the opposite direction of the SWICKLEY ALARMS car. He was already trying to lose them—he was smart, at least.

"Please pull over," the driver's voice boomed through a loudspeaker. That small, pathetic light flicked around as the man did an awkward three-point turn, knocking over some garbage cans.

"Arden Place. It's that—"

"Dead end. Yeah, I know it. Why there?"

"I don't know?" I fumbled for the lyric book just as Kipps took another hard turn, squishing me against the passenger door. "Something about a red house . . . that doesn't mean anything to you?"

"I think part of that street is along the outside wall of the set. She might be leading you to an exit. But I don't know how she thought you'd get there alone. They are not happy."

He checked the rearview mirror as two bicyclists appeared and went all Tour de France on us. Another SWICKLEY ALARMS car came down the block. The driver rolled down his window and waved, signaling Kipps to pull over, but Kipps just gave him a thumbs-up and kept driving.

"You're going fifty," I said, but before I could finish the sentence the speedometer passed it. Fifty-two, fifty-five . . .

"We have one chance, and this is it," Kipps said, his eyes moving from the rearview mirror to the intersection in front of us. A young mother pushed a double stroller across the street. Kipps didn't even slow down.

I kept thinking he'd brake, he was obviously going to brake, but we were heading right toward them and if anything, he was speeding up. The woman had headphones on, her Walkman clipped to her belt. As she stooped down to tie her shoe she let go of the stroller and it drifted further out into the intersection, right in our path. It was in the middle of the street and she still hadn't noticed.

"Kipps—you're going to hit it. You have to stop. Kipps. Kipps!"

But he didn't stop. He just swerved, clipping the front of the stroller, exploding it into a dozen pieces. I turned back, my breath trapped in my chest. The mother screamed over the pile of blankets and twisted plastic.

"Pull the car over, I want to get out," I said.

"You didn't recognize her?" Kipps took a turn so hard I thought the Land Rover would flip. "She's the cashier at Sassy Shoes. And Principal Haverford's wife. And the

Swickley Times reporter who interviewed me at school, and who knows what else. Fake—it's all fake. They probably didn't even bother to put dolls in there."

I turned back but the woman was already out of view. The bicyclists and SWICKLEY ALARMS cars were still there, racing to catch up with us. I pulled open the glove compartment and took out the Land Rover's user manual. When I thumbed through the pages they were all blank. The cover was a color print pasted onto a notebook.

"You think that's Mr. Rutherford's place? That crazy old guy?" Kipps said as we sped past the broken-down house on the corner of Fox Lane and Route 24. The shutters were peeling and plaid sheets were tacked to either side of the windows, creating makeshift curtains. I'd seen kids throwing rocks at it just the other day. "That's technical support. You need an extra camera placed or a rush set decoration, you go to the bathroom at the gas station. The third stall, the one that always has the OUT OF ORDER sign on it—there's a door that leads right into Rutherford's backyard."

It was the only EXXON in town. I had the sudden memory of Kristen pumping gas one morning on our way to school. I'd just unbuckled my seatbelt when she asked me where I was going. *Ew, that bathroom's disgusting*, she'd said. *I can't believe Amber uses it. Just wait until homeroom.* But I didn't listen. I walked in as Amber was coming out of the OUT OF ORDER stall. She looked surprised, then nervous, then said something about checking to make sure it was still broken.

"Fortune House," I said, remembering the Chinese food place on Arbor Mist Road that had been closed for over a decade. "It was never a restaurant."

"That's the production headquarters for the show. Like-Life Productions—they have a few shows on now. This is the flagship."

"Chris Arnold," I said, realizing. "There's no way that guy is sixteen. He's like the abominable snowman. He looks like he's in his thirties."

"I think he's twenty-nine. And yeah, he and Amber actually dated in real life. Only he cheated on her with Queenie Mar, this pop legend. It was a whole thing."

"But you're . . ."

"You think I'd stay here if I was eighteen? Four hundred and eleven days until my birthday. It's not like I'm counting and re-counting, or in a perpetual state of anxiety over it."

Arden Place, the dead-end Sara had led us to, was just a block away. It didn't matter that the SWICKLEY ALARMS cars were still tailing us, that every time we slowed just a little bit the bicyclists reappeared in the rearview, their fingers flitting to their ears, whispering . . . what? Updating the producers on where we were?

I fumbled through my purse and pulled out the small round gray thing.

"This was in the box."

"A key fob," he said.

"There must be a door, then. That's where she's leading us. The red house, the maple tree . . . maybe something behind it?"

"It's possible, but I've only ever gone out an exit on the east side, and that was over four years ago. In that strip mall with the Baskin-Robbins? The adult video store has a back room—"

He was looking at me when we heard the series of quick, sudden pops. Then the rush of air as it left the tires. I turned back and saw a rubber strip on the road behind us. It kind of looked like a speed bump, but with knifelike blades angled back, ready for destruction. Both alarm vehicles slammed on the brakes before hitting it.

"Shit." Kipps pounded his fists on the steering wheel as the Land Rover rolled forward, then stopped. "We'll have to run. Take everything, let's go."

I didn't move at first. Kipps was already out of the car, already sprinting ahead, but I watched the rearview, wondering how far they'd go to keep us from leaving. I just sat there, frozen.

Kipps yelled something, and his voice brought me back.

This was it. If I was going, I had to go—now.

The cul-de-sac was visible ahead. As we got closer a huge man came toward us, walking a Rottweiler. He must've been six five, his hair gelled up in the front. The bicyclists who'd trailed us for so long had stopped back at the rubber strip and were now jogging toward us. We were surrounded.

"Which house?" Kipps said, as we turned into Arden Place. "Where?"

I nodded to the one that stood in the center of the horseshoe, directly in front of us, not wanting to be obvious. But Kipps didn't get it. It took me darting ahead for him to follow. When I turned back, glancing over my shoulder, the man with the Rottweiler fumbled with its leash, then dropped it, and the dog chased after us.

"Come on, move," I said, willing Kipps to go faster. The house's backyard was fenced in, and I focused on the tall, latched gate, hoping we'd make it. Somewhere behind us, the SWICKLEY ALARMS car started up again.

"Stop where you are. Please await instructions."

I made it through the gate first, keeping it open just enough so Kipps could slip into the yard. He was almost inside when the dog reached us and bit onto the back of his jeans. It got the tiniest bit of fabric, but it was enough that we struggled, pushing the gate to block it, then finally ripping free. The thing jumped and barked, its claws scraping against the other side of the fence.

"I don't even know what a maple tree looks like," I said, scanning the backyard. There were three big trees, and a pile of firewood in the corner.

"That one, it has to be," Kipps said, pointing to a larger one with reddish leaves. When we got to the trunk it had that same strange, plastic feel as the fake ones in the park. I took out the gray key, or fob, or whatever it was called, and pressed the button on the top of it. A stream of light shot out a pinhole in the front.

I scanned the light over the front of the tree, thinking it must connect somewhere. It wasn't working. I pulled out the lyric book and pressed it into Kipp's hand.

"There's a code, you start from the back," I tried, but

when I glanced over my shoulder I saw the two bicyclists coming toward the fence. The dog was still snarling against the gate, and it was only a matter of time before its owner reached it and set it after us again. "It should tell us the next thing after the maple tree. Maybe it says how to open it, where to put the key."

Kipps thumbed through the book, trying to parse out the last of what Sara was trying to tell me, but it all felt so useless. It didn't work. Whatever this key was, it wasn't the right one, it didn't match up. Or I'd misread the code somehow.

"Come on, please," I whispered under my breath.

There was nothing after this. I couldn't just pretend for the next year, waking up each day and going to school inside the set, as if this was all normal. I couldn't wait until I was eighteen to leave. This wasn't the way it was supposed to end.

"Kipps Martin," a voice called from outside. "Leave Jessica alone. Come to the front of the house immediately."

"This is fucked," Kipps said, and when I glanced over I noticed his hands were shaking. He hadn't even gotten the book open.

The two bicyclists reached the back gate. They whispered into their earpieces, frantic, relaying what was happening in the backyard. I took a few steps behind the tree and saw the hinge of a door. It was painted brown to blend in, but it stuck out half an inch. I could see the seam in the plastic. I passed the key along the side of it, then to one of the knots in the middle. The sound was so subtle I could barely hear it. A quick, low beep.

Then a door in the tree trunk popped open. In front of us was a steep, narrow staircase, disappearing into the darkness below.

25

I turned and bolted the door from the inside, hoping that would hold them back long enough for us to get through. The walls of the tunnel were rough and cold to the touch. I could hear Kipps racing along beside me. I kept my hand out, feeling for a light switch, as if I could will one into existence. It wasn't until the stairs were far behind us that we saw any signs of life.

The tunnel bent to the left and a row of lockers appeared. A man sat on a bench beside them, changing his shoes. I rubbed my eyes, letting them adjust to the overhead lights that now dotted the ceiling. *Principal Haverford*. He'd swapped his suit and tie for a denim jacket and tight pants. He laced up a bright white high-top and looked at me, then behind me, like I'd appeared in a blast of smoke and fire.

"What the actual fuck? You're not . . . you're . . ." he said.

I didn't respond. Instead I picked up my pace, cutting in front of Kipps.

"He must be getting off his shift," Kipps whispered.

We passed three vanities and some salon chairs, which were scattered with colorful makeup palettes. Shelves of accessories, racks of clothes. Nurse's uniforms, police uniforms, postman's uniforms, a TCBY shirt and one for Sassy Shoes. Ripped denim, plaid, Doc Martens, butterfly clips, and some J.Crew dresses I'd admired but never actually bought. I recognized a patent-leather flight crew bag from the Delia's catalog.

As we got closer to the end of the tunnel I could hear it clearly, the words coming from somewhere above. *Fair wages, power*, the chant started. *Fair wages, power.* After a few seconds there was a break, and another chant began. *Hey-ho! Hey-ho! Fair pay for extras on your show! Hey-ho! Hey-ho! Fair pay for extras on your show!*

"Those are the people striking?" I said over my shoulder. "I heard them some mornings. Only it sounded like 'Forages.' I didn't know what it was."

"Yeah, it's been on and off for over a week now. They brought in a bunch of scabs to try to repopulate the set, but it's still obvious, right?"

"I guess there's only so long that half of Swickley can have the flu."

I glanced back at the tunnel. I kept waiting for someone to appear behind us, for someone to yell for us to stop, to wait. But we kept moving until the tunnel bent to the right, leading to a narrow flight of stairs. The chants were much louder now. When I pushed the trapdoor at the top, it pushed back. I tried the key again.

"The door at the other exit—the lock was right at the center," Kipps said, pointing to a circular metal piece where the two doors met. I waved the light over it and it took a second to catch, but it finally spun clockwise, open. The doors fell back, the sky a brilliant blue above.

"Fair wages! Power!" the chant filled the air.

Dirt stretched out in front of us, stopping at a two-lane road. We could just see the backs of the buildings on the other side. I glanced over my shoulder. A tall, chain-link fence towered over us. Barbed wire lined the top and a sign read: SHOCK WARNING: ELECTRIC FENCE. 7000 VOLTS. Beyond that was the cinder block wall—the set's perimeter.

"Now what?" I asked, scanning the buildings ahead. "I refuse to believe it's that simple. They're not giving up that easily."

"No doubt." Kipps turned back and stared up at the electric fence. "I've never been out this way. Your guess is as good as mine."

"Let's just find cover. We're too exposed here."

I closed the trapdoor and made sure it locked. There was a second chain-link fence with barbed wire, but this one wasn't electrified and opened easily with the key. The area around the set was a barren strip of land, broken in places by overgrown grass or scattered trash. What looked like a single bus stop, complete with bench and metal shelter, sat five yards from the trapdoor. I took off toward the nearest building, a strip mall with its back to us.

The actors were a football field away. There were hundreds of them, standing right in front of the second fence, but they didn't seem to notice us. They held signs and banners. Some were marching in a line, a collective pacing back and forth. Others waved their signs as though someone above might see them.

I thought the world outside might look and feel different, but it was as if we'd stepped into an alternate reality, this one a bit dimmer than the one I'd known. Crinkled wrappers and soda cans accumulated by the curbs. Trash piled up at the back of buildings, the stores faded, paint peeling away from the stucco. Kipps kept going, but I turned to look at the wall behind us.

Like that, it was all gone. My parents, Sara. Swickley High and band concerts and afternoons at the mall. Just last week I'd spent a half hour obsessing over which top I'd wear, because it was Thursday, the day Tyler and I had study hall together. It had all felt so important, as if that decision alone could sink me. I wanted that girl back, the one who didn't know what was coming for her. I'd give anything to care about a sweater clashing with my jeans.

"Move it or lose it," Kipps called out. "Come on, hurry."

I shook out my hands, trying to calm my nerves, but it didn't help. I ran to catch him and we moved as fast as we could, walking along the back of the strip mall where no one could see us. We peered around the corner and into the parking lot. There were only a few sleek, egg-shaped cars, nothing like the huge clunky ones I'd seen inside the set. The pizza place had a line at the counter. The bank next to it was closed.

"This is . . . New York? Where are we?"

"Yeah, technically Long Island. The set was just a town where they bought out every single resident, and they built a wall around the perimeter. They made it look really vintage."

"Vintage?"

A sleek white car nearly ran us over as we crossed the lot. The pizza delivery guy in the front seat was sleeping. He only blinked open his eyes once the car was in park. He got out and walked right toward us, but his head was down as he poked at a screen in his hand.

"That guy . . ." I asked. "He was sleeping. How was he sleeping?"

"The car is a newer model. Self-driving."

A few more sped past, and we pressed against the side of the building so no one would see us. There was a supermarket and a couple of car dealerships down the street. One said SILVERLIGHT 2400 in neon script. We passed a burger place called Charlie's that smelled like bacon grease. All the customers were facing the back of the restaurant, watching a giant screen above the counter.

Kipps stopped at a side window and waved for me to come closer. A dozen or so people were scattered throughout the restaurant, their backs to us, heads bent as they watched something in their laps. Most of them had earpieces, and occasionally they'd adjust them, only half paying attention to the giant screen on the wall. The restaurant was playing a live feed from inside the set. There were shots of the cul-de-sac, which was now filled with people. My parents were there, plus the bicyclists who'd chased us and a bunch of people barking orders into their headsets. A caption scrolled across the bottom of the screen.

The phrases BRING HER BACK and THE END moved past on an endless loop, followed by the words VOTE NOW and a timer that ticked down from thirty seconds. The audience leaned 88 percent BRING HER BACK, with only 5 percent for THE END. The rest were undecided. Two commentators started unpacking the results, gesturing animatedly, but we couldn't hear what they were saying.

"People vote? Why?" I asked. "That's beyond twisted."

"The producers started doing it about five years ago," Kipps said. "They think it helps the audience feel more invested."

"Well, who cares if they want me back?" I said. "It's done. They can accept it or not, but it's over. I'm not going back there. They think I'm just going to, what? Play along? Pretend the last two days never happened?"

Kipps rested his forehead against the window. His breath left a small half-moon on the glass.

"Kipps?"

"We don't want to go back, so we won't go back."

"But . . . ?"

"It doesn't seem like they're just going to accept it," Kipps said.

"So what? They drag me back, kicking and screaming?"

"They'd probably try to make it part of the show. You rebelling against your family, confronting them. You feeling trapped, betrayed, struggling with life inside the set. You reuniting with Sara after realizing she was just playing your sister, that you were never actually related. It's just more entertainment. Hours of it."

"Well, they have to find us first."

"We have to be smarter than them." He was still watching the screen as he spoke. "I'm telling you, eighteen—that's the magic number. Count down the days. Once we turn eighteen, we're free; they can't legally keep us inside the set against our will. We won't need a guardian's permission to leave."

"Let's go, come on," I said, tugging Kipps's arm as I started across the parking lot. I felt a sudden jolt in my stomach and I swore I could run forever. My gaze scanned the different side streets, but there was no obvious exit.

"No—look." He didn't move.

When I went back to the window, they'd just posted another question for the audience to vote on. USE ANY FORCE NECESSARY or DON'T HARM HER, EVEN IF SHE GETS AWAY. VOTE NOW.

Again the timer ticked down.

Neither of us spoke. We just watched the seconds slip away, until the results flashed on the screen: 47% USE ANY FORCE NECESSARY, 41% DON'T HARM HER, and 12% UNDECIDED.

"They can't actually mean that," I tried, but it sounded pathetic, even to me. "They just want to make it seem more dramatic, probably. Do those votes really matter?"

Kipps was silent. He wiped the foggy half-moon off the glass and turned away.

"Yeah, they matter," he finally said. "They really matter."

26

"We need to find a bus stop like the one by the fence," I said. "We need to get as far away from the set as possible."

"That was a shuttle stop for people who work inside," Kipps said. "Actors, crew, the extras—at least before the strike. I don't know if they even have public buses here. We need an Uber."

"What?"

"When I lived outside the set you used to be able to get a ride off your device, but the producers confiscated mine last year. Uber—it would pick you up and take you wherever you wanted to go."

"How do we get it then . . . this Uber thing?"

"We can't if we don't have a device."

"What the hell is a device? Why are you talking in code?"

The minutes were ticking away, and I could feel my anxiety rising. The producers knew we'd left the set and they were coming to bring us back. We only had so much time before they found us here, and Kipps was using all these random words I'd never heard before. Where exactly *were* we?

"What about those car dealerships next door? Maybe that's something," I said.

"So . . . what? We just steal one?" But Kipps was already walking in that direction, crossing into the supermarket parking lot. It wasn't like we had any other leads.

"We ask to take it for a test drive." I said.

"You, Jess Flynn, ask to take it for a test drive," he said. "Walk me through that."

"Chime in at any time with a better idea. Really, any time. Like now . . . or now . . . or—"

"I'm thinking!" Kipps snapped, but he said it way too loud. A couple loading groceries into their trunk turned and stared at us. Kipps brought his hand to his hair, shielding his face, and they squinted against the setting sun, as if they weren't quite sure what they were seeing. I grabbed his arm and pulled him toward the supermarket's entrance. The last thing we needed was someone recognizing us.

It was unlike any store I'd seen before, with every item behind a towering wall of glass. A woman with a pixie cut parked her cart in a recess in the glass wall. She punched some numbers into the keypad beside it and a mechanical arm behind the shelves sprang to life. It grabbed a box of cereal, bringing it to the end of the row and then straight down, where it deposited it gently into the cart. She kept typing away, and the arm darted up and over the different shelves, plucking out bags of pretzels and boxes of cookies.

A dad was there with two kids—one tucked in the shopping

cart and the other trailing behind him, mesmerized by the robot. Everyone was alone in their own separate world, typing on a screen posted on the front of the cart, or on a portable one they carried with them. I kept thinking they'd turn, they'd see us, but most people had their heads down as they passed. I brushed shoulders with someone watching the feed from the set, and she didn't even give me a second glance.

"How do we get one of those?" I whispered to Kipps. I pointed to the tiny screen the dad had in his hand. He kept jabbing it with his finger. "Can we buy it here?"

"Negative," he said.

"Those were the devices you were talking about."

"Yeah, but it's not that simple," he said. "There are accounts associated with them. It's a whole thing."

I checked over my shoulder to make sure the couple hadn't followed us inside. Then we went straight to the back of the store, as far away from the parking lot as possible. We turned down another aisle and I saw a familiar face. My mom was staring back at me from the cover of a book.

RETRO DESIGN was scrawled across the top in neon letters. She was standing in our living room. There were two other books beside it, a memoir titled *Living in the '90s* and one that said *10 Steps to Building Your Brand*. The shelves were stacked with plates, dish towels, curtains, and wallpaper in bright pink, turquoise, and purple patterns, all with a Helene Hart stamp on the label. This whole time my mom actually had been working, just not at the house around the block. There were Helene Hart spatulas, lemon zesters, "mom jeans," and hair ties.

Next to my mom's home goods line was a section called STUCK IN THE '90S. You could buy my face on a tee shirt, on a hat, on knee-high socks.

"What? No, no, please no . . ." I said, pressing my palm against the glass. They'd chosen my seventh-grade class picture for some of the merch, which was particularly mean. Seventh grade was the year I'd attempted to shave my bangs instead of growing them out, and I'd walked around with a full inch of peach fuzz on my forehead for all of September. Of course (of course!) it was right in time for photos. I'd hunted down every copy in my house and destroyed it, but they'd found one. They'd even put it on a mug.

But it didn't stop there. They'd found a way to monetize all of it.

Want Amber's Kipling backpack? Need a compilation of all the covers I'd performed in the last five years, including the song from the Swickley High talent show? A workout video from my dad, Carter Boon? Swickley High Varsity Baseball cards? Posters of Kipps shirtless? Kipps pouting at the camera? How about a SAVE SARA tee shirt?

They made stuffed animals that looked like Fuller. A block of Baby-Sitters Club books that opened in the back and had Ring Pops, Nerds, and Fun Dip inside. It was like someone had walked through my bedroom and mass-produced everything in it—the lava lamp, the comforter with tiny lavender flowers, the corkboard with daisy pushpins, the string of white Christmas lights. They even had bottles of GAP Dream perfume.

"Stuck in the '90s," I read out loud. "That's the name of the show?"

The cars, this store, everything I'd seen outside was all a little off.

"Kipps, what year is it?"

He gritted his teeth, like someone had just wired his jaw shut. "Errr . . ."

"Tell me."

He looked away. "2037."

"*2037?*" I repeated. "You're joking."

"I'm not. I swear, I'm not. I didn't really want to be the one to say it but . . ." He gestured at the wall of merchandise. "I guess it's kind of obvious we're not in the '90s, huh?"

"Who else was going to say it? You think we're going to run into some therapist who's going to sit me down and, like, gently break the news to me?" I asked.

Kipps pressed his lips into a straight line.

"So, Bill Clinton? He's not the president?"

"No, he's dead," Kipps said.

"Alanis Morissette? Puff Daddy?"

Kipps cringed. "I don't know? I think they might be alive still? People don't really listen to Alanis Morissette anymore, no offense. Not when Izzy Pike is making music."

"That means . . ." I tried to do the math in my head. "Ew. How old is Scott Wolf? Like . . . 70?"

I couldn't shake the visual. Scott Wolf, *my* Scott Wolf. Old. Wrinkled. GRAY.

"Who is Scott Wolf?" Kipps said.

"Bailey from *Party of Five*?"

It was useless. I kept imagining him with saggy jowls and stooped shoulders. Scott Wolf with a grandpa pancake butt and white hair. "Gross. That is truly repulsive."

I looked up at the screen hanging from the ceiling. Different advertisements scrolled past. "So not only were they lying to me about the set, but I'm not even in the right decade."

I kept thinking about that Jamiroquai video, "Virtual Insanity," where the floor shifted beneath his feet. Furniture slid to the right and then the left and he was pulled down a padded hallway with cockroaches climbing up the walls. Everything kept changing on me, and I couldn't keep up. I didn't have the moves. I was in a pile in the corner, a couch crushing me against the wall, cockroaches tangled in my hair.

"If it makes you feel better, *Stuck* gets the highest ratings of any Like-Life show. That's why they have all this merch."

"It doesn't."

"Whoa." Kipps leaned in, examining his poster. "They airbrushed my abs."

I couldn't help it, I cracked a smile. He definitely looked more chiseled in the photo than he did in real life.

"I thought being ripped was, like, your thing."

"Ummm . . ." He stared at the ceiling. "No."

"What do you mean, no? Everyone talks about how you're, like, this superstar athlete. That you're captain of the varsity soccer team and blah, blah, blah."

"Feel this," he said, and he clapped himself on the shoulder. I brought my hand up beside his and pressed down. There were at least two inches of padding inside his black and red fleece jacket. I laughed as I felt down his arm, where the padding extended, creating a fake bicep. "They tried to get me to work out but I refused. Out of principle. I mean, it's not fun. And I've never liked to sweat. Gross. So then they tried to get me to drink these protein shakes." He bit down on his tongue, like he was choking. "I used to pour them down the sink."

"So you've never played soccer? How is that possible?"

"Stunt double."

I'd almost forgotten where we were, but then I noticed a girl staring at us from the other end of the aisle. She was our age and wore acid-washed jeans with a neon-yellow sweatshirt. She smiled at me like we were friends.

Kipps noticed her the same moment I did, and we both turned and started weaving toward the exit. I tried to tell myself it was a good sign she hadn't said anything, that it might still be okay, but my hands had gone cold. We needed to get out of here.

The automatic doors opened into a courtyard with a clothing store and a sushi restaurant with outdoor tables. A group of guys laughed as they picked at a plate of sashimi. The side of the brick building had four different screens projected onto it, but our set was the only one I recognized. They were still running the live feed from the cul-de-sac.

We crossed the courtyard to one of the car dealerships. The only thing that saved us was people's phones, their "devices" I guessed, which held most of their attention. Everyone was looking down, checking something on their screens, or turning them to show someone else.

The car place had three garage doors made of glass, and one on the side was open, revealing a row of colorful vehicles.

They were all egg shaped, and the seams disappeared, so you could hardly see where the door handles were. A pink-haired woman in the back of the store talked loudly into a headset while simultaneously typing at her desk.

"We can adjust that, sure, let me just run the numbers again . . ." She clicked her tongue against her teeth as she typed.

"What's the move?" Kipps asked, as we circled a glossy black car in front of the others. I traced the spot where the door met the carriage, finding what looked like a handle. When I pushed it in, the door opened, and the vehicle started beeping.

"Would you mind holding for a second?" The pink-haired woman was watching us from across the showroom, but we kept our backs toward her, pretending we were fascinated by the car. "Can I help you with something?"

"We wanted to test-drive the new SL522 . . ." Kipps just read the letters and numbers off the front of the hood. In an even stranger move, he made his voice two octaves lower than it normally was, but he sounded more like a cartoon cowboy than a grown man. I glanced sideways at him, trying to get the message across: Be cool. Play it down.

I could feel her staring at us still, clocking my plaid baby-doll dress and Doc Marten boots. Kipps's North Face fleece and Sambas. Kipps gestured to a cord stuck into the side of the vehicle and a row of lights on the dashboard. *It's on*, he mouthed. Then he said something about it charging.

"You know, I'm going to have to get back to you on that,"

the woman said, returning to her conversation. I heard her chair roll out from under her as she stood. "We don't call it an SL522. It's a NextGen Cloud. Nothing like a Land Rover, that's for sure . . . Patrick."

Patrick. We were statues, that word alone enough to cement us in place. She recognized us. She knew exactly who we were. When I glanced back she was typing away on the screen in her hand.

"Yeah, you're not going to believe who's here . . ." she said, laughing. She touched her earpiece with two fingers. "Jessica Flynn and Patrick Kramer."

Whoever she was talking to responded, and I could only imagine the snarky comment, because the woman threw her head back and laughed even louder this time. I glanced over my shoulder at the crowd in the courtyard. One of the giant screens now had JESSICA FLYNN FLEES STUCK IN THE '90S SET scrolling across the bottom of it as a reporter interviewed a Swickley Alarms guy. My chest felt tight. Kipps was still staring at the pink-haired woman, like he couldn't believe what had just happened.

"Yeah, post it. Sure," she said.

"Let's just go," I whispered, nodding to the car. It was right there, and we didn't have a chance without it. Now that people knew where we were, we'd be completely trapped if we didn't leave now.

Kipps didn't respond, just jumped into the passenger side door and pulled on his seatbelt. I stared at him, waiting for him to realize what he'd done, but he sat there, his hands in his lap.

"I only have a learner's permit," I said. "You're the one who knows how to drive."

"Yeah." He nodded. "A 1995 Land Rover. We couldn't afford one of these."

"Nuh-uh," the woman yelled. "Game's over. Get out. That vehicle's worth more than your life."

She darted out from behind the desk, but I ran around the front of the vehicle and climbed inside. Nothing was the same as my dad's Flynn Pest Control van, the only other car I'd ever practiced in. Those handful of times he took me to the parking lot behind Home Depot, there was always the ignition key, the two pedals, and the gearshift in the center. It was Kipps who found the door locks by hitting the wide screen on the dashboard.

"Enough. Come on, get out," the woman said, reaching us a second later. She pulled at the handle twice, then yelled for someone across the courtyard.

"Where's the gearshift?" I ran my fingers over the center console where it would've been. "How do I put it in drive?"

Kipps scrolled through options on the dashboard screen, swiping this way and that with the tip of his finger. The two pedals were there, beneath my feet—gas and brake. But how was I supposed to use them? Wasn't the car supposed to drive itself?

"Hold on . . ." Kipps said. He pulled up a menu on the screen with a few different options, then pressed one marked *D*. "Try that. Hit the gas."

I pressed down hard on the pedal and the car went skidding out of the showroom. The charger ripped right out of

the wall, creating a long rubber tail that clattered along behind us. We clipped the edge of the garage door on our way
into the parking lot and the glass pane exploded into a thousand pieces.

27

We skidded out into the lot, the broken glass raining down around us. The NextGen Cloud flew off the curb and hit the ground hard. I swerved, trying to avoid a parked car, and slammed right into a brick wall.

"It's fine, it's fine, it's fine." Kipps was running on repeat, glancing at the rearview, then over my shoulder at the small crowd emerging from the courtyard. It wasn't fine, though. The front bumper had made a loud, horrible crunch when it hit the wall, and now it was folded in on itself. Part of the headlight skidded across the ground.

"How do I reverse?" I asked, but as soon as I said it I saw the R on the screen, right beside the D, and pressed it. When I put my foot on the gas again we spun back over the pavement, nearly knocking into a lamppost. I hit the D again, my finger shaking as I touched the screen. But then we were moving forward. We were pulling out onto the main road, speeding away.

It was four lanes wide, with just enough room for someone to pass us. The car was impossibly light. I barely had to
touch the wheel, guiding it through the boxy clip of stores
and restaurants. The small suburban town was similar to
Swickley, only every place was bustling and every parking lot
was full. People clustered outside of bars or lined up at a Chinese take-out window, even though it was getting dark. The
7-Eleven was still open. There were cars in front of us and
behind us, zooming past in both directions. A high-school
baseball field was lit up, a single player racing around the
bases, his gold jersey glittering under the spotlights.

"I'm ready for the part where this thing drives itself,"
I said, my palms slick against the wheel. "When's that going
to happen?"

"You have to opt in, then set a destination," Kipps said.
"It's too risky to be in the system, though. If the car is re-
ported stolen, which it will be, they'll know exactly where
we are."

"Are they following us?" I couldn't bear to check the
rearview mirror.

"I think we're good," Kipps finally said. I didn't know
where to go so I just kept racing forward, trying to get us as
far away from the set as possible.

"So this is the real world . . ." I slowed down for a red
light. A dance studio was lit up, and a few young girls in
tutus pliéed at the barre. "There are people everywhere. It's,
like, bursting with people."

"Yeah, the set's kind of lonely . . . that's the first thing
I noticed when we moved inside permanently. It was bad

enough before, but especially since the strike. And nothing's open after eight, unless you count the diner and the movie theater . . . which is only open if you're there."

The light turned green. Kipps pointed to a sign that said 495 WEST.

"That's the expressway, I remember. If we can just make it there, we have a shot."

We turned left off the main road and into a neighborhood, headed for the highway. It was a version of my life except somehow more vivid, more real. The trees seemed bigger, twisting over us in electric greens, and a boy scrambled up the branches into one. A guy in a Yankees hat mowed his lawn. A teenage girl played tug-of-war with a leggy brown puppy. I had the giddy, floating feeling of falling in love.

I'd never needed things to be perfect. I still saw the missing shingles and the dented trashcans turned over near the curb, and I knew life outside the set would have its own problems. I didn't know anyone here besides Kipps. I only had three dollars in my wallet, and even if I could get one of those device things, I had no idea how to use it.

But racing forward, out over the potholes and broken concrete, my small town and my parents and that hospital felt far away, like it was a story I'd heard about someone else. I let the speedometer climb above thirty, which I'd never done in the Home Depot parking lot. The car responded to even the slightest weight on the pedal, every tilt of the wheel. I was in control.

"You're smiling," Kipps finally said. I didn't notice, but he was staring at the side of my face. "Don't do that, you're scaring me. We're on the run. This is serious business, Jess Flynn. Keep your head in the game."

"My head is in the game."

"Good, because we can't slip up."

"Why are you saying it like that, like I'm the one who'll slip up? Maybe you're the one who's going to do something stupid. You ever think of that?"

"It's not out of the realm of possibility. I had to go to urgent care once after chugging a bottle of Crystal Pepsi."

"That's repulsive. Why would you do that?"

"My brother dared me."

I rolled my eyes, about to get into it with him, but as we approached the highway entrance I saw the bus. It was on a road perpendicular to ours. It sped into the intersection ahead, cutting us off. The logo on the side read LIKE-LIFE PRODUCTIONS in cheerful blue script.

"Shit," Kipps said, the same time I was thinking it. "The producers. That's it—they're not going to let us leave. They blocked off our exit."

"What is that, the shuttle bus?" I said, squinting at the tinted windows. There were people inside.

"Yeah, it's one of the ones that runs to and from the set. There's at least one person from the security team on there. Sometimes more. They have to keep the fans away."

I thought about making a U-turn, but there were already cars behind us, and there was nowhere to go but back. Stores and strip malls penned us in on either side. There must've been three large apartment complexes between us and the on-ramp.

The bus doors opened. Two men in dark shirts got out and stood to one side. They had holsters at their hips . . . Guns? Tasers? Everyone on the bus was watching, and a woman who looked suspiciously like Miss Olivera, Kristen's field hockey coach, pressed her hand to the window. I kept my foot on the gas as we sped closer, but I'd have to brake eventually.

"They're calling my bluff. They don't think I'd hit a bus full of people," I said.

"Yeah, because you wouldn't. It's over."

Kipps gripped the center console with one hand and had his other palm on the side of the door. He wanted me to slow down. I didn't.

"Jess?"

"We can't give up now."

"But there's nowhere to go."

I kept my hands exactly as they had been on the steering wheel. I kept the pressure exactly the same on the gas, even as we got closer to the bus. When we were so close I could see the security team's stunned expressions, I swerved to the right, over a driveway and onto the vast lawn of an apartment complex. I crashed through some bushes and over a small hill before swerving back onto the road, the bus somewhere behind us.

"You did it," Kipps said, turning back. "I can't believe you did it!"

I yanked the wheel hard, to the right, and pulled onto the highway.

28

I'd never been on a highway before, but there was no point in me saying that out loud. Of course Kipps already knew I'd only driven in the Home Depot parking lot, just like he knew about the hamsters I had when I was seven, Rocky and Bullwinkle, and the time I cried in the gym storage closet because Ben Taylor said my eyes were too far apart.

I still really hated Ben Taylor.

Kipps must've known about all of it: the time my mom bought my first tampons, and then my dad mentioned it and I screamed for an hour, because why on earth would she share that with him? Kipps knew I had loved, or at least thought I'd loved, Tyler. He'd probably seen that footage of us from Jen's party. Every time I thought of something to say I realized it had probably already been told to him, that he knew things he couldn't unknow, even if I wanted him to. I was overcome with that horrible, sinking feeling I'd had when my diary went missing in eighth grade. It had fallen behind my bed but for that hour I was so sick I'd nearly thrown up. I kept imagining walking into homeroom and everyone laughing at me, or Chris Arnold reciting passages to our math class.

My secrets and hopes and quirks had been out there for over a decade, for everyone to consume whenever they'd wanted, as cheap and filling as popcorn. They'd made hats and tote bags and lava lamps, monetizing every part of it, but I'd left the set with nothing. My mom had this huge home décor empire and my dad had written books and I'd never even gotten an allowance. I was supposed to work at the Swickley YMCA this year, for the second summer in a row, making five fifteen an hour.

"Could you maybe slow down?" Kipps gripped the handle above the door. "You're not a great driver. No offense."

"Should've taken the wheel when you had the chance."

I checked the rearview, then the side mirrors, which felt like a responsible thing to do. The other vehicles on the highway gave us a wide berth. Every now and then the car made this beeping sound when I drifted over the dotted white line.

Kipps double-checked that his seatbelt was buckled. It was the third time he'd done that in the last twenty minutes. "I don't want to risk the self-driving setting. It's not worth it. Seriously, we'll be lucky if there isn't a tracking device in this thing."

"You think they're tracking us?"

I could barely get the words out.

"Maybe, maybe not. It's hard to know. Some of the newer models had tracking devices, but then there was this whole uproar over privacy, and so they made it opt-in. But it's possible the showroom models have it switched on. Let's just take it as far as we can."

"This is nerve-wracking."

"Which part? Being chased by security people who want to drag us back into a set where we're filmed twenty-four seven and have, oh, zero freedom?"

"Yeah, that."

"Maybe we should get off and take local roads. They're going to catch up with us on the highway. We'll just keep heading west toward the city."

"New York City?"

"Yeah. I've only been twice, when I was a kid, but there are ten million people there. I just think it would be easier to lose them. In these smaller towns we're too exposed."

That sounded right, but I couldn't be sure of anything anymore. We passed a sign for Lakeville Road. I hadn't figured out how to use the turn signals, so I just pulled into the right lane. The driver behind me leaned on their horn.

"See my bag?" I said, pointing to it on the floor by his feet. "Check the book in there. Sara made marks by the different letters. I didn't get a chance to decode it all. There was more."

I went down the ramp too fast and had to slam on the brakes. Thankfully there was no one was behind us.

"I can't read in a car. It makes me sick."

"You're serious?"

"Do you want to see the sandwich I had for lunch?" Kipps raised his eyebrows, his forehead moving like it was made of rubber. Somehow, in the past half hour, he'd morphed into a completely different person than Patrick Kramer. His voice was different. His mannerisms were more exaggerated. He was even a little . . . he was weird.

"Were you just, like, acting the whole time?" I said. "Every time we talked. You were playing Patrick Kramer? What, did they give you a whole pamphlet on me before we met? Something to give you a competitive advantage? *She loves scary movies, raspberry cheesecake, summer weekends at Maple Cove*, blah blah."

He let out a long, shuddering sigh. "Whoa. That's pretty narcissistic."

I tried to keep my expression neutral, but my neck felt itchy and hot. I don't know how much time passed before he finally laughed.

"Jess, I'm kidding," he said. "I've watched the show since I was eight. My family was obsessed with it, especially after the fifth season, when your parents got in that car crash and Lydia took temporary guardianship over you? Everyone was tuning in every week, freaking out about what would happen next."

"Yeah, riveting . . ." I rolled my eyes.

It had happened in the spring, on the night before Easter, and we'd found our unfinished baskets scattered on the floor of our parent's walk-in closet. They must've been building to the finale. Every year there was another catastrophe, another drama, and that one had been small, more manageable, in comparison to the tornado or Sara's diagnosis.

"But yeah, they still made me research you after they

decided I'd be the love interest. Except it wasn't a pamphlet, it was an email with like five thousand attachments and an interactive slideshow and all this crap. I read through your psychological profile and all your likes and dislikes, and then they made me take a test at the end."

I turned left onto a main road. The sky had darkened, slipping into a hazy pinkish blue, and there weren't as many cars out. I just kept driving west, like Kipps said, trying to imagine what my psychological profile would even consist of. What did they have slides of, my favorite foods? The music I listened to?

"You couldn't say no?" I asked.

"My parents aren't really into hearing *no* anymore." Kipps was quiet for a minute, then he rested his forehead on the window. I thought he might say something else, but instead he changed the subject. "What is that, a mall? What town are we in?"

I noticed the building he was talking about, a towering complex with stores on the first floor. The upper levels looked like apartments. We caught glimpses of a man in a tank top cooking dinner and a family huddled in front of a giant screen. ALL TIME MARKET read a sign on the bottom floor. It had the same logo as the supermarket we'd passed through less than an hour before.

"I have no idea . . . "

"We'd never even been to Long Island before we moved onto the set," Kipps said. "I lived in Pennsylvania my whole life. There has to be a map somewhere . . ." He jabbed at the dashboard screen, then dragged his finger right, but he couldn't figure out where to find it.

"We've been going west, for sure," I said.

"How do you know?"

"Doesn't the sun rise in the east and set in the west? Or is that a lie too?"

I pointed to the horizon line, which had the last remnants of the sunset, a few streaks of sherbet pink and orange. I'd pulled down the front visor to block the glare.

"I think that's true," Kipps said.

"I mean, if you're right, we just keep heading this way until we hit the city."

We passed a sprawling golf course. The greens were completely dark, the parking lot empty. I pulled into the right lane to let someone pass when something sounded on the dashboard—a low, steady beep. But the screen was still saying we were in DRIVE. Everything looked exactly the same as it had a few seconds before.

"What is that?" Kipps asked, when it didn't stop after a minute or so. He swiped through the dashboard, eventually stopping at a panel with a red, blinking image of a battery. 5% LEFT.

"Please do not tell me the battery is running out," I said.

"Well, it is, but don't worry," he said. "It says something about a replacement battery. It's probably in the back."

He climbed over the center console and into the cramped backseat, his scrawny butt bumping me in the shoulder as he went. Despite being tall, he was narrower than most guys our age, and he moved completely differently now that he wasn't on camera. His limbs seemed floppier, wild almost, compared to the rigid, buttoned-up guy I'd talked to at Jen Klein's party.

He fiddled with a panel in the backseat. When he finally opened it, a silver battery was inside, with two cords coming out of the top. I watched in the rearview mirror as he examined it.

"Is that the spare?"

"Um . . . bad news. I don't think there is a spare."

"So what does that mean?"

"It means we're going to have to ditch this thing."

The beeping was incessant. I hit the button on the screen, where it said 3% LEFT, but nothing stopped it.

"And what are we going to do with it?" I said. "We can't just leave it on the side of the road. Whoever finds it is going to know we're here, in . . ." I scanned the shoulder and spotted a sign that read LAKESIDE GOLF CLUB, EST. 2002. ". . . Lakeside."

Kipps was still in the backseat, and he went from window to window, surveying our surroundings. I'd barely moved my hands the whole time I'd been driving. The car was slowing down, from forty miles an hour to thirty-five, and falling still. It didn't matter how hard I pressed on the gas pedal. Nothing helped.

"There's no one behind us right now," I said, glancing in the rearview mirror. "Maybe we just pull the car onto the golf course and leave it there. They won't find it until morning. It'll at least buy us some time."

"Sure, great." Kipps peered out the back windshield, then the front, checking for oncoming cars. "Go now."

I turned the wheel to the right and our front tire hit the curb first. The impact threw us back in our seats, but we kept going, breaking through a bush and out onto the golf course. The hill we were on sloped down and we picked up speed. We hadn't counted on the lake that split the green.

"Turn the wheel, just go around," Kipps yelled.

"I can't."

I tried to guide the car off to the left, but the momentum was too strong. When I braked we just skidded over the damp grass. We went down one more slope and crashed into the lake, water splashing over the front bumper.

"This is not good," Kipps said, as the vehicle floated out, slowly coming to a stop where the water was deep. I went to roll down my window but couldn't. I banged on the glass, my heart alive in my chest. This wasn't how it was supposed to end, not here. Not like this. I wasn't going to drown in some nasty golf course lake.

Think, think, I repeated silently. Kipps said something but it was somewhere beyond me. It was a few seconds before I came up with anything.

"We have to open the doors, just let the water come in," I said. The hood was already submerged, and the vehicle was starting to tilt to one side. "Then get as far away from it as possible."

"Really?"

"I saw it on *Rescue 911*."

"Cool, I guess. I trust William Shatner," Kipps said.

"On the count of three. One, two . . ."

I never made it to three, I just nodded, and we pushed the doors open at the same time. The water was relentless, rushing into the Cloud and sinking it twice as fast as before. I kicked off the frame and swam as far out as I could. I'd completely cleared the car when I realized what I'd done.

"Oh no . . . my purse," I said. "I need it."

"You do not need your purse. Have you lost your mind?" Kipps yelled. He was on the other side of the vehicle, swimming toward shore. The water rushed over the roof. Then slowly, gracefully, it slipped below the surface.

"It has the book—the code Sara left," I said.

I took a deep breath and dove under before he could argue with me, swimming fast toward the sinking Cloud. The water was a murky greenish color, and it wasn't until I was only a few feet away that I was able to see the outline of the thing. The door was swept back and tilted up toward the sky. I had to wrench myself on top of it to get in.

The purse wasn't near the steering wheel like I thought it might be. I'd hoped it had floated up as the Cloud tipped on its side. Instead I had to go farther into the car, diving down into the well beneath the passenger seat and feeling for it there. I still couldn't find it. My lungs were hurting now, and I could hear my pulse in my ears. I knew I wouldn't be able to last much longer and still have enough air to get back to the surface. I felt around the back seats before pulling myself out.

I was swimming away from the Cloud when I caught sight of it, drifting along the bottom of the lake. My chest felt like it might explode. Part of me wanted to get to the surface and take another breath, but what if the bag was gone by the time I came back? I dove several feet down, the pressure in my head growing. As I looped the strap around my arm, I could no longer see the surface. The sky had gone completely dark and it all looked the same—up, down, sand, stars. I wasn't even sure where the car was anymore. I could feel panic taking over—that need for another breath.

Then I felt Kipps's hand on my arm. He tugged and we were both moving fast toward the surface, him kicking wildly as I floated behind him, clinging tight to his hand.

29

"That was bad. Really, really bad," Kipps repeated. "We have to be more careful."

"What did you want me to do, leave it there?" I asked. "I still haven't figured out the last pages. I don't know what Sara was trying to tell me. There's more to it, there has to be."

I pulled my hair into a ponytail, squeezing the water out through the ends. My baby-doll dress stuck to my legs. It didn't matter how many times I twisted the hem or shook out my denim jacket, they were soaked. We stood in the middle of the golf course, trying to steel ourselves against the night air, but everything inside me was trembling. It must've been fifty degrees.

"What now?" Kipps wrung out his fleece with both hands. The padding was more obvious now—there were lumps around the top of the jacket sleeves. Without it his arms were long and elegant, like a dancer's.

I looked up at the golf complex a hundred yards off. It was possible they had security cameras. Even if they didn't, someone driving by could've seen the break in the bushes, the tire marks. It was impossible to know how much time we had.

"Let's get out of here," I said.

But where were we supposed to go? We had no money, there was no obvious place to go, and the woods around the golf course were dense. I trudged up the hill in front of us, moving away from the clubhouse and toward a cluster of trees. Kipps's footsteps squished in the grass behind me. *We have to be more careful*, he'd said, but all I'd heard was *you have to be more careful. You almost got me killed*. It hadn't been a choice, though, not really. If I left the book I never would've known what Sara needed to tell me, if she was outside the set, if there was any way to see her again. Kipps already had answers about who he was. I needed mine.

When we got to the tree line I turned back, studying the lawn. In the moonlight the lake was a flat silver coin. The car was completely submerged. The only sign that it had sunk was a steady stream of bubbles breaking the surface. Two lines of grass were ripped up where I'd tried to brake.

We started through the trees. We could barely see in the dark, the golf course was getting farther away with each step. My clothes were cold and stiff against my skin, and even though I crossed my arms inside my jacket I couldn't hold on to any body heat. My fingers and toes were already numb.

"This is beyond creepy," Kipps said.

"It has to be better than walking along a main road."

"We didn't come all this way to freeze to death in the woods."

"We won't. See? What do you think that is?"

I already knew, I didn't need him to answer. There were two lights about a hundred yards off. Porch lights. It took a few more minutes before we passed a wooden fence, and I saw some houses through the trees. Huge, stately brick things, with high fences and covered pools. One had white shingles and columns that framed a porch. Most of them had lights on inside, but when we passed one that was dark, I pointed to the back door and the shed beside the fence.

"What about that one? No one's home, at least not right now. We could try the shed."

"The cameras, though . . ." It took me a minute to realize what he was pointing to. A plastic dome was perched on each house. "We have to find one that doesn't have a security system. Not like that, at least."

It took us another ten minutes to find a house without cameras. Every window was completely dark, and the backyard had a covered pool with a guesthouse. We peered through the glass door. A couple with two young kids stared back at us from a framed photo on the wall. If I wasn't freezing and hungry, I might've felt guiltier. But my shoes were soaked through. I had on one layer of wet clothes and I could feel it getting colder. We had to do this.

"You ready?" Kipps asked. He tried the doorknob but it was locked.

"Are you?" I turned back to the main house and checked

the windows again, making sure no one was there.

"I guess. I've never broken into someone's home before."

"It's technically a guesthouse, so maybe that's better?"

We both knew it wasn't. He pressed his elbow against the glass square closest to the doorknob, then wrapped his other hand around his fist. He hit the glass pane twice before it broke. Then he reached his hand over and popped the lock. We slipped inside, shutting the door behind us.

I held the lyric book above the stove, just out of reach of the blue flame. I'd been drying it out for a half hour but its pages were still rippled and warped. I'd tried to save the photo strip, too, delicately pinching its corners as I moved it closer and closer to the heat. It had only kind of worked. Sara and I looked fuzzier than before, and I'd accidentally smudged my mouth off in the bottom picture.

"It's very possible this is going to save us," I said. "This is the thing that's going to tell us what to do next."

"An Alanis Morissette lyric book," he said, staring at it.

"That's right. Technically it's not just any lyric book, it's *Jagged Little Pill*."

"Just wanted to be sure."

"You have any better ideas? I'm open."

Kipps felt around one of the top cabinets, but there was only a stack of paper plates. He moved on to a set of drawers. We'd found some pool towels and robes in the bathroom, where we'd hung our clothes to dry. The guesthouse had a tiny kitchen and a loft bed, but the fridge was empty, unless you counted the bottle of ketchup and loaf of moldy bread.

"I still have uncles who live outside the set, an aunt, a bunch of cousins," Kipps said as he checked behind some cutlery. "We could try to call them, but it's a risk. The producers have probably paid them off already."

"Paid them off? Come on, you think they'd actually tell them where we are?"

Kipps raised one eyebrow. "If it meant fifty grand? A hundred? Yeah, of course they would. People are desperate. My Uncle Roo hasn't worked in five, six years. The trade wars started, then the economy tanked. The unemployment rate has skyrocketed. It's pretty bleak out here." When he got to a lower cabinet he smiled. "Yes!"

He held up a bag of pretzels and a six-pack of Heineken. It wasn't much, but it was something. He examined the top of the bag and scrunched his nose.

"The expiration date was in 2035. Not ideal."

"Sounds fine for a girl from 1998." I opened the bag and tried one. They really didn't taste stale. "I'll pass on the beer though. It doesn't do anything for me."

Kipps stood and hugged the six-pack to his chest. "Well, I think you'll feel differently about these. These are very, very special Jess. They have alcohol in them."

I tried to read his expression, not sure if he was joking.

"You're telling me I've never actually had alcohol? Every single drink I've had was fake?"

"Correct."

I was going to say something about the wine coolers Amber always lifted from her basement fridge, but then I realized they were part of the set too. It was all part of the set, and they couldn't give us alcohol with millions of people watching. It was weird to think the actors might've been pretending to be drunk when they weren't. Or maybe they actually were drunk, and they'd just snuck in their own liquor supply. I'd spent so many parties surveying the room, wondering why I wasn't laughing as loud as the rest of them. Why didn't I ever feel like dancing on the couch or sliding down Jen Klein's banister?

"So Chris Arnold . . . ?" I said out loud, not really talking to Kipps, to anyone.

"Not a drinker—he's just that good. Plays a wasted dude like nobody's business."

Kipps cracked open a can and passed it to me. He opened one for himself and clinked it against mine. "To your first real drink. I'm sure it would be better cold, but us scavengers can't be picky."

The first sip tasted like the nonalcoholic version, but when I swallowed it down it stung a little bit. I didn't mind that it was room temperature. We were in robes, and with the stove going for the past half hour, the place suddenly felt cozy. Comfortable.

"This isn't your first drink?" I asked.

"I'd sneak one every now and then from my parents' supply. At some point they stopped saying anything about it."

"It tastes just as bad as the nonalcoholic kind," I said. "Except it's kind of worth it?"

Three sips in and I already felt the warmth spreading out in my chest. I left the book open beside the stove and sat on the couch, pulling my knees up beneath me. The cushions were so soft it was like sitting in a cloud. I leaned back and my whole body sunk into them.

"About what you said before, how it's bleak . . ." I pointed out the window at the front house, with its manicured lawn and stone facade. "It doesn't look so bleak. Everything here seems really . . . nice."

"This is a bubble." Kipps passed me the pretzels, then took a long swig of his beer. He'd curled up on the floor across from me, his back against the wall. "Most people aren't living like this. It's hard to make decent money, even if you have a job at a big company. That's why working inside the set is such a draw. All of a sudden, you get health insurance and a pension, a salary, and all these other benefits. They put my family up in a three-thousand-square-foot house with a hot tub and a wine fridge. I didn't even know wine fridges were, like, a thing."

"But they weren't paying the extras well," I said. "Otherwise, why would they strike?"

"It's all relative," Kipps said. "The audience doesn't have sympathy for them because those jobs are so hard to get, and they can't understand why anyone would jeopardize having steady work. But I see it, I know. The extras don't have the full benefits that a guest star does, and then they have to commute into the set on top of that, and some of them are working twelve, fourteen-hour days, six days a week. It takes a lot just to populate the town. There's a rumor that everyone who was part of the strike is done, fired. Chrysalis Remington—the creator of the show—she apparently said she'll never let them come back."

"So, what? She was just going to replace half the school and hope I didn't notice?" The beer went down easy, and my cheeks felt warm to the touch. The tension in my back released. It wasn't so bad, this whole drinking thing.

"In fairness," Kipps laughed, "you didn't notice when they replaced the actress who plays Kristen's stepmom."

"Wait . . . what?"

Tess Stavros owned the diner where Kristen worked. It had supposedly been in her family for over thirty years. I remembered the exact moment she looked different, how we'd come in one night and she was behind the counter wearing these thick black glasses. Her hair was down even though she usually pulled it back, the hairnet visible when she was standing directly beneath the overhead lights.

"Kristen told me she'd just lost some weight. And she needed the glasses for reading." I tried to laugh, but I could already feel the heaviness of that particular betrayal, how easy Kristen had rambled off an explanation. She was too good a liar. "This is beyond messed up."

"Welcome to the world in color," he said, taking another sip of beer. "We're not in Kansas anymore."

I looked out the window, checking the backyard. The main house was still dark. We only had one light on above the stove, but I got up and pulled the curtain shut so it was less obvious we were there.

"You know what I always wondered about?" I leaned forward, my elbows on my knees. "That guitar teacher I had. Harry?"

"His real name was Arthur Von Appen," Kipps said.

"So you knew him?"

"The whole world knew who Arthur was."

"Because he tried to tell me. That time we were alone the den," I said. "I never saw him after that."

"No one saw him," Kipps explained. "It was like he vanished off the face of the earth—because he did. They were sending a message."

"You think they killed him?" I asked. "They make TV shows. They're not the mafia."

Kipps held up his hands. "Let's just say . . . I don't think they *didn't* kill him."

"Come on, Kipps. You can't seriously believe that."

"*Stuck in the '90s* is their highest rated show. There are viewers all over the world. It's our last gasp of global influence," he said, pulling the robe tighter around his shoulders. "They're not going to let anyone jeopardize those advertising dollars. People who threaten the show are at risk. It's that simple. Like-Life Productions uses ex-military for their security team."

The mention of the security team made me uneasy. I could still picture the two men standing in front of the bus, and the authority with which they moved, as if they deserved to be there more than anyone else. It was possible that one choice—taking guitar lessons—had pulled Arthur into my orbit, and trying to help me had cost him his life. I wished I could somehow undo it, that I could somehow go back.

"You think they'd . . . what? They'd kill us?"

The question floated there between us. Kipps let out a long staggering breath.

"Kipps?"

"I don't know. That's the truth."

"No, they can't," I said, but I had a sick, unsettling feeling in the pit of my stomach. "They need us. I'm not some random neighbor. You aren't a substitute teacher or one of those fake doctors. Isn't your family getting their own spin-off show?"

"They can do whatever they want." He was usually so light with everything he said, but this was different. Now his tone was flat and even. It unnerved me. "I don't know how far they'd take it. Nothing surprises me anymore. Besides, you know they're going to draw this all out. I can't even imagine what the ratings have been like this week. That shot of us dodging the bus?"

"Entertaining, yeah," I said, rolling my eyes.

I got up and checked on the lyric book. It was still damp in places, but you could see the markings under the letters, even if they had faded a bit. I'd be able to go through it in the morning.

I tried to push away the idea that the producers might take things further than they already had. We couldn't know where the bottom was, how deep and dark it would go, what kind of extremes they might inflict on us. I told myself Kipps was exaggerating, that they were making a TV show—it was about entertainment, that's all it was.

But part of me kept pushing back. They were the ones who'd signed off on the Guignard's Disease storyline. They thought it was fine, ideal even, for me to watch my sister die. For me to suffer through those three vicious years, spending anxiety-stricken weeks waiting for test results, or organizing and outfitting Sara's room, trying to make it somewhere she didn't hate spending all her time. It had been torture, death by a thousand paper cuts, and my parents hadn't done a thing to stop them.

"Just for the record . . . I didn't want to lie to you. That wasn't my choice," Kipps said. "I was never supposed to be a lead. It didn't start out that way."

"So what happened?"

"My family and I were extras on the show, and a few years in I had the grave misfortune of being 'discovered.'" Kipps made quote signs with his fingers. "One of the producers was all, I like this guy's cheekbones. He polls well with the audience. Let's prep him to be the love interest."

"That was ninth grade, huh?"

We didn't really talk back then, but even I'd realized Kipps had changed, that he was different somehow. In middle school he hung out with the video yearbook kids and was editor of the school newspaper. I always saw him in the computer lab playing Oregon Trail. Then he'd started hanging out exclusively with the athletes. Suddenly everyone was talking about how he was the fastest soccer player on the team, or spreading rumors about him and Julie Pinski hooking up in the woods behind the gym. Soon there were three guys trailing behind him wherever he went, as if he'd started his own boy band.

"So you don't play any sports?"

"None."

"What do you talk about with those guys then? They're all so . . ."

"Dumb?" he said. "I've met poodles that are smarter than Ben Taylor. Outside the set he goes by Golden. Just one name: Golden. He hawks some kind of protein powder."

"He said my eyes were too far apart."

"That wasn't acting. He really is a dick."

"What did you do in the set, then? If you didn't play sports and you didn't go to the Wolf Den and you didn't talk to those guys you spent all your time with?"

"My brother Reed and I play Dirt Road, this VR game." He sat up straighter, gesturing with the beer can. "Oh, and there's this fantasy series called the Voyage of Laggerbath. Nine books. I've read them all five times, no joke."

"The Voyage of Laggerbath," I repeated. "One of the many other things I missed. At some point you're going to have to catch me up on the last forty years."

I hadn't meant it to come out the way it had. Self-deprecating and a little sad, like I was an animal who'd never seen the sun. But there were whole decades I knew nothing about. Television shows and movies, presidents and wars. My existence had been limited to a five-mile radius, to that small town and all the manufactured drama there. I'd never even been to New York City before, never seen the Statue of Liberty or the Brooklyn Bridge, and we'd lived less than an hour away.

"Everything feels so warped," I said. "Like, I should be happy, right? That I'm away from my parents, from two people who not only lied to me about the show but about my sister dying. God knows how long they were going to keep it a secret. Maybe forever. It's like they had no concept of what that would do to me, how it would send my life careening off in this whole other direction." I turned the book to a damp page and held it closer to the flame. "But it's not like this will be any easier. In almost every way, it'll be a million times harder. We're like . . . runaways."

"You're saying you want to go back?" Kipps tilted his head to the side, studying me.

There were things I missed already. Those mornings when my bedroom window was open just a crack, and I was warm underneath my comforter, Fuller curled up on the end of the bed. I missed the lasagna Lydia made, and how when she was cooking the whole house smelled like tomato sauce. My mom loved playing board games, in this way that really must've been impossible to fake, and she'd challenge me to Guess Who? long after I'd outgrown it. She was always doing things to try to fake me out, make me think she had someone she didn't, like ask all the questions she didn't want me to ask (*Does he have a mustache? Is he a blond?*). Even now, I missed the way she laughed. It didn't happen often, but when she did she couldn't stop, and she sometimes doubled forward, covering her mouth with her hand.

How had it gone so far? How had we gotten to this place, where I was in a stranger's house, in stolen clothes, drinking a beer with a boy I hardly knew? My parents had been making money off the show, lots of it. And part of me understood the need to document our life, to enter it into some formal record, as if that made it count in a way it couldn't otherwise. But they had hired someone to play my sister. I kept turning that over—they hired a child actor to play my sister. They'd staged a car crash and a burglary, her illness and death. At what point had that life fumbled out of their control? Was there a moment when they could feel themselves slipping, saying yes to things they shouldn't have? Did they regret it at all?

"Sometimes I think I was just like a prop in my parents' life. Another thing for them to sell. I want to be wrong about that, I do, but they need to show me. If they want me to come back, let them show me they understand what they did wrong. Let them prove they love me, that at least that much was real. I mean, they should be able to prove that, right?"

It was probably naive, but the idea of going back inside the set and living by their rules, of having to listen to them and pretend they deserved my respect . . .

"I guess that's what I wanted to say before," Kipps said, pushing the beer tab back and forth. "I'm sorry. You know, that I was part of it. It was wrong and I always knew that, I guess. I always knew."

I waved the book in the heat, flipped over another page and dried that too. I wasn't sure how to respond. He should be sorry; he should feel awful.

"You don't have to say anything," he tried.

"I know I don't."

"But if you wanted to give me a sense, or even a number, from one to ten, on how big of a douchebag you think I am . . . ten being the Biggest Douchebag in the World and one being Not a Douchebag at All, then I—"

"Four."

"Four? Not bad."

He seemed momentarily pleased with himself.

I set the book down and sat on the floor across from him, my legs folded to one side. I took a few more sips of beer. "What if you're right, what if I'm just being optimistic. What if we can't rely on Sara, or whatever her name is. What if we've got nothing besides the three dollars in my wallet and these bathrobes."

"We try to figure it out?" Kipps gestured with the can. "Think of it this way, if I have over four hundred days until I'm eighteen, and you have . . . ?"

"A hundred and sixty," I said. "Something like that. Assuming my birthday is actually my birthday."

"We just have to make it that far. Then we come out and give our sides of the story. We can write books, do the whole talk-show circuit. I mean, whether we want it or not, we're going to be recognizable for a long time after this. We might as well cash in and make it work for us. On our terms."

I groaned out loud, like he'd just punched me in the gut. The thought of being on camera again, after going through so much to escape the set? I didn't care if I was getting paid for it, or I was telling my side of the story . . . it was a hellish prospect.

"I'm just saying," he tried, "it's an easy way for us to make money."

"Okay, say we do that, which I'm not actually agreeing to. Where do we go until then? We can't stay in New York. The city is still too close to the set, even if there are a gazillion people there."

"They're going to think you're headed to Los Angeles. All that LA talk," he said.

"No, definitely not . . ."

I didn't want to be Jessica Flynn anymore, star of *Stuck in the '90s*. The thought of being on stage at the Troubadour, in front of some massive audience, had lost all appeal. I could still feel people's eyes on me, even when I was in the privacy of a bathroom, and I'd started turning the lights off every time I changed my clothes. It was going to take years before I trusted a mirror. I still checked them from all different angles, trying to see if they were even the slightest bit transparent.

I didn't want to go to some big city, where I'd fight through sidewalk crowds and be stuck in bumper-to-bumper traffic, or have to face dozens of commuters on the subway. I didn't even really want to go to New York, but I knew it was the right choice.

"There are hundreds of trains and buses leaving the city every day," I said. "All we need is to make it onto one. Let's go somewhere remote, somewhere where there aren't a lot of people."

"Antarctica?" Kipps smiled.

"There aren't trains to Antarctica," I said, and held up a finger. "But yes, you get the idea. Somewhere beautiful. Somewhere remote. Somewhere where no one will look at me ever."

"I can't promise I won't look at you. That would be very, very hard."

When he said it, there was something else there. Then he smiled and I tried to ignore the heat in my cheeks, the sudden awareness that he thought I was pretty.

"I'm serious, Kipps. I don't want to go somewhere where people will recognize us, or come up to me in the street and start trying to talk to me. I know 99 percent of the world wants to be famous, but it sucks. It isn't actually fun. Let's find a cheap place in northern California, somewhere by the beach. Maybe New Mexico or Vermont. We'll just find somewhere and wait out the time however we can."

"Together."

Kipps stretched his hand out for me to take. It hadn't been obvious before that, that we'd stay together, no matter what. But we only had each other now. We both knew we'd never make it alone.

I pressed my palm to his, and his fingers clasped mine. He squeezed. The light was streaming in from the glass door, and for the first time I noticed the way his nose angled down to the left, just the slightest bit, this perfect imperfection. He'd rinsed off in the shower and his hair was still damp. A few curls fell over to the side of his forehead, framing his face.

"What?" he asked, narrowing his eyes at me.

"Nothing."

He squeezed my hand again and held it there. I tried to fix my expression into something normal, something that betrayed nothing, but I knew he'd already seen it. I couldn't stop myself even if I'd wanted to.

He'd seen my googly love eyes.

30

We sat on the floor, our backs against the couch. Kipps was fiddling with a sleek white remote control, jabbing at a button on the top and then shaking it, trying to get the battery to work. We wanted to check the news to make sure no one had found the NextGen Cloud in the lake.

"I've never used one of these things," he said.

"Let me try."

"It's not intuitive."

"Uh, I think I'll be able to figure it out," I said, reaching for the remote. "Don't say it like that. *It's not intuitive.*" I mimicked his voice.

He pulled the remote away and we wrestled for it, my arm stretching out behind him, our faces inches apart. After the second beer I felt bolder, and I didn't pull away when we fell to the side and rolled over the carpet, our bodies smushed together. I held the remote high in the air and pressed the button in the center. When that didn't work I tried another button on the side.

A hole in the wall opened and a small black lens appeared. In an instant, it projected an image on the smooth, flat wall across from us.

"Ah-ha!! And you said it couldn't be done!" I threw my arms in the air and did a little dance.

"You are a genius," he said, bowing. "And I am nothing."

"That's right."

I took the last swig of my beer and stared up at the screen. The center button on the remote spun counterclockwise, and when I pressed it with my thumb a guide popped up on the wall. There were hundreds of channels. Every time I turned the button, dozens more appeared.

"Whoa," I said, scrolling down. "There were four channels inside the set. Four."

"You only had four channels on your specific TV," he said. "But we got all of them. They were trying to control what you saw."

There had been a news channel I never watched, a sports channel that ran different football and baseball games on repeat, and then the SWB, which played all our favorite shows. *Party of Five* and *90210* and the TGIF lineup, which we'd watched religiously when we were younger. The fourth channel played movies all day long, some classics and then newer stuff like *Ghost* or *Clueless*. One day they played *The Poseidon Adventure* from 1972 on repeat for twelve hours straight, and Sara and I watched it three times in a row.

"Ooh, there," Kipps said, and pointed to something at the bottom of the list. The title said *Stuck in the '90s: The Aftermath*.

"I don't want to see anymore *Stuck in the '90s* coverage," I said. "I've had enough."

"It's not coverage, it's one of those post-show things where they have some of the actors on," Kipps said. "We should just see who they're interviewing. It would be good to know what they're saying."

I scrolled down and clicked into it, and suddenly my parents and Sara and Lydia were all there. Sara wore an iridescent blue blouse and hoop earrings. Her dark hair was styled in big barrel curls that spilled down in front of her shoulders.

"Oh my God," I said, sitting up on my knees. "Sara looks so good. She looks healthy."

I hadn't seen her like that in years. She was still a little thinner than she was before she'd gotten diagnosed, but her cheeks had color to them. She was wearing real clothes, not the flannel pajamas she'd spent every day in. She was sitting up straight with her legs crossed. She looked so grown up.

The host must've been sixty-five or seventy, his hair gray at the temples. When he spoke, you could see deep dimples in both of his cheeks. He looked suspiciously familiar, though I couldn't figure out why.

"Let me ask you, you've come under fire for your choices these past three years concerning Sara," he said. "And we know there was a rift between you and Charli over Sara leaving the show. What do you have to say to those critics?"

"Charli Dean," Kipps explained. "That's Lydia's real name."

My mom glanced down at her hands. She twisted her bracelet back and forth before she finally spoke. "I'm used to the critics. People say I'm a bitch, I'm cruel. I'm a bad mother. I've heard it all. But we made the choices—and let me remind you it's a *we*—it's me *and* Carter."

"It is a we," my dad echoed. "They always come at her, but we make decisions together. I'm not as laid-back as I play on the show. People should know that by now."

"It's all internalized misogyny," my mom said, "this rage that is solely directed at mothers, but that's another discussion. What people don't fully understand is that this choice we made over seventeen years ago, to bring Jess into the show—we're still feeling the weight of that choice. And Carter and I agreed it would be better if we waited until she was older to disclose the nature of the show. Every year it got harder. You tell yourself, maybe we'll just wait one more year, maybe when she's sixteen. Maybe now's the time to do it, but it's a hard call."

"It never felt like the right moment," the host said.

"No, it didn't," my dad jumped in. "We agreed with Chrysalis, the creator, that eighteen was a good time. When she turned eighteen. That way she could decide what she wanted her life to look like after, if she wanted to leave the show and go to college or continue on in some capacity."

"Or because every year that went by that I didn't know, you were all profiting. The status quo was good. You were all making money," I said.

Kipps pumped his fist in the air in solidarity. "Truth."

"And the feud with Charli?" the host asked.

"Charli and I have had our disagreements," my mom said, nodding.

"Yes, we have," Charli agreed. "And we will continue to have those disagreements."

"Why's that?" the host asked. "That sounds intense."

Charli straightened up in her seat. Her bright blond hair was pulled back, and she was wearing a neon-pink shift dress she never would've worn inside the set. Her gray eyes were lined with lash extensions.

"I think Sara and I," she started, "we ultimately realized it was our time to leave the show. That this was right. It's just . . . at a certain point our hearts were not in it."

"What do you mean?" the host asked.

"We just started to look forward more to the end of the show than the day-to-day, if that makes sense."

"And I think for me," Sara said, as the name SARA FLORES appeared on the screen below her, "my role has been so limited there isn't a lot to miss. I'll hate not seeing Jess, of course. We really were sisters. That part you can't fake."

"I think we all felt that," the host said.

"My mom and I are really excited about what's next. As you know, Mario, this is our last public appearance." She glanced into the camera. "I think we could both use some time to ourselves. Out of the public eye."

It was the way Sara said it that made me feel like it was just for us, some kind of clue.

The host let them sit there, hoping the silence might force them to say something more revealing. After a minute he turned back to my mom and dad. It was only then, looking at his profile, that I realized who he was. Mario Lopez—A. C. Slater from *Saved by the Bell*. He'd become a talk show host.

"You know I have to ask, now that Jess has left—fled the show . . . do you regret anything?" Mario Lopez asked. "If you could change anything, would you?"

"We have every reason to believe this is temporary," my dad said. "They're already narrowing down her location."

"And if it's not?" he went on.

"It is, we know it is," my mom insisted.

"You've both been so open about the difficult childhoods you had," Mario went on. "Helene, you've talked about how abusive your parents were. Carter, your mother died when you were young and your father left when you were three. You bounced around between different family members. One of your goals with this show was to give Jess the childhood you never had. Seeing the 1990s through a different lens, as you would have wanted it to be. Do you think you succeeded?"

"I do," my mom said. She turned to my dad. "I really do. I think most of Jess's childhood was idyllic."

"I agree. And we're excited to make more memories together," my dad said.

There was an awkward look between Sara and Charli. They would not be included in those memories, that much was clear. Something had happened between the four of them, but I couldn't tell what, exactly. It seemed like they truly hated each other.

Mario Lopez said something about the producers looking for us, but he didn't give any specific details, and no one said anything about the lake or the NextGen Cloud we'd crashed. Then the show cut to a local news story about a fire in a scooter factory. It was just eleven o'clock.

"Well, that was thoroughly depressing," I said. "God, all that stuff about my parents' childhoods . . ."

I closed my eyes, trying to push down my feelings. It didn't excuse any of it, of course it didn't, but I hated the idea of my dad moving around every few months, or my mom being in an abusive home. They'd always told me my grandparents were dead. When they did talk about their childhoods it was only the brief mention of Grants Pass, Oregon, where my mom grew up, or some story about how my dad's dad had sold vacuums.

"I'm sorry," Kipps repeated.

I shook my head. "It's not your fault."

I hit the remote and the lens disappeared into the wall. The room was dark except for the light streaming in through the door. I looked at the loft bed. My head hurt from thinking so much. I just wanted sleep.

"I need to shut my eyes. This day . . . it's too much."

"I can take the couch. You go, sleep."

Kipps collected the beer cans from off the floor and tossed them in the trash. He fixed the sofa so the pillows were straight, and I could tell he was just a little bit drunk, his movements different than they normally were. I didn't think I'd say it until I did.

"There's enough room for both of us, I think. But if

you're going to be a prude about it we could sleep head to toe, like the grandparents in *Willy Wonka*."

What the hell was wrong with me? Couldn't I say something cool, even if it was only this one time?

Kipps just smiled. "I am not being Grandpa Joe, I'll tell you that much. Maybe the other grandpa. The one everyone forgets about."

I turned off the stove and fanned the lyric book out so the rest of it could dry. Kipps was right behind me as we climbed the ladder to the loft, and when I got to the queen-size bed I tossed him one of the two pillows. He lay down with his head by my feet, and he stayed on top of the blankets, snuggling the long terry-cloth robe around him. We both stared up at the ceiling.

"Goodnight," he finally said.

"Let me know if you need some blankets."

"I think I'm good."

I closed my eyes and listened to him breathing. The loft ceiling was so low that my whole head filled with the sound. A minute passed, then ten, but I felt more awake than I'd been all day. Every time he shifted on the bed I opened my eyes a crack, trying to check if he was sleeping.

His eyes were still closed. He'd turned over onto his side, curling in on himself. It was weird, being this close to him, when just a week ago he was someone I was trying to avoid. I stared at his face, how his cheek smushed against the pillow. Suddenly he felt as unfamiliar as the room we were sleeping in. Did I know him? Could I really trust him? After Tyler, part of me wanted to swear off boys entirely.

"Jess . . . I can't sleep."

He didn't open his eyes.

"Me neither," I said.

He stuck out his elbow, propping his head in his hand so he faced me. "I guess I'm not used to sleeping in bed with girls."

"You make it sound so scandalous," I said. He looked down, embarrassed. "But yeah, I guess I'm not used to sleeping in bed with boys."

"It's weird, right?" He seemed genuinely thrilled to acknowledge it.

"I mean, I just watched my parents on a talk show, telling A. C. Slater why they lied to me for my entire life . . . so . . ."

"Yeah, it's all relative." He pulled his robe up around his neck, and we were both silent for a minute. "What are you thinking?"

"Right now?"

"Yeah."

"I was wondering . . . if I could actually trust you. It doesn't feel like I can trust anyone anymore."

Kipps stuck out his bottom lip and nodded, like he was considering it. "You'll have to wait and see."

"Kipps!" I nudged his leg. "The answer is: YES."

"I mean: YES!" He smiled. "But you can wait and see."

"I just don't understand how it went that far, you know?" I said, tracing a seam along the pillow. "How did my parents agree to it all?"

"This might be hard to hear, but the show isn't all bad," he said. He waited, but when I didn't respond he kept going.

"When I was eight, my dad lost his job. He was drinking a lot. My brother and I started watching it for the first time. You and Sara had just found Fuller behind the bowling alley."

"They'd stuck him in that cardboard box."

"Yeah . . . and you'd take him into your backyard and play with him for hours. You'd dress him up in doll clothes and pretend to serve him tea, and he'd jump in that pile of dried leaves and roll around, and you'd laugh and laugh. Anyway, we loved watching the show. It made us feel normal for that hour. Like things might be okay."

He smiled, and in that moment I noticed everything about him, like I was looking through a camera lens that had suddenly come into focus. There was a tiny mole just below his right cheekbone, and his eyes narrowed so much when he was smiling I could barely see what color they were.

"I know how evil the show is, I do," he went on. "And even when my family was making all these choices inside the set, and I knew they were wrong, I felt the tiniest bit conflicted about everything. Because people love the show, and they love it because it makes them happy—if only for an hour every day. Outside the set, it's all some people have."

"And you think my parents knew that? That that was part of why they kept going?"

Kipps shrugged. "Maybe. I'm not sure."

He fell back so he was staring up at the ceiling again. He tightened the robe around him.

"I guess, just . . . thank you," he finally said. "For that."

I adjusted the pillow so I could see him better. He stretched out his hand toward me and I took it, letting our fingers fold into each other. His eyes closed first, and I watched him for a long time, how his chest rose and fell with each breath. Kipps was careful with what he said to me. He didn't just talk to talk, and I knew that was a good thing, even if everything else felt unsure. We'd gotten this far, hadn't we?

We were still holding hands when I finally gave in to sleep.

31

For that first minute before I opened my eyes, I was back in my bed in Swickley, the comforter pulled up around my neck. I could almost feel Fuller at the end of the bed, tucked to the left of my feet. My alarm clock on the nightstand beside my head. For that one minute, I was able to forget.

It was the sound of the train horn that finally jolted me out of it. Somewhere, just a short distance away, it blared once, then twice, cutting the still silence of the morning.

"Pssst." When I opened my eyes, Kipps's hand was on my shoulder. "We have to get up. We should get out of here."

"What time is it?" I asked.

"Six."

I groaned, and Kipps started laughing at me. He was still in his terry-cloth robe. There were creases across his forehead.

"Do you hear that?" I pointed into the air. "There's a train. Somewhere close."

Kipps leaned forward, straining to listen. It was like the train was purposefully quiet. Kipps just shrugged.

"Come on," he said. He squeezed my shoulder again.

He climbed down the ladder first, and I was right behind him. I went into the bathroom and checked my clothes. The denim jacket was still a little damp, but my baby-doll dress and tee shirt were completely dry. The tee shirt had gone from white to this murky light green, though. I closed the door and started getting dressed, knowing there was nothing I could do about it now.

"Okay. Important question," I called to Kipps through the door. I could hear him just outside, erasing all traces of us. The sink ran for a second, then stopped.

"Hit me."

"If it's 2037," I finally said, pulling the tee shirt on, "how'd you know how to live in 1998? If it's so different inside the set."

"There's all this training," he said. "Before you're even allowed in the set you have to learn all this stuff. Pop culture, movies, music. TV shows. The type of clothes everyone wore, the hairstyles. I got really into movie quotes. I thought that would be my thing. 'YOU CAN'T HANDLE THE TRUTH!' 'Hasta la vista, baby . . .' That way if I didn't have anything else to say, or no one thought I was funny, I could use those lines. It only kind of worked."

I stepped out of the bathroom, but the morning air gave me a chill. All the warmth from the stove was gone.

"Did you ever hear someone say 'Talk to the hand'?" Kipps put his palm between us, blocking me out. "Or 'Talk to the hand 'cause the face ain't listening'? I really wanted to use that one, and I managed to do it a bunch as an extra, but then as soon as I got the guest-star part, they told me to stop. Told me it was too much, that Patrick Kramer would never say that."

"I've heard it, yeah," I said. "Jen Klein used to say it sometimes, and a bunch of the kids in my lunch period last year."

He disappeared into the bathroom to change. I heard the clinking of his belt buckle, his feet on the tile floor as he hopped into his jeans.

"I might try to start using it, if that's okay."

"Knock yourself out."

"Well, I can't right now. It would be out of context. Maybe even a little rude."

He came out of the bathroom in his fleece, only it was turned inside out so only the lining was showing, making it look like it was all black. His hair stuck up in the back. He was really cute . . . and funny. If only the producers had let him be more him, less Patrick Kramer.

"I'm going to check if there's anything in the storage up there, under the bed," he said. "We could use some extra clothes. You especially."

He pointed to my baby-doll dress, and the weird greenish tee shirt underneath. The hem of the skirt was caked with mud.

"I know, I know. I look like butt."

"Never." He smiled that smile, and I couldn't help it, I smiled back. Then he climbed the ladder to the loft.

I held the lyric book up to the light. There wasn't much else to decode. Just a few last pages. It took me twice as long as it normally would because the marks were much lighter than before. The paper had taken on a different texture as it dried, and it wasn't easy to see each one—I had to hold it at just the right angle.

IM ALREDY OUT

CALL WHN SAFE

WLL COME FR U

Then there was a phone number in the front pages of the book, split in twos.

32 35 55 94 23

I immediately opened every cabinet and drawer, checking them again for a phone, but there wasn't one. At some point the pen had fallen out of my bag so I just repeated the numbers in my head until they were a part of me. We'd call Sara once we were safe. Even if we couldn't contact anyone else, we had one ally. She'd gotten us this far. Maybe she could take us a little further.

When Kipps came back down the ladder, he was wearing a baseball hat that said MICHELOB. A gray sweatshirt was slung over his shoulder, and he tossed it to me as soon as he got down.

"I found some things. You have that."

I pulled it on and immediately warmed up. I didn't even care that it was three sizes too big, with a peeling yellow logo on the front.

"Sara gave me a number to reach her at. We can try it when we get to the city. We have to at least try it, right?"

"Yeah, if she can help. How do you want to get there?"

I heard it again, far off at first. The train horn blared once, then twice. If we were talking or not listening for it, we would've missed it. Then it was gone.

"There's a station nearby. Come on. Let's go."

32

Someone was at the door again. This time it was a loud, authoritative knock. I gave Kipps a wide-eyed nod. This was his cue.

"One minute," he said in a choked voice. "I'm sorry, I'm just . . ."

Then he made a loud, hacking sound, like he was vomiting into the toilet. He kept going for another minute, moaning and doing this weird gurgling thing with the back of his throat. Eventually I waved my hands, signaling for him to stop. We wanted people to think he was hungover, not dying of Ebola.

"Good acting," I whispered. "It's like you've been practicing for years."

He curtseyed, then the train jerked forward and he fell into the wall. I had to cover my mouth to keep from laughing. We'd found a backpack and a canvas boat hat in the guest-house closet, and we'd stolen those too. It was just enough that I felt guilty, but not enough that I felt safe. Kipps still looked like Kipps, and when I caught my reflection in the scratched-up mirror on the bathroom wall, I still looked like me. The hat helped, but it only covered the top half of my face.

The train braked, and I had to hold on to the bar beside the sink. The station had only been a ten-minute walk from the house. When we got to the platform we knew it would be too risky to sit with the other passengers. Besides, each seat had a device to scan your ticket and these weird bumper things that prevented you from sitting down until you did. We'd spent a half hour crammed inside the bathroom, which reeked of Lysol and urine. Kipps pretended to puke every time someone came by.

We waited for the automated voice. People plodded past outside the door, rolling suitcases in their wake. *This is the train to New York*, the voice said. *The next and last stop is Octavia Station.*

"Octavia Station? That's the final stop?" Even though I'd never been to New York, I'd heard about Grand Central. Penn Station. The Statue of Liberty. I'd never heard that name, not once.

"There's this billionaire, Olivia Octavia. She came in and built this whole complex in the center of the city. It was all over the news. It has transportation, dining, apartments. Everything."

Kipps checked his baseball cap in the mirror, then curled the brim down so it hid more of his face. I tucked my hair up under the canvas hat, just to see if it helped, but I still looked a bit odd. The men's sweatshirt came halfway down my thigh.

"We just need to get to a phone," I said. "There must be pay phones on every corner. We find one, call Sara, and see what she says."

Kipps shook his head. "No dice."

"No dice? What do you mean, no dice?"

"Pay phones aren't a thing. Like, I've kind of heard of them, the same way I've heard of typewriters or VCRs but—"

"VCRs aren't a thing? Since when?"

"Since Netflix. And Hulu and BeeBop. That Blockbuster in Swickley, they just built it as part of the set, to make it more authentic. No one actually rents videos anymore."

"Okay, whatever," I said, annoyed. "I've been living in 2037 for one day. I can't be expected to know everything."

The train braked and we steeled ourselves against it. We waited until it came to a complete stop before opening the bathroom door a crack. Men and women in business suits filed past.

"Our best bet is borrowing someone's device," he said. "But, sidenote: I'm going to need some food."

"I know. I'm starving. I've been thinking about that triple-decker club sandwich they had at the Cresthollow Diner. With those french fries . . ."

"I always got the onion rings. That place was legit, for a fake set restaurant."

When Amber and I visited Kristen there, she always made a big show of the dessert menu. For some reason they'd made plastic versions of every slice of pie and cake they had, and they were all on a giant silver tray. I could picture it so clearly, Kristen showing it to different tables, trying to entice them to try something, or letting the younger kids poke at the fake food. It was still so vivid. My mouth started watering thinking about their raspberry cheesecake. Kipps and I had split the last of the pretzels this morning, but it hadn't been enough.

We waited until a whole line of passengers streamed out of the car, then we ducked onto the platform. Something opened up inside me. It was freeing, to be lost in a vast sea of people, just another anonymous face next to a dozen others. We were packed shoulder to shoulder as we stepped onto an escalator. Everyone was staring straight ahead, enduring the commute, or typing away on their device.

I looked back, making sure Kipps and I didn't get separated, but there was a middle-aged man between us, with a single patch of gray hair in the center of his bald head. Before I could say anything Kipps reached his hand up the railing for me to take. When I grabbed it, it didn't feel the way it had when Tyler and I held hands. I wasn't nervous. My palms didn't sweat. It felt good, right—like we were always meant to be this way, joined as one. When I squeezed, he squeezed back.

The escalator climbed one flight, then the next. As we traveled up the glittering white tunnel, the station came into view above. At first I could hear the rush of the crowd, see glimpses of the neon advertisements projected onto every flat surface. But it wasn't until the escalator spit us out onto the main concourse that I understood the scale of it. The ceiling was hundreds of feet high, a towering dome with a skylight at the very top. Dozens of faces looked down on us from different screens. A young couple modeled swimsuits while a man with salt-and-pepper hair did a shaving demonstration. It wasn't long before I recognized some of them.

Amber was on a screen above a place called Coffee Craze, only the caption said her name was Kiki Wilder. Inside the set she was the preppiest of the three of us, with crisp collared shirts under sweaters, or pleated plaid skirts and shift dresses. She always wore pearl earrings. Now she weaved through an audience in a patent-leather halter dress, high-fiving kids who looked about my age. She was hosting some kind of talk show. WELCOME BACK, read the caption that scrolled past. I'M KIKI WILDER AND WE'RE COUNTING DOWN WITH THE DANDELIONS. THEY'RE COMING IN AT NUMBER SIX THIS WEEK. The screen cut to three girls with spiky blue hair singing on the roof of a skyscraper.

"Kiki Wilder? That's her real name? Since when does she have her own television show?" We moved through the crowd, trying to find an exit. A dozen tourists in matching blue sweatshirts stood in the middle of the concourse, taking photos, oblivious to the people maneuvering around them.

"Kiki doesn't just have her own television show. She has a clothing line and I heard she's developing a makeup line too. This is supposed to be a riff on *Total Request Live*, that MTV show from the nineties with Carson Daly," Kipps said. "Ever since she and Kristen became producers on the show, their careers have taken off."

"*Producers?*" I could barely get the word out. I'd thought

they were just reporting to the producers, or Chrysalis, or whatever her name was. I remembered Amber's expression after she'd followed me into the park. And Kristen arguing with me about the phone that had fallen out of Amber's bag. There'd been levels upon levels of manipulation. I didn't know what was true anymore, what was real.

"I thought you knew . . ." Kipps whispered. "I'm sorry."

"No, don't be. I should've known. That makes sense." I took a deep breath, trying to push away any feelings about it. The idea that our entire friendship had been faked. It was easier, thinking they were supporting actors like Kipps, that they'd been urged on by Chrysalis or my parents. I hated to think about how much time I'd wasted, all the thought and energy I'd spent caring about them, when they'd cared so little about me.

We turned a corner and walked down a wide corridor, passing a wall with more screens, more advertisements. There was a smiling Jen Klein, her hair in perfect spirals down her back. She held a bottle of what looked like purple vitamins. LULU HAIR GUMMIES, the screen read. SHINE ON, GORGEOUS. We passed a few more ads, some animated, and then there was my mom, doing a cooking demonstration in a kitchen I didn't recognize. *Cooking with Helene Hart*, read the chyron underneath. I'd always wondered why she'd been so meticulous, writing down everything she cooked at home. I'd find scraps of paper in the utensil drawer, with recipes named things like Ten Minute Chicken Piccata.

We passed an ad for a big-budget action movie. A buff middle-aged man swung from the bottom of a helicopter, his shirt blown back, revealing his six-pack.

"Is that . . ." I asked. "Mr. Henriquez? Our tech teacher?"

"Yeah, he's a huge star," Kipps said. "A lot of people inside the set have whole other careers. Kristen's been doing really well with this podcast network she started, and then she has two different stand-up specials out. Millions of You-Tube followers."

Podcast network? YouTube? I didn't even bother asking.

We turned the next corner, which was lined with shops and restaurants. There was an All Time Market, like the one we'd found just outside the set, and a store devoted to something called a "selfie stick."

I'd felt good, better, after our walk to the train. We'd used the time to go over all the basics of iPhones, iPads, and social media, and how the show had aired five nights a week, an hour of all the best footage from that day. It ran most of the year, ending in late spring and picking up again in the fall, though they sometimes did summer specials. Kipps recounted the whole first book of the Voyage of Laggerbath and confirmed that yes, the Harry Potter series was actually a really big deal.

But now I couldn't walk three steps without seeing some phrase or reference I didn't recognize. Kipps was cool about answering questions, and he didn't do that infuriating, stereotypical guy thing where he turned the answers into mini lectures, like he had a PhD in the twenty-first century. I just didn't want to be the girl who asked. I'd been on Principal's List, honor roll. When our family computer broke I was the one who took it apart and replaced the hard drive. I'd never needed anyone's help before, and I didn't like that I needed it now.

"Let's call Sara as soon as we can," I said, starting toward an exit. I scanned the shops, hoping one might sell phones, but there weren't any.

"Roger that," Kipps said. We passed a group of tourists in sweatshirts and baseball caps. Beside them, Kipps and I looked normal. We blended in.

We passed a sports bar, its door propped open with a bucket of these plastic cartridges I'd seen everyone smoking. Several screens inside were playing clips from *Stuck in the '90s*. The moment I took my first steps toward my parents, my dad capturing it all on his camcorder. Sara and me running circles in the backyard. My mom zipping up my seventh-grade formal dress, and Jason Chin breaking up with me on the bus home from middle school. As Kipps and I stood there watching, the scenes cut away to a woman with a stiff, plastic expression.

"In a few minutes we're going to go live to a vigil being held in Boston, Massachussetts. Jessica Flynn and Patrick Kramer have decided to leave the set, and according to a recent statement the producers released, they've supposedly decided they're done being filmed on the show. Like most of us, people in Boston are holding out hope that Jessica and Patrick will be brought back to Swickley safe and sound. The Like-Life Productions team encourages you to be on the lookout for them, particularly if you live in and around Lakeville,

Long Island, where they were last spotted. There's a $500,000 reward for any information leading to their return, and remember: if you do see them, livestream all encounters on the *Stuck in the '90s* fan channel, along with the location."

"Don't worry," Kipps said, pulling me away. "We're not going to be here long. In and out."

"Of course I'm worried," I whispered. "They just put a bounty on our heads."

"Let's try that place." Kipps pointed to an unassuming storefront a few doors ahead. It looked like a post office, with cardboard boxes piled high in the front windows. We both adjusted our hats so the brims dipped down, covering more of our faces, then pushed through the front entrance.

The store had three different rows, made entirely of metal cages. Each cage contained hundreds of cardboard boxes in different sizes, all stamped with the same AMAZON logo. A screen in the corner was blinking a neon-blue sign that read STAND BY.

"Last name and date of birth?" a man with a white ponytail called from behind the counter. His green-and-black polo shirt was streaked with a weird brown stain. He didn't bother looking up from his device.

"We're not here to pick up anything . . ." Kipps said. While he approached the man, I circled the back of the store, making sure no one else was there. The guy stared at his device. Every now and then he'd take a long, slow sip of his soda.

"This is crappy," Kipps said, "but I lost my phone—I've literally been going back and forth to the platform trying to find it. No luck. You mind if I borrow yours to make a call?

It'll be quick, two seconds?"

"What about hers?" the man nodded toward me.

"She doesn't have one on her. She's doing one of those seven-day device cleanse things, they're really popular right now . . ."

The man just shook his head and pointed to a screen in the corner.

"Can't," he said. "It's almost time to vote."

"Oh right, sorry," Kipps said, seeming to understand. "I'll try you later?"

"Sure."

Kipps looked back at me, then nodded to the exit. It wasn't until I was at the door that I saw what the man was talking about. IT'S THAT TIME AGAIN, a graphic on the screen in the corner read. TIME TO MAKE YOUR VOICE HEARD. MEET TODAY'S CONTESTANTS. Peppy electronic music filled the store, signaling the start of . . . what? A TV show?

I tried to stay behind Kipps, out of the man's line of sight, but I quickly realized it didn't matter. He never looked away from the screen. A gray-haired woman in a cape danced around a decrepit kitchen, producing doves from under her arms, inside her pockets, and behind her back. Before long she had eight birds lined up across her shoulders. Some weird stats hovered in the corner of the screen during her performance, then a prompt urging people to VOTE NOW. A timer counted down thirty seconds. As soon as the timer was up the woman disappeared, and a teenage boy appeared. He was sitting on his bed playing a harmonica. It was so terrible it made me wince.

"What is this? Vote for what?" I asked.

"People are competing for a chance to work inside the set," he said. "They film these auditions themselves, and if they get enough votes, they start them off as extras. It's a paid job. Especially now, with the strike, the producers are probably looking to fill hundreds of new positions. They're already anticipating us coming back."

"Boo, you're nothing. Get him off." The man behind the counter laughed at Harmonica Boy. He kept tapping his device, voting as many times as possible.

A caption on the screen displayed a series of details: YOU-TUBE FOLLOWERS: 278, DOMINION FOLLOWERS: 22, INSTA-GRAM FOLLOWERS: 1905. NUMBER OF TIMES AUDITIONING: 4. WHY I DESERVE A SHOT: I WANT TO PAY OFF MY MOM'S MEDICAL BILLS.

After the vote counted down, it went to another shot, this time a family with three kids all under the age of ten. They'd put together an amateur contortionist act, where the kids stacked themselves in elaborate shapes and pyramids. All five of them were decked out in shiny, sequined blue spandex with their last name, Tannuzzo, printed on the back.

"This is weird," I said. "Who would humiliate themselves like this? It's embarrassing."

We stood there, watching the next audition. A twenty-something blond woman in a bikini made seductive faces at the camera. That was it—just faces—she didn't even bother saying anything, and she still somehow got 58 percent of people voting to advance her. I turned to Kipps, about to make a joke, when I noticed his cheeks were flushed. He was staring at the floor.

"Kipps?"

He wouldn't look at me.

"That's not how your family got on, right? I thought . . ."

I waited, hoping he'd fill the silence between us, but he didn't. Instead he pushed out the door and started down the corridor.

33

"Hey, wait up," I called to Kipps's back. He didn't turn around. He just hopped on the next escalator, and we both sailed up toward the street. I had to maneuver past a woman and her giant I-may-have-a-corpse-inside-this duffel bag to get to him.

"Come on, Kipps, talk to me. I'm sorry, I shouldn't have said that."

"It's fine. It's whatever."

"It's not whatever."

The escalator spit us out onto a bustling city street. The sidewalk traffic was thick and fast in both directions, and several people bumped my shoulder before I managed to catch up. Kipps was right beside me now, and I held onto his arm, even though it didn't seem like he wanted me to. We couldn't afford to get separated here. It would be a disaster.

Office buildings, apartment buildings. A theater with a glittering marquee. Sleek cars raced past in both directions while people on bicycles and scooters zipped along the edge of the street. Everything towered above us. Fifty stories, a hundred. I felt like we'd shrunk somehow, miniature versions of ourselves inside an elaborate, polished maze.

We passed a tourist superstore filled with NEW YORK CITY hats and I LOVE NY mugs and Lego replicas of the Statue of Liberty. Just beyond it I saw a sign for City Eatery. The asymmetrical building was all glass, and the cafeteria inside was a glossy white from floor to ceiling. Dozens of white tables and chairs set against a glittery white floor. Everyone was watching giant projections on the back wall, casting their votes for the auditions. We found a table in the corner, away from the crowd, and I made sure we sat facing in, so people passing on the sidewalk couldn't see our faces.

I grabbed the menu, thankful to have something to focus on. It had this glossy front that said CITY EATERY but when I touched it nothing happened. I turned it over and pulled at the edges, but it wouldn't open.

Kipps smirked. "It's just like an iPad . . ." He drew a line with his finger in the air.

I drew a line over the front of it, using the same motion he did, but it didn't do anything.

Kipps laughed. "You have to actually touch the screen, like swipe at it."

He scooted his chair closer to me, and we each held the menu with one hand. He put his other hand over my finger and showed me how to swipe to the drinks, to the desserts. The screen changed over each time we traced a line across it.

"That's actually pretty cool," I said.

"Yeah." Kipps hit a few buttons, ordering a burger and milkshake. After he helped me place my order, he finally spoke. "About before, you were just being honest."

"I was being judgmental."

"I shouldn't expect you to understand."

"I can try."

He glanced sideways at the crowd in the back of the café. Most people ate as they voted, occasionally pausing to order something else from the electronic menu or refill their drink at the beverage machines. Two little girls played with their dolls. They kept looking in our direction, but I told myself they were too young to watch the show, they couldn't recognize us.

"You spent your whole life inside the set," he said quietly. "In Swickley—this made-up town you've always wanted to leave. But out here, it's just not as simple. The same rules don't apply to everyone. Nothing is easy. There aren't a ton of opportunities. Working inside the set is a good job; it's stable. It pays."

"Pennsylvania, where you grew up," I said. "It's nothing like this? Nothing like New York?"

Kipps picked at the menu's leather case. "We're from this tiny town most people have never heard of. Wyattsville. There are just a few places to work, and they laid off a ton of people when the recession hit. My dad was out of work for two years. You know how many times we auditioned to get on, just to be extras in the set?" Kipps asked. "Twenty-eight times. As a family. My parents were obsessed with it—we'd come up with these elaborate parody songs. My dad wrote a really complicated one about living in the nineties and that's the thing that finally got us a break. That silly, inane song.

"It really was great at first, it was. All this stuff is taken care of. My mom had been working for this delivery service called ASAP. It was long hours and barely any money. Zero benefits. And then suddenly all we had to do was go to the set every day and just . . . live our lives. For ten, twelve hours every day. Go to school, dress the part, not say anything stupid or give anything away. It was easy. My mom was talking about building this following out of all the books she was reading on set, like a special book club or something. But you can only spend so long living in a world that's not real before you start to lose something."

"What do you mean?"

"Yourself. What you believe. I don't know."

We sat there, watching as the auditions continued. A trio of break-dancers made it through and were heading to the semifinals at the end of the week. An all-girls a capella group got 38 percent of the vote. The audience hated a skinny, gray-haired guy who sang Frank Sinatra, and as soon as he saw the results his face crumpled and he turned away from the camera. It was difficult to watch.

"You regret leaving?" Kipps pretended to study the menu, to be absorbed in all its details. He seemed nervous, though. "I wouldn't blame you if you did."

It would be easier not to care, to just explain away what had happened, and every lie my parents had told me, just so I could have my old life back. My bed, and the comforter that always smelled like lavender laundry detergent. My guitar and keyboard, and the case of CDs that I could flip through with my eyes closed, always landing on an album I wanted to hear. The steady routine of school, friends, dinner, homework, school, friends, dinner, homework . . .

What would I lose?

Yourself. What you believe. I don't know.

"I don't want to go back," I said. "I'm here. With you."

I don't know what made me do it, but I pulled the menu away and grabbed his hand, taking it between my own. He looked nervous at first, but then his lips twisted into a smile.

"What?"

"I'm just relieved," he said.

"Me too."

He smiled and rested his forehead against mine for just a second. It was so quick, I wondered if I'd imagined it.

One of the customers a few tables over stood and turned toward the exit. I slipped my hands away, tucking them under my thighs. Kipps and I leaned toward each other. Then we both pretended to study the menu, keeping our heads down as he passed.

34

The food we'd ordered was the only thing keeping us in those seats, that promise of a hot meal. Water. Coke. I kept waiting for someone to turn around and recognize us, or for the Like-Life Productions security team to appear in the doorway. I didn't want to think about it, but it was possible a surveillance camera had already captured us. It felt like they were everywhere—at the train station, on our train, tucked in the corners of doorways or perched on the edge of houses and lampposts. I adjusted my hat, pulling it down another inch.

They had three different screens projected on the back wall of the restaurant: two with captions and one with audio that streamed through the entire place. The coverage of the show was relentless. Even as the auditions barreled on, with people twirling color-guard flags and playing the clarinet, another screen aired something called *Couch Commentators*. Two women in their late twenties drank pink wine as they sat cross-legged on an oversized gray sofa, theorizing on what might have happened in the park, when I'd gone off camera.

"Oh God, look . . ."

Someone changed the screen above the beverage machine to an interview with Tyler. We couldn't hear the sound without an earpiece, but I followed the captions. It was some kind of talk show, a panel of women grilling him. SO I HAVE TO ASK, one of the hosts said, WHAT DID YOU SAY TO JESS THAT WAS SO DISTURBING SHE NEVER WANTS TO SPEAK TO YOU AGAIN? PEOPLE HAVE BEEN TALKING ABOUT IT NONSTOP, SAYING YOU CONFESSED SOME HORRIBLE SECRET, AND YOU KNOW, THERE'S A WHOLE CONTINGENT OF PEOPLE WHO THINK THAT YOU WERE ACTUALLY THE ONE TO TELL JESS ABOUT THE SHOW. WHAT DO YOU HAVE TO SAY TO THAT?

Tyler's expression dimmed, and he put both hands on the table in front of him. I TAKE THIS STUFF TO HEART, he said. NONE OF THAT IS TRUE, OBVIOUSLY, WHAT HAPPENED BETWEEN ME AND JESS WAS JUST A MISUNDERSTANDING. SHE WAS REALLY UPSET ABOUT HER SISTER, AND I JUST THINK SHE WASN'T HEARING ME RIGHT. I DON'T EVEN KNOW WHAT SHE THINKS I SAID. I WISH THAT HADN'T BEEN OUR LAST CONVERSATION, BUT IT WAS. He turned and stared straight into the camera, biting his lip like he might cry.

"He's so disingenuous," I said. "It's infuriating."

I'VE BEEN TRYING TO TELL MYSELF, IF YOU LOVE SOMETHING, LET IT GO. SHE WAS MY BEST FRIEND. AND IF SHE NEEDS TO BE WITH PATRICK RIGHT NOW, THEN SHE NEEDS TO BE WITH PATRICK. I DON'T TRUST THE GUY, AT ALL. THE PRODUCERS ARE SAYING THEY HAVE HOT-MIC CONVERSATIONS OF

HIM CONVINCING JESS TO LEAVE. AND I'M WORRIED ABOUT
HER, I REALLY AM. BUT I CAN'T CONTROL WHAT'S HAPPENING,
IT'S BIGGER THAN ME. BIGGER THAN ALL OF US.

"Enough with the unrequited-love storyline," I said.

"That guy is shameless," Kipps laughed. "The hair and
makeup lady told me Roddy—that's Tyler's real name—he
spent all of ninth and tenth grade sucking up to Chrysalis
Remington. He'd find out when she was going to stop by
tech support, and then he'd create an excuse to be there. Like,
he needed an extra camera placed or his makeup needed a
touch-up. He worked on her for two whole years, trying to
get her to see him as your love interest."

"Sounds like Tyler. He wanted me to pretend like nothing
happened, just so he could stay a guest star."

"There's a rumor that you hitting him with that ball in
fourth grade wasn't an accident," Kipps went on. "One of
my friends was there and he swears Roddy ran as fast as he
could into the ball. He just wanted to interact with you."

I didn't want to think about it. It was bad enough that
Tyler—Roddy—had been scheming for the last few years . . .
even the way we'd met had been staged?

"Do you know he's been auctioning off your half-eaten
food online?" Kipps continued. "Old Snapple cans, chewed-
up gum tucked in a crumpled receipt, sandwich crusts. They
haven't been able to prove it's him, but everyone knows. It's
so obvious."

"No, stop." I covered my ears with my hands. I shook
my head back and forth, wishing I could unhear it. "That's
revolting."

I turned just as the food runner approached, dropping a tray in the center of our table. He had another tray balanced on his forearm. He said nothing, just threw down some extra ketchup packets and darted across the café.

"You sure we're not going to get in trouble?" I asked. As hungry as I was, I didn't want to touch anything until I knew it was safe.

"I did it a bunch of times when I lived outside the set," Kipps said, and took a bite of his burger. "Especially when it's busy like this. We'll just leave without closing out the check. They won't notice until it's too late."

"It just feels . . . wrong."

"We already broke into someone house. We stole a car." His eyes went wide as he popped another french fry into his mouth. "A car, Jess. And now you're having a moral crisis?"

"I see your point," I said.

Kipps was already halfway through his fries. He was methodical about the ketchup, emptying the packets like toothpaste tubes, rolling the ends until every last drop was added to the fries. I glanced across the café just as the food runner disappeared into the kitchen. The burger smelled so good, and as I picked it up my mouth puckered, saliva bursting at the back of my throat. The patty was a thin, dry thing, but the taste of the bread and cheese and pickles brought me back to life. I couldn't get it down fast enough.

"No one has let go of their device," Kipps said. "Even for a minute. There's no way anyone will lend us their phone until after the auditions are over."

"Who knows when that'll be, though."

Tyler's interview had ended, and now the screens were showing a remote interview with Kristen and Amber, who were recording from Kristen's bed. It was strange, seeing the room I'd been in hundreds of times before, with its blue-checked comforter and the *In Living Color* and *Clueless* posters on the wall. Kristen never got rid of her collection of troll dolls, and the small army was lined up on the shelf behind them, a rainbow of tufted fur.

Someone yelled for the staff to turn the sound on. The auditions went silent, and suddenly Amber's voice cut across the room.

"These past two days have been tough," she said.

It's been tough? I wanted to say. *Did you and Kristen almost die when your car skidded into a lake? Did you walk a mile in soaking-wet clothes, in fifty-degree weather?*

A talk-show host appeared on the split screen. "We all saw you go into the park after her, and the harrowing scene that unfolded as she fled the set. What was going through your head in that moment? Can you tell us a little about what happened between you two, what that conversation was like?"

"It was really hard. One of the hardest conversations I've ever had," Amber said. "She was really confused, and obviously just devastated about Sara. I was trying to calm her down but she seemed really off."

"We've both spent a lot of time going through things she said, things she did, wondering if there were warning signs."

Kristen was wearing a pair of overalls she'd borrowed from me last month and never given back. It was the ultimate Fuck You.

"You must've heard the fan theories." The host leaned forward as she said it. "People are talking about that scene in the locker room, when you dropped your phone. Some people think it was more than a mistake, that maybe you were trying to tell Jess something was wrong. Warn her about the show."

"Well, that's ridiculous," Amber shot back. "I would never violate my contract. People say a lot of strange things and you can't believe it all. As much as I care about Jess— and we both really do care about her—I'd never do that."

"It would be understandable, really," the host went on, "if the guilt got—"

"Next question," Kristen laughed. "Seriously."

"I don't have to tell you this," the host said. "But there are people who are critical of you both since you took on roles as producers last season. They called it a conflict of interest, that you'd be both her best friends and producers on the show. And there are, of course, people who think Chrysalis took the Sara storyline too far by killing her off, that it was cruel. Maybe even abusive. What do you say to that? Does that concern you at all?"

Kristen glanced sideways at Amber, that look I'd seen between them a hundred times before. They were trying to figure out what to say before they said it.

"We love working on this show," Kristen said. "One of the reasons I have my podcast network is because I love media, and Like-Life Productions has created some of the most innovative media of this century. All storylines go through Jess's parents, Helene and Carter, and have to be approved by them. I don't have to remind you, Helene is an executive producer on the show. So if Jess's own parents are approving it, I can't say I have any ethical problems?"

The host waited a moment to see if Amber would jump in, but she didn't.

"So what's next for you two? Chrysalis seems confident the show will restart soon, that this is just a brief hiatus, but . . . any updates on your makeup line? Tour dates for the *'90s Life* podcast? Any more stand-up specials?"

I couldn't follow their responses because a small, persistent voice was in my other ear. When I turned around, Kipps was fiddling with the electronic menu, trying to turn it off. A red light on the top was blinking.

"What is that?" I whispered. But it only took a few seconds before it repeated.

"We request that you close out your bill at this time," the voice said. "Please scan your thumbprint now."

"She asked if we wanted anything else, and I said no. But then she keeps telling me to close out the bill. She's said it twice." He flipped the thing over, running his fingers along the sides in search of a button, but there wasn't one. "I haven't used one of these in years. Most people pay with their thumbprint—it stores your payment info. You just have to press down on the screen."

"Can you get it to stop?" I said, as the volume on the device doubled.

"Um . . ."

That was a no.

"Where I grew up, you had to actually ask to close out the bill, it didn't just start demanding you pay. It won't shut up."

A high-pitched beeping now accompanied the voice's instructions. A redhead in the back of the café studied us, then glanced through the window into the kitchen, waiting for the food runner to emerge again. A young mom with two small children turned around, and she smiled when I accidentally made eye contact with her.

That smile. Like she knew me.

I'd barely had the thought when she started screaming.

"Oh my God, oh my God!" She stood, turning to the family eating next to her. Then she pointed right at us. "It's them! It's Jess and Patrick Kramer!"

35

The woman aimed her device at us like it was a weapon. Within seconds, the rest of the café had craned their necks to see what was happening. Some joined in, holding up their own devices. One boy began frantically typing something into his phone.

"Does that mean I get the reward money?" the young mother asked, glancing around. "I get the reward money, right?"

I hadn't even reached the door when the screens in the back changed over, one by one. Then Kipps and I were right there, in our stolen hats and clothes, beside our table of crumpled napkins and wilting fries. LIVESTREAMING FROM NEW YORK CITY, read a caption below us.

"Jessica Flynn and Patrick Kramer have been found, safe, in a restaurant in New York," a voice said. "Members of the Like-Life Productions security team are on their way to retrieve them. We're livestreaming now, with the help of some of our audience members."

I reached the door first and broke off to the right; a crowd had formed at the other corner as they waited for the light to turn green. Kipps ran beside me. We kept our heads down as we took another right, sprinting several blocks before crossing over to a residential street. The apartment buildings towered above us. It wasn't until we crossed another main street, one called Park Avenue, that I spotted two different screens, animated billboards on the brick facades above us.

One showed the clip from City Eatery, with Kipps and me ducking out the door. Another was shaky footage of our backs as we ran up the street. Park Avenue was packed with people, and some stopped on the sidewalk to watch the live feed. We pushed into a crowd crossing the street, hiding in the middle of the pack. No one seemed to notice us. Almost everyone was watching their device or one of the screens above.

I darted ahead of Kipps and turned down another street, trying to find somewhere that wasn't so busy. But it was impossible to escape the crowds. As we walked farther east I spotted two more billboards up ahead.

We were halfway down the block when I looked up and saw a girl with pigtails, around eight or nine, leaning out a third-floor window. "That's them. Mom, they're coming this way!" she yelled to someone inside.

We doubled our pace, my legs burning from the effort. We had nowhere to go, but we ran anyway, taking a right and then a left up another residential street. Sometimes I caught glimpses of the screens above. More people had emerged from their apartments. They stood on balconies and leaned out windows, and a few spilled onto the sidewalks. We had to run beside cars to get around them. As we ran past a bar, two drunk guys stumbled out the door and right in front of our path, coming at us like linebackers, ready to take a hit.

"Give me that five hundo Gs!" one yelled, and the other started laughing.

Kipps grabbed my hand and we slipped between two parked cars and into the street, dodging a woman on a scooter.

They were streaming clips of our backs as we disappeared around a corner, and there was a consistent overhead shot from someone filming from a roof. I kept glancing up at the screens, hoping that at some point they'd lose us, but there were too many people with cameras. We were almost never out of view.

We approached another wide street. We slowed our pace just a little and two men approached us on our right, jogging beside us to get closer shots. For a second I thought they might've been sent by the producers, but I didn't recognize either of them from inside the set. Kipps held up his hand to block their devices.

"Which way?" he called out.

"I don't know. Let's just keep moving," I said, but I could feel the panic setting in. We were completely lost inside a vast stretch of stores and apartment buildings, and there was no obvious place to hide.

I sprinted ahead toward a complex with several apartment

buildings. In the center was a stone courtyard with a play-ground and swings, but no one was there. Most people had gone to the busier streets to look for us. We walked around the back of one of the buildings. The alley was so narrow that the apartments faced in, with no view, and all of the windows were shut. A fire escape hugged the concrete facade and there were three metal doors marked EMERGENCY EXIT on the ground floor. One was propped open, a brick jammed where the door met the frame.

I waved for Kipps to follow me inside. When I pulled the door open, I didn't get more than two steps before I came face-to-face with a ruddy-cheeked guy who was at least a foot taller than me. He had on suit pants and a crisp button-down shirt.

"I told you, Elsbeth," he called to someone behind him as he strode into the alley. I backed away and knocked right into Kipps, his toes under my heel. The man used those few seconds to his advantage, stepping around us, closing off our exit.

A woman with a coiffed blond bob followed him out. She wore an elegant knee-length dress and suede slippers, as if she hadn't had time to find real shoes. She extended her arm out, holding a device in front of her. "I'll never doubt you again," she said, laughing. "Everyone went one way and we went the other. And that made all the difference."

"I love that you're quoting Robert Frost right now. Did we start? Are we starting?" The woman held up a finger, then nodded, and the man stared directly into the camera. "We are holding Jessica Flynn and Patrick Kramer here, in the Rosewood Apartments on Twenty-ninth Street. We'll await instructions from the producers on what to do with them."

As soon as I heard the address my whole body stiffened. Kipps ran his hand through his hair and tugged at the roots, the way he did when he was nervous. They'd told the producers where we were. Our exact location. If we didn't get out of here soon, we were done.

"We've been fans of the show for years." Elsbeth glanced at me over the device. She said it almost as an apology, like they couldn't help themselves. I didn't get it. They were both dressed nicely, and she had a fat stack of diamond rings on two different fingers. They didn't seem like they needed the reward money.

The man stalked forward and positioned himself between Kipps and me. Kipps was taller than him, but it didn't matter, the man was broad shouldered and muscular. I wasn't afraid of the couple—they didn't seem like they'd hurt us. But now that the Like-Life Productions team were on their way, all bets were off. Maybe if I cooperated, I'd be allowed to go back to Swickley, to its manicured lawns and backyards pools, to the beach at Maple Cove and my pleasant, but completely false, existence. But what if I didn't want to? How far would they go to make me? Would they threaten me, bribe me? One thing was certain: they'd never let Kipps back into the set. Maybe they hadn't released our hot-mic conversation to the public, but the producers had obviously heard what he'd said to me in the Land Rover; they knew everything that had happened that day. I never would've escaped had he not helped me.

Kipps grabbed my hand and squeezed. Then, without a warning, he dropped it and rammed the guy with his shoulder, hitting him so hard he flew back into the brick wall. I heard the sharp sound of his breath leaving his body. He stumbled, trying to catch his balance.

"Run, Jess—go!" Kipps yelled.

But I couldn't move, I couldn't leave him. The man's face was already fixed in a tight, angry expression. I thought he was going to punch Kipps but instead he pulled something from the back of his belt. He had a small silver gun. I'd only seen them in movies—it didn't look real.

Kipps didn't notice it right away. He was still hunched forward, and he charged the guy again, jamming his shoulder into the man's gut. "I swear I'll shoot you," the man said, and then Kipps realized what was happening. He turned and looked up, but the guy already had a handful of his shirt, holding him in place, and his other hand clutched the gun. Kipps tried to grab it from him, but the guy jerked back, maneuvering so it was out of reach.

The gun went off.

Everyone stopped. Elsbeth let out an animalistic shriek. Even the guy seemed stunned, and he studied the gun, turning it to the side, like he wasn't quite sure it had really happened. The popping sound rang in my ears.

Kipps stood and stared at his left bicep. His shirt was torn away at the side, and even though he pressed his palm against it, trying to stop the blood, a dark red stain spread out around his fingers. He winced, pressing harder, but after a minute he hunched over in pain.

"You saw what Patrick did," the woman said into the camera. "My husband was just acting in self-defense. He didn't mean to."

I didn't realize at first who she was talking to. She'd turned around and was now standing beside her husband. The camera on the device was filming both of them.

"Everyone saw what happened," he said. "That was not intentional. I only brought the gun to scare them, this was all a mistake."

He started rambling on about just wanting the gun as a prop, just in case, and the woman stood behind him arguing that Kipps was being aggressive, and they should still get the reward money because they told Like-Life Productions exactly where we were. They kept on, arguing their case into the camera.

I don't know what else they said. As soon as both their backs were turned Kipps and I took off down the alley, ignoring them when they yelled for us to stop, when they yelled for us to come back.

36

We found a fire escape on the back of the next building. I yanked down its metal ladder and made Kipps go first, but it was almost impossible for him to climb with his injured arm. I stood right under him, and for the first few rungs he used my hands as a stirrup, pushing off of me until he managed to drag himself onto the initial landing, groaning and wincing the whole time. Once we got up to the stairs he was slow and methodical, favoring his right arm as he took the narrow metal steps one by one. We didn't stop until we reached the top floor.

"I can't believe you did that," I said, pulling off my sweatshirt. He sat back against the wall and let out a long, slow breath. "Kipps, you shouldn't have done that. Why did you do that?"

But when he looked at me, his dark eyes serious, I knew why. He didn't have to say it out loud. He did it for me—he wanted to give me a chance to get away.

I rested my hand on his. "Let me see . . ."

He winced as he picked the fabric away from his skin. The bullet had just grazed his arm, but it was enough to take out a chunk of flesh. The wound was still bleeding badly. I pulled off my sweatshirt and ripped at the cheap fabric, tearing off one sleeve. I wrapped the long strip tight around his arm, putting pressure on the wound, then tied it.

"Let me guess." He smirked as he watched me finish the knot. "*Rescue 911?*"

"No, I learned that in my after-school first aid certification class." I got right in his face. I wasn't going to let him know-it-all a know-it-all. "It's, like, first aid 101."

"Is that right?" he said, moving an inch closer.

We stayed there, so close our noses almost touched, until I couldn't take it anymore. I was the one who let my eyes fall to his lips, who closed the space between us. He brought his palm to my cheek and kissed me hard, just once, then rested his forehead against mine. He was cradling my face like it was a rare, precious thing.

"This feels real," I said. "This is good."

"This is very real."

There was no wishing or wondering in it—it was true. True in the way that all simple facts are: grass is green, 2+2=4, *this is real*.

He leaned down and kissed me again, and this time we both gave into it, letting it take us somewhere else. I tried to remember his shoulder, but I wanted so badly to touch him. My hands were on his neck, running down his sides, my fingers combing through his hair. He pulled back and rested his thumb on my chin for a moment, staring at me. Then we started all over again, his tongue warm against mine.

I don't know how much time passed, but when I broke away, his cheeks were pink. His lips were red and swollen. At some point he'd unzipped the front of his fleece so I could slip my hands inside it.

"I'm glad we established that," Kipps smiled. "Now we need to get the hell out of here."

We looked down at the street below. The apartment building must've been five, six stories high. From where we stood, we could see people running past, their devices out, checking each street for signs of us. A giant billboard two buildings over was livestreaming the scene. Audience members swept through restaurants and stores, checking and double-checking back patios and aisles in search of us. Several groups had stopped by the courtyard of Rosewood Apartments, trying to find out from Elsbeth and her husband which direction we'd gone in. One guy pushed into a public restroom only to find a woman changing her baby's diaper.

"Hold on," I said, turning to the narrow ladder that led to the roof. The vertigo hit me as soon as I stood up. We were so high above the city I felt its spinning pull, and I gripped the railing with both hands, thinking I might fall. I was slow as I climbed the extra story, then crossed to the far end of the building and looked around. There was water on both sides of us, and a giant patch of green was visible to the north. We were on the east edge of the city toward the south, but knowing where we were didn't do us any good. Every sidewalk was packed. It was as if every single building had been evacuated. People spilled into the streets, horns blaring as cars skidded to a stop. The traffic on Third Avenue was barely moving.

"We might be able to get to the eastern shore, by the river," I said, climbing back down. "It's a possible escape route. It's not too far off."

Kipps stared at me, waiting for me to continue. ". . . but?"

"But every single street is packed. Crowds everywhere. It's a huge risk," I said. "They know we're in the area. They're looking for us."

"I would give anything to have my phone right now," Kipps said.

"Sara must've seen the broadcast. She must know we're here."

"Yeah, but we could be anywhere. And even if she wanted to come get us, she couldn't. She'd have to fight off half of New York."

I knew that, but didn't need to say it out loud. Our situation was starting to feel desperate, and I had to remind myself to keep breathing, to think good thoughts and stay positive and all that other BS people say to make themselves feel better when things are really, really bad. I told myself we could wait out the crowds, but I knew Kipps was in bad shape. His color had changed in the last half hour. His complexion was dull. Every few minutes he'd tense up, steeling himself against the pain.

The broadcast cut away from the livestreams to go to another talk show. Sound was being piped in from somewhere, but I couldn't figure out where. A tall, slim woman with intense eye makeup sat cross-legged in an armchair. She wore a bright purple leather jacket with a high collar and was almost expressionless as she spoke.

"That's Chrysalis Remington, the creator and executive producer. The one I was telling you about, who Tyler was trying to suck up to."

I recognized the host from another talk show. The rail-thin girl leaned forward, peppering Chrysalis with questions. The volume was just loud enough that we could hear.

"Is it true that the audience in New York has lost track of Jessica and Patrick, that they don't currently know their location? How do you expect the Like-Life Productions team to bring Jess back to the set if they don't know where she is anymore?"

"Well, we do know where she is," Chrysalis said. "Not precisely, but we have narrowed it down. And as you saw from that one disturbing livestream, Patrick is now injured. Which is one of our immediate concerns, getting him the help he needs. This is a very serious situation."

"Absolutely. No matter how you feel about Patrick Kramer, we can all agree that we don't want anyone getting hurt." The host glanced at a card in her hand. "What would you say to Jess, if she's listening?"

Chrysalis stared into the camera. She had sharp features, high cheekbones and a small beak-like nose. She cleared her throat before speaking.

"Jess . . . you might not know me, but I know you so well. I've been with you every moment of every day of your life. It's really that simple. And I have always allowed your parents to make decisions for you." She took a deep breath and continued. "I understand how jarring it must've been to discover what was outside the set. To realize that there was a lot more to life, to society, than what you knew. But the choices your parents made for you were theirs to make. And I think if you talked to them, if you really gave them a chance, you'd learn more about the hows and the whys. Look. The world isn't a perfect place, and this isn't some perfect story about perfect people. Part of growing up is realizing the adults around you have faults and flaws. They're not infallible. And no matter what they did, your parents miss you, they're distraught. Your friends miss you, your community misses you. It's time to come back."

"And if she doesn't?" the host asked. "Are you okay if she chooses to live outside the set? That seems to be what her actions are saying, right?"

"Well, she's a minor. A runaway, technically. Jess's parents are deeply concerned, and we'll do whatever it takes to bring her back to them. Right now we're focused on getting Patrick the medical attention he so desperately needs. We hope Jess realizes the gravity of the situation and doesn't try to handle this on her own. That would be a huge mistake."

The host thanked her, and Chrysalis stared into the camera one last time. She smiled, just a cold, tight little smirk of the lips. Somehow I knew it was meant for me.

37

We hope Jess doesn't try to handle this on her own.

That would be a huge mistake.

"Maybe she's right," I said, staring down at my hands. The blood had dried under my fingernails. "Maybe this is where it ends for us and I just need to accept it. I'm going back to the set. We're going back. What if I just turned myself in, then you could see a doctor? Go to a hospital?"

Kipps stared straight ahead. "I'm not letting you turn yourself in, not for me."

"Come on, Kipps, you're hurt," I said, pointing to the makeshift bandage. "We can't go on pretending like this is going to be okay. We haven't even been able to find a phone to call Sara. I'm not going to let you bleed to death here, on some rando fire escape."

"I don't feel like I'm going to bleed to death?" Kipps said it as a question, like he wasn't entirely sure it was true.

"Kipps!" I squeezed his knee. "See? This is bad."

"No, I mean . . ." Kipps said. "I think she was just messing with you. Trying to get inside your head. If she can convince you I'm about to die, then she has some serious leverage. You'll have to take me to the hospital, expose yourself. You'll have to call her and beg for help. It's all about control."

Kipps *had* been shot, though. He was bleeding, and even if it did look like a surface-level wound, I wasn't a doctor. I didn't know for sure. But it was a more convenient story, the one where Kipps was gravely injured and we had to turn ourselves in. In that version I was small and helpless.

Then there was the thing she'd said about my parents. *They miss you. They're distraught.* Chrysalis didn't need to tell me the world wasn't perfect, that much was apparent. It wasn't beyond my ability to understand how it could happen, how the show might've started as one thing and turned into something else entirely, and my parents had just kept on every day, making hundreds of these small concessions that had destroyed us. They could be distraught, they could miss me. They could be human. It didn't change how much it hurt.

The truth was, I didn't want to go back. How could we stop now?

"I'd never forgive myself if something happened to you," I said, my voice unsteady. "All these people have been hurt because of me, and I—"

"All these people? Who?" Kipps asked.

"You said they killed that guy Arthur."

"I'm not a hundred percent sure?"

"That doesn't make me feel any better," I said. "I don't

want to be responsible if you . . ."

"Okay, seriously, that's just dramatic. Besides, I don't want to go back. I might have a chunk of my arm missing, and we might be broke and on the run, but I don't want to. I bet my parents already sold me out. They were probably all, *Chrysalis, what do we have to do to stay in this sick-ass house? Just say the word and we'll disown him.*"

"Come on. Your parents aren't sociopaths."

"Ehhhh . . ." Kipps tilted his head, like he had to really consider it.

The screen across the way had changed over to the same *Couch Commentators* show that had been playing earlier in the café. Now the two girls with pink wine started hypothesizing that Patrick was actually a "creep" with a "smarmy smile," and why had they ever thought he'd be a good boyfriend?

"I'm not going back, Jess," he repeated. He stared up at me, his hazel eyes catching the sun. "Seriously. So let's figure out what's next. Because we don't have much time."

"Please, please don't die," I finally said, and I let out a long, rattling breath. "I cannot handle that, on top of everything else."

"I'll try my very best."

I peered down into the alley below. The height was dizzying, that heady, uneasy feeling taking hold of me.

"I'm going to get us out of here." I said it out loud and it felt more certain, like I could will it to be true. I turned to the window next to the fire escape and peered through the curtains. I couldn't see any movement inside, but it was hard to be sure. We waited for a few minutes and still didn't hear anything. I pressed both palms on the glass, then pushed against the frame, but it was locked. I took my wallet out of my bag and grabbed my Swickley High ID card, slipping it along the frame to try and unhook the latch. It didn't work.

"One of these has to be open," I said. "Just wait a sec."

Kipps leaned back against the wall as I squeezed past.

"I'm happy to sit right here," he said. "Trust me."

There was another window one story below. This one had sheer curtains, and it looked like there was a bedroom beyond it, but it was empty. When I pressed my hands against the frame, it slid up an inch. I waited, listening for voices, but it was quiet.

"Come on," I called to Kipps. "It's empty."

He held on to the railing with his good hand as he came down the stairs. I climbed in first, intending to turn and help him. But the sight of the room sent my head spinning, and I had the strange, immediate sensation of coming home. It was a teenage girl's bedroom, only the walls were painted the same pale purple that mine had been. She had the same comforter with tiny lavender flowers, and she'd found a similar desk, the corkboard over it lined with pictures and a vintage *Seventeen* spread of Scott Wolf in *White Squall*. The glow-in-the-dark stars were in almost the same exact arrangement as mine, and the Christmas lights were tacked onto the wall right above a guitar.

Kipps bypassed the bedroom completely and went straight

to the door, exploring the rest of the apartment. When he came back he was still holding his left arm.

"I don't think anyone's home."

"She has *YM* magazines, *Seventeen*, Delia's catalogs. Where'd she get all of this?" I asked, examining a stack on her nightstand. Some of the issues dated back to 1997, 1998. Her dresser wasn't the same wooden one I had, but she'd positioned it in the same exact place—right next to the door. She even had a lava lamp on it, except it was blue instead of purple like mine.

Kipps spun around, checking the guitar beside the corkboard to see if it was real.

"This is the best re-created set I've ever seen. They used to do contests for this type of thing. She could've easily won." He came beside me, studying the magazines I'd found. "You can buy some of these vintage. There are a bunch of sites out there that sell them. I always loved the vintage baseball cards—and the Pogs. Do you think anyone actually played with those?"

"I never did."

"Anything from inside the set goes for a lot more than the replicas," he said.

I spotted the piggy bank across the room. It was the same kind my dad had won for me at the Swickley carnival—a blue plastic thing with a rubber plug in the bottom. It was perched on a shelf above the bed.

"No way. Don't even tell me," I said, reaching for it. It was lighter than it would've been if it was filled with coins. I popped the rubber plug out and shook the Warheads into my palm. She had three different kinds—watermelon, apple, and blue raspberry.

"These are my favorite," I said, holding them up to Kipps. I squeezed a blue raspberry into my mouth and threw him an apple. He'd plopped into the inflatable armchair in the corner. That was one of the differences between this room and mine. I'd always really wanted one of those stupid things, even if they were completely hideous.

"You think she has an extra device somewhere?" I opened the top drawer of her desk, but it was filled with markers, rubber bands, and other junk. "I saw some guy at the café with two of them. People can have more than one, right?"

But Kipps didn't answer me—someone else did.

"Yeah, I have more than one," an unfamiliar voice said. "Now will you stop going through my shit?"

A girl stood in the doorway, holding her device in her hand. She looked a year or two younger than me, but we were the same height, and she was wearing one of my favorite outfits—a black baby-doll tee and plaid skirt. She even had on a pair of boots like mine, with a chunky heel and laces up the front. Her dark brown hair was parted in the same exact place, with the same exact cut. She pinned back her bangs with two snap clips, one on each side.

"You're . . . Jess Flynn?" Her eyes trailed from me to Kipps, who stood when he saw her. "You're in my room. Jessica Flynn and Patrick Kramer are in my room."

She raised her device, about to capture us both on camera.

"No—please wait," I said, running toward her. "Don't livestream this. No one can know we're here."

"But everyone's looking for you." She gestured outside.

277

"There are thousands of people on the street, waiting for you. Everyone wants you back."

"But we don't want to go back," Kipps said.

The girl narrowed her eyes at him. I noticed she was wearing the same shimmery purple eye shadow I wore, and the same lip gloss I usually carried in my purse. I'd lost it at some point since we left the set.

"Is it true?" she said, turning back to me. "Did he make you leave? What did he say to you to get you to go?"

"He didn't make me leave. We're friends."

I moved closer to Kipps, so our shoulders were almost touching.

"And we need your help . . ." I tried to look past her, into the living room. "No one else is here, right? You're alone?"

"I live with my aunt and her boyfriend," she said. "But they're waiting with some of the crowds on Twenty-fifth, over by Madison Square Park. I just came back to get my jacket."

"We need to get in touch with a friend," I said. "We're trying to find her."

The girl didn't respond. She kept glancing down at her phone, like she hadn't quite decided if she was going to record us or not. Outside a quick, cruel ripple of laughter rose up from the street. I imagined them showing old clips of me plucking my mustache, or voting on whether I should get a nose job.

"They're going to find you anyway," she finally said. "Like, I could be the one to tell them where you are, or someone else could, but the security team is already in New York. They got here, like, five minutes ago. Helicopters, vans, production trailers, everything. You don't really have a lot of options . . ."

"And let me guess," Kipps shot back. "It would be nice to have five hundred thousand dollars."

The girl smiled, revealing a small gap between her front teeth.

"Well, yeah. That too."

Our chance was slipping away. Maybe I'd been stupid to think she'd help us. Why would she, when just one video could turn her into a celebrity in her own right? When she could have hundreds of thousands of dollars sitting in her bank account?

I pulled my purse in front of me and dug through it.

"Look . . . what did you say your name was?"

"I didn't. It's Mims."

"Mims, great," I said, turning over the contents in the bottom of the bag. "I'm sure right now you're thinking about all the different things you could get with that reward money. Maybe you think they'll give you a cameo on the show, or you'll get some great sponsorship deal, blah blah."

I finally found the photo booth strip. Sara stared back at me, her brown eyes bright. In the middle picture she was making this face she always did when someone photographed her. Her lips were twisted to the side in a funny smirk. I knew she thought it made her look pretty, but she was already pretty.

I told myself that it didn't matter, that it was just a stupid photo booth strip. One of the pictures was smudged now, and it was still warped from when I'd gotten it wet. But I'd carried it with me to the park that day. I'd taken it through the tunnel and out of the set. It had survived the NextGen Cloud and that terrifying moment in the lake. It was hard not to assign meaning to it, as if the photo strip alone had saved Kipps and me—as if this tiny piece of paper had been the thing that helped us get this far.

"Here," I said, passing it to her. "You can have this. That's definitely worth something. I took it from the collage on Sara's wall."

Mims studied it, then handed it back to me.

"It's not worth five hundred thousand dollars, that's for sure."

"If everything goes according to our plan, and we're able to get out of here, then *Stuck in the '90s* is over. The show will end, and the value of all the memorabilia will go up. I don't know how much it'll be worth, but it's something."

She paused, then tucked the photo strip in the inside pocket of her jacket. "What else you got?" she asked, nodding to my purse.

I turned to Kipps, seeing if he had anything good. I wasn't expecting her to ransack us.

"Uh . . . I have a fake driver's license that says Patrick Kramer," he said, digging into his pockets. "And a sticky Tic Tac. Or it's an old Tylenol—I'm not really sure."

"I'll pass on the Tic Tac," Mims said.

I thumbed through my bag, ignoring the lyric book. It had Sara's note in it, with the phone number she'd given me. I couldn't risk letting Mims see it. The other stuff I'd had forever, but I didn't necessarily want to give it up.

"I have this Keroppi change purse," I said, passing it to her. "It still has a bunch of quarters in it. And you can have my wallet, too. That has my learner's permit and some stupid cards and stuff. I think there's a gift certificate to Topkapi. And my old YMCA time card."

I handed her the entire purse, tucking the lyric book in my jacket pocket when she wasn't looking. She still didn't seem satisfied. She kept rooting around the thing, like there might be some other hidden treasure inside, something I hadn't yet mentioned.

"Can we use your phone or not?" Kipps finally asked.

She tossed him her device. He looked at me, then at the phone, the same flat black thing everyone had filmed us with. He clutched it to his heart and closed his eyes for a few seconds, as if it were hugging him back.

"What was the number?" he whispered.

As I said it back to him, from memory, he typed it in the device and hit a green button. Then he showed me how to hold it so I could hear it ring. The microphone was somewhere in the bottom of it, but I couldn't see it. I couldn't see any of the speakers either.

I ducked down the hall and found a bathroom, closing the door behind me. It rang four times before someone picked up.

"Hello?"

It was Sara's voice. The sound of it made me laugh, this quick, gasping breath of relief.

"Oh my God, Jess?" she said. Then she called to someone in the background. "It's Jess—Jess is on the phone."

"I'm okay." I tried to keep my voice even, but it was no use.

"Jess, I'm so sorry," she said, and now her voice was quaking too. "For everything. I didn't know until I knew, and then it was too late. They told me you were, like, method acting or something. That year you went to sleepaway camp, the producers and Charli—Lydia—they took me aside and told me everything. That Charli was my mom. That we'd all been playing this game of pretend. I thought you knew it was a TV show. I always thought you knew."

"I definitely did not know."

"Yeah, I get that now. Obviously. It's this whole thing between me and my mom—she didn't tell me until two weeks ago, until after you started asking about the protesters and the strike. You said that thing about the chanting, and then Amber's phone falling out of her backpack. I'm still angry with her, it almost . . ."

I heard a muffled voice in the background, then Sara started arguing with someone. She must've put me on mute because the call dropped out for just a few seconds.

"Fine, you hid the box and the key fob for me. That was the least you could do, though," she said to someone in the background. She took a deep breath. "I'm just—I really am so sorry, Jess."

I tried to count the tiles behind the sink even though my throat tightened and my eyes squeezed shut, the tears coming on fast. I tried to steady myself but it was no use. I was crying harder than I had in years.

"I know," I choked out.

"I'm coming," she said. "Are you still near the Rosewood Apartments? Where Kipps was shot? You're still in the city?"

"Yeah, we're safe for now," I said. "Some girl let us borrow her phone. But I don't know how to get out of here. The streets are packed. Everywhere we go, people start filming us. There's a highway close to here, right on the east side."

"We're already on our way. It says we'll be there in . . . forty-eight minutes. Can you get to the exit at Twenty-third, the FDR? It's on a map I'm looking at."

"Yeah, if we have to," I said. "I'll figure out a way."

When I tried to say something else, the words got stuck in my chest. I could barely breathe. I felt like I had a golf ball lodged in the back of my throat and I was sobbing, really sobbing now.

"Jess?" she said after a minute.

I made a small, squeaking sound, and she knew that I was still there.

"I love you," she said. "I'll see you soon."

I don't know how much time had passed. I was still holding onto the phone, pressing it against my ear, when I realized she was gone.

Kipps was waiting for me right outside the bathroom. I'd splashed water on my face and managed to turn it into something other than a pink, tear-stained mess, but when

I met his eyes it was clear he knew I'd been crying.

"What happened? You okay?" He said it low, soft, then checked over his shoulder to make sure Mims wasn't listening.

"Yeah, I'm fine. I have a plan. We're going to meet Sara in . . ." I looked down at the phone, which was apparently a watch, too. "Forty-four minutes."

"How are we going to get there?" Kipps asked.

I walked back to Mim's bedroom—my bedroom—where she was sitting on the bed, flipping through a Delia's catalog.

"We already made you rich," I said. "How would you like it if you were famous, too—if everyone knew your name?"

"What do you mean?" When her brows drew together, a deep line appeared between them. "Is this a joke?"

"Here," I tossed the device to her. "You can start filming now."

38

I didn't recognize myself in the mirror. Mims had dug through her aunt's closet and given us super serious, corporate looks. I had on a blue pantsuit that was two sizes too big, with a silk scarf tied at the neck. Kipps looked like a psychotherapist in his argyle sweater and slacks. We'd wrapped his arm with a fresh bandage and a plastic bag, so the blood couldn't seep through. His Sambas were the only giveaway. The men's shoes Mims had in the apartment were three sizes too big, and Kipps never would've been able to run in them.

"The wig works," I said, brushing the black bob into place with my fingers. Mims had worn it for a Halloween costume, playing a superhero named Asteroid Amos, whoever that was. It was simple, but it was a better disguise than anything else.

"It's not going to matter what we're wearing if we get there late," Kipps said, checking the time on Mims's device.

"We need to go. Like now."

I could've spent another hour with Mims, running through the videos we'd filmed and when to post each one. I wasn't inclined to trust her, a random stranger who'd demanded every last personal item I had, but we didn't have a choice. She agreed to follow our plan. I had to take her at her word.

"You have to post the first one—"

"Once you clear the building," she interrupted. "I know. You told me five times. I'll go to the roof and wait until I can't see you anymore. Then I'll call the news station and upload it."

"And then the second video once you're on your way. Ideally when you're only a few blocks from Times Square."

I'd left all my clothes out on her bed. It didn't look like much anymore, the denim jacket, baby doll dress, and stretched-out tee shirt. The scuffed Doc Marten boots. But it's what people would expect I'd be wearing. It was supposed to give us the head start we needed.

"Jess, let's go. I'm serious," Kipps said, grabbing my hand.

"Don't worry, I got it," Mims said before closing the apartment door in my face.

He reached the stairwell first, and I raced down behind him, hugging the metal banister at each turn. When we got to the bottom, one of the first-floor exits led to a back alley. We hurried down it and turned the corner onto a wide street. I could hear the crowds to the west, along Twenty-third Street.

Just as the livestreams were used to track us, now I could use them to track the audience. There was an electronic billboard on every other building. Screens everywhere. Some of them had sound, and they showed audience members lined up along the road or watching a line of Like-Life security vans arrive on the north side of the city. There were a few shots from viewing parties around the country, and more of people sharing their personal accounts of what had happened in the café. A particularly rowdy group had assembled in the alley where Kipps had gotten shot. They were drinking and listening to that couple retell the story.

When we got to the bigger, more exposed intersections we kept our pace steady, and sometimes I fell back so it didn't look like Kipps and I were together. He was the one who'd found the spot on the map. While Mims and I were preparing our disguises, he'd looked at several overhead shots on her device, then memorized our half-mile route. We'd just passed a church when all the screens changed over, broadcasting the same thing.

"We have breaking news," a short, muscular host I didn't recognize spoke into the camera. The audio was being piped in from so many places there was a faint echo after every word. "Our studio has just been sent a video from an audience member on Twenty-sixth Street. She says she encountered Jessica Flynn and Patrick Kramer just moments ago. Take a look."

I knew we needed to keep moving. But I could feel myself slowing, wanting to pause every few steps to watch. One billboard was in clear view to our right as we headed toward the river. There were still dozens of people on the street. Some sat on the curb so they wouldn't miss anything, while others walked, frantically typing into their devices, looking for updates.

The video started and there I was, in Mims's bedroom—our bedroom—facing her device. The shelf and the blue piggy bank were in the background.

"Hi, I'm Jess Flynn. But everyone already knows that," I started. "I wanted to address everyone's concerns about me, and Patrick, and assure everyone I'm safe. Patrick never did anything to hurt me, and he only tried to help me do what I asked him to. I'm making this video because I want to come back to the set. I want to return to my family, and my friends, and everyone in Swickley. I want to return to you, the audience who's watched me grow up—who followed my every breath, my every action."

I couldn't help but smile at that line. I'd made Mims film it twice because I had such a hard time making it feel believable. But I was happy with the final result—it read as earnest, heartfelt. I seemed real.

"I want to meet the Like-Life security team in the center of Times Square. I'll be there at noon," the video continued. Kipps had stopped next to me. I knew he wasn't happy about the delay, but he seemed vaguely mesmerized. We had both been worried about how the video had turned out, and if Mims would be able to pull off the plan—the timing and order of everything.

"I ask for the audience's help to get home. Please," I said into the camera. "If you see me making my way through the city, clear a path so I can get through. Don't stop me and try to get a photo or the perfect shot with me in the background.

I miss my parents and I'm ready to be home."

The video cut to livestreams across the city. A whole restaurant broke into applause, people cheering and hooting as they raised their glasses in a toast. Some shouts echoed down a nearby street. Some of the people who'd been sitting on the curb had already gotten up and left, heading north.

Kipps grabbed my hand and we started moving again, this time running. We took a right, moving closer to Twenty-third Street. I could hear the dull rush of the highway up ahead.

"Just a little farther," Kipps said, and he squeezed my hand.

The sound of the broadcast still drifted out of windows, though most people seemed to have left their homes hours ago to be in the middle of the action. The roads were strangely quiet. As we turned down another street I saw my mother's face on a screen over a drugstore. She and my dad were here, in New York, standing beside one of the Like-Life Productions vans. They were waiting for me.

It was almost enough to get me to turn back.

But when my mom jumped down from the SL4500 production van, she held up both hands and waved to the gathering crowd. There were a few thousand people assembled along the sidewalks and on a set of risers in the center median. Policemen were already there, with metal barricades that sectioned off the crowd.

She didn't stop there. My mom and dad walked out to talk to their fans. My mom leaned over, scribbling on something, and it took me a moment to realize she was giving out autographs. Hats, tee shirts, and posters—she scrawled her name across all of it. Someone stretched out their arm and she signed that, too. My dad posed with a group of elderly women in tee shirts that had a picture of his face and read WE SWOON FOR CARTER BOON.

When we finally reached the highway ramp, there was no sign of Sara and her mom. We stood on a narrow strip of land, pretending to wait for the light. A few cars raced past. The brown, brittle grass was hard beneath our feet.

"What time is it?" I asked.

Kipps felt around his pockets, forgetting he didn't have any way to know.

"Mims should have left by now," I said. "Where's the next video?"

"She'll post it," he said. "Why wouldn't she?"

"Where is it, then?" I asked. I moved to the left, trying to get a glimpse of another screen.

"Maybe she's waiting until she's a block or two away."

But the footage had already switched over. There was a shot of Mims running down the street, her own one-person marathon, making her way to Times Square. People high-fived her and chanted, "Jess! Jess!" as she passed.

She had bigger eyes and a narrower face, and she was much skinnier than I was. But no one in the crowd seemed to notice or care.

"Everyone thinks she's me," I said.

"That's great," Kipps said. "Wasn't that the plan? She distracts everyone so we can get away?"

"It's only great if she plays that second video," I said.

The second video I'd recorded was a direct address to the audience. Mims was supposed to play it as she got close to Times Square. It was a three-minute video where I stared into the camera and told the audience how they were all complicit in my parents' lies. Every single person who'd tuned in, watching me crawl, then walk, then talk. Watching me flirt with Tyler and kiss Tyler. Watching me watch my sister die.

I told them I'd lied—that I'd never go back to Swickley, that I would never again allow myself to be used like that. My life didn't exist for their entertainment. I wanted bigger things for myself, and they weren't entitled to any of it. They never had been, and they never would be. Kipps thought the recorded lecture was vicious, but good. Really good.

"It's only great if everyone realizes she's not me," I said. "It was supposed to be a middle finger to the producers, the audience, to my parents. All of them."

As Mims approached Times Square she reached a barricade. Chrysalis Remington cut across the median and walked toward her. She was flanked on either side by two security guards in Like-Life Productions polos, holsters on their hips.

"Chrysalis is going to realize," I said. "It's game over. She hasn't even played the second video and it's already over."

A third security guard, a short, plump woman with dirty-blond hair, rushed in and pulled back a section of the barrier to let Mims inside. The camera was so far away I could barely make out the girl's features. They never zoomed in, even as Chrysalis and Mims came together and Chrysalis reached out her hand for Mims to take. Chrysalis leaned over and started whispering into Mims's ear, and that was it. They just kept walking. Chrysalis was taking her to see my parents.

"Are you kidding?" Kipps said. "There's no way she thinks it's you. She's, like, two inches from her face."

"Yeah, she didn't notice that I shrunk an inch? We don't even have the same color eyes."

But they were walking and talking. Chrysalis even laughed when Mims said something. She fucking laughed.

"I think this is Sara, she's here," Kipps said from somewhere behind me. "Forget it, Jess. Forget them."

I took a few steps back, turning toward the highway. A shimmery red NextGen Cloud raced towards us going eighty miles per hour. It stopped in seconds, just a few feet from where we stood. I looked back one last time, hoping that maybe she'd still do it. Maybe Mims would still play the video. But Chrysalis had an arm around her now. Mims wasn't even holding her device. The last thing I heard was the dull roar of mass applause, spreading out over the city.

39

Sara looked more like herself than she ever had inside the set. Her skin had this dewy glow to it, and she'd styled her long black hair in a cool braid that ran down the side of head, then tied around a bun in the back. Her mom, Charli Dean, was wearing a neon-blue tracksuit with little rhinestones. Her hair was blonder than it ever was before and still styled from the special the night before, though it was frizzy after a night's sleep.

"Sweet ride," I said, climbing into the back seat.

"We got a really good severance package." Sara laughed.

From where I was sitting I couldn't hug her, not really, so I gave her my hand and she held it tight. Her eyes were watery, and she swiped at them, trying to stop the tears.

"Jess, you know my mom, Charli . . ." Sara trailed off. She rolled her eyes. Then mouthed the words *I'll tell you later*.

"Hi, sweetheart," Charli said, her long pink fingernails

rapping on the wheel. "I'm sure you hate me almost as much as Sara does right now. That's okay, I can take it. I made my choices and I'll own up to them."

"I don't hate you," I said. It was true. I didn't know why Charli had lied to us for all those years, but she was here now, wasn't she? That counted for something.

"Can you guys talk once we're moving? We've got to go." Sara checked the rearview for oncoming cars. "We shouldn't draw attention."

We were about to close the door when I realized Kipps hadn't climbed in. He was still standing beside the car, his right hand clasped around his left shoulder.

"Kipps, come on," I said. "What, do you need a formal invitation?"

He looked from Charli to Sara, then rubbed the back of his neck.

"Seriously, Kipps," Sara said. "Now's not the time to be shy. Get in."

But it was Charli who took it a step further.

"Jess is our family, whether she wants us or not," she said. "So you're our family now. Who cares about those idiots."

She waved her hand, which glittered with gold rings. She was gesturing to the screen on the dashboard. I hadn't noticed at first, but they'd been watching the footage of Mims as she reached Times Square. Mims ran up the last block and right into my mother's arms. I waited, counting down the seconds it would take before my mom realized it wasn't me. She was holding a Jess imposter. My mom pulled back and stroked Mims's hair, brushing her bangs out of her eyes.

If there was a moment of hesitation, or worry, her face never revealed it. Instead she whispered something into Mims's ear, then sandwiched Mims right between her and my dad, leaning down so their foreheads touched. They were clutching her so tight it was impossible to get a good angle on her. They cut to one of the plasticized hosts from before.

"A family reunited," she said. "It's going to be a long road back to normal for them, I'm sure. But Jessica Flynn is on her way home. She's safe."

Charli turned the screen off. I stared at it for a minute before I finally registered it was dark. That was it. It was over.

Why hadn't I realized? The show would go on without me. Maybe they would dye Mims's hair a shade lighter, like mine, or close the gap between her teeth so we had the same smile. But it would just go on.

Part of me expected it from Chrysalis. The success of the show had hinged on me coming back. To the creator who'd built the franchise, I guess it didn't matter what version of me did, as long as the show could continue, along with the constant revenue stream. But my parents? How far gone were they, how desperate to hold on to what they had, that they'd accept someone who wasn't me? I tried to tell myself they were just performing for the cameras, that they'd still be working behind the scenes to get me back. I tried to tell myself it wasn't what it seemed.

But a sick, quaking feeling overtook me. The show, their brands, that stupid '90s design book and Helene's memoir, my dad's workout videos—it all meant more to them than I did. Even now, after I'd left, they were still choosing the show over me. They would always choose the show.

"Come on, Kipps," I said. "Let's get out of here."

Kipps slid in beside me. Then we were off, speeding north, the city slipping past outside our windows. Charli was almost as bad a driver as I was. She swerved in and out of lanes, cars blaring their horns in her wake. When the buildings around us turned to warehouses, then unbroken stretches of trees, she went twice as fast, until the road opened up and we were free.

"We bought a place up north, outside the city," Sara explained. "You're going to love it. You walk out the door and it's ocean for miles."

"Very few people," Charli agreed. "Very quiet."

"You can stay as long as you want." Sara turned around to look at me, then Kipps. "You both can. We already agreed we're giving you half of everything we earned on the show. Right, Charli?"

"I know it doesn't change anything." Charli didn't meet my eyes in the rearview. She gripped the wheel tighter, her head down.

The mannered part of me almost said thank you, but I stopped myself. It was the least they could do. Now Kipps and I would be able to take that money and do something meaningful with it. We could actually wait out the time until we were eighteen, without struggling. We could decide our own future.

"I could use somewhere quiet. I think we all could," I said.

"It's just . . ." Charli bit her lip, and she looked like she was trying to figure out what to say. "When people are desperate, they do desperate things. Sara's dad died before she was even born. It was a car crash. I didn't know what . . . I wasn't prepared."

"Let's save the whole sad story for later," Sara said, an edge to her voice. "Jess doesn't need to hear that right now."

"I'm trying to apologize," Charli shot back, with a similar edge.

"Then apologize."

Charli took a deep breath, then let it out in a giant heaving sigh. When she finally looked up into the rearview, her eyes were watery. "I'm sorry."

She was the same person who'd sat at the dining room table and helped me with my math homework, and tucked me into bed when my parents were working late. It had been Lydia, not my mom, who'd picked me up from school when I broke my wrist in gym class. She was always there—even now. She was the one showing up.

"Okay," I said. "It's okay."

Kipps grabbed my hand and held it for a moment, just to remind me he was there. We stared out the windows. Brown, winter-scorched grass stretched out on either side of us. The few buildings in the distance were falling into disrepair. Whole neighborhoods looked as if they'd been abandoned, and the ones that didn't were filled with piles of trash and the rusted shells of old cars, smoke rising into the sky from the occasional fire. No one spoke.

At some point the exhaustion of the past few days

overtook me, and I rested my head on Kipps's good shoulder. My eyes fell closed. I could hear each of his breaths, and then Sara put on music, but I was too tired to ever ask her what it was. The sky went dark. For miles, it felt like we were the only people on the road. Charli said something about a constellation and astrology, and Kipps was polite and launched into this whole thing about being a Taurus.

I don't know when I drifted off, but it was easy. Comforting. I'd never felt so safe—not even in Swickley, when I was home.

ACKNOWLEDGMENTS

This book would not exist without the support and enthusiasm of several people. First and foremost, to John Cusick, agent extraordinaire, who loved this from its first pages. Thank you for all your insights and encouragement while I was shaping this story—it is so much stronger because you were its first reader. A huge hug and thanks to Alex Arnold, who can talk Bachelor Nation and character development in the same sentence, and who made this book better with all her sharp, creative notes. You really GOT Jess on every level, and I am so grateful. To the entire team at Quirk, but especially Brett Cohen, Jhanteigh Kupihea, Nicole De Jackmo, Moneka Hewlett, Andie Reid, and Jane Morley—you always knew just what this book could be. Thank you for championing the weird and wonderful.

I'm grateful for my friends and family, who encouraged me during the year it took to write this book, and the two years before that, when I struggled through a manuscript that may never leave my drawer. Much love and thanks to Jenny Han, Jen Smith, and Morgan Matson, for writing retreats and boat rides and heated games of Anagrams. Thank you to Lauren Kate Morphew, Anna Gilbert, Julie Kraut, Nicola Yoon, Brandy Colbert, Robin Benway, Julie Buxbaum, Connie Hsiao, Robin Wasserman, Lauren Strasnick, Maurene Goo, Elissa Sussman, Talia Osteen, and Melva Graham. Love and gratitude to my parents, Tom and Elaine, and to Annie, Jimmy, Kevin, Yas, Doc, and Harry. Most importantly, thank you to Clay, my partner and best friend, who made me laugh, and took me out for deep dish pizza, and has been my cheerleader and confidant every day for the last five years. I love you.

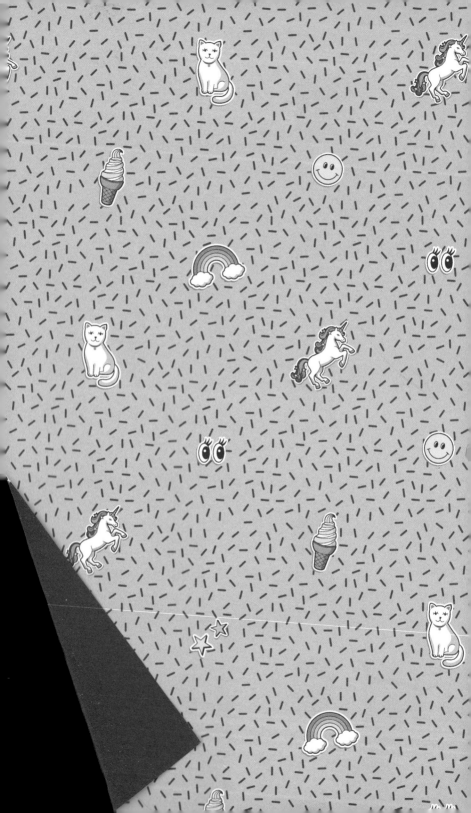